BODY IN GRACE

A RITA PATEL MYSTERY

By Catherine Cooper

Body in Grace
Copyright © Catherine Cooper 2017

This book is sold subject to the condition that it shall not, by way of trade or otherwise, be lent, resold, hired out, converted to another format or otherwise circulated without the publishers' prior conjunction in any other format other than that in which it is published.

The right of the author to be identified as the author of this work has been asserted in accordance with the Copyright, Designs and Patents Act 1988

ISBN 978-1-910779-72-9

This story is a work of fiction and the characters and events in them exist only in these pages and in the author's imagination.

Typeset and published by
Oxford eBooks Ltd.
www.oxford-ebooks.com

Chapter 1

"A gun is no more dangerous than a cricket bat in the hands of a mad man."

HRH Prince Philip

Introduction

Saturday 25th April 2015 5.30pm

"Congratulations Rita! And thanks!" Detective Inspector Jamie Bridge of the Leicestershire Police smiles at a room full of friends and relations of Rita Patel, studying at Warwick University; "Reading history and solving mysteries" as she likes to say.

Several phones are pointing towards her, and Rita tries to brush her unruly brown curly hair out of her face to look better for the pictures shortly destined for an appearance on Snapchat, Flickr or Instagram. Absorbing the acclaim of the room, Rita tried to recall how she had first heard about the mystery of the death at the cricket ground, why she got involved in trying to solve it, and the mistakes she had made.

It was all the fault of her older brother, Mohal, Rita thought, as she remembered what a tumultuous and dangerous time her second term at uni had turned out to be. She would never have thought of investigating what happened to Farah Ahmadi, whose lifeless body was found last summer on a fire escape, but for Mohal and his excitement about the inquest.

Saturday 7th February 2015 7 am

"You'll never guess Rita! The verdict was unlawful killing! My first inquest! The paper is bound to use my material now!" Considering this was shocking news about a death, her brother, who was hoping for a traineeship with the local paper, had sounded inappropriately pleased, Rita noted.

She had listened to the voicemail just before she boarded a vehicle with her friend Rohan to take part in a fundraising exercise. Soon she was being propelled to an unknown destination, prevented from seeing where she was going and forbidden to speak, giving Rita plenty of time to recall the family meal which had taken place on her last visit home, when the subject of the inquest had been discussed.

Sunday 1st February 2015 7pm

"City need a win" Nayan, Rita's younger brother, had said as her family had sat together round the white table in the grey and white state- of- the- art kitchen which Rita's mother, Padma, had insisted upon installing in their home at 10 Elm Drive. It was no surprise that Nayan was concerned about the local football team. Nayan had been ecstatic when Leicester City gained promotion to the Premier League at the end of the last season, Rita recalled, and had run round the house and garden shouting out the news. Neither would Rita would forget in a hurry the euphoria of both her brothers when Leicester City had beaten Manchester United by five goals to three in September. Since then, however, a win against Hull and a draw with Liverpool had been notable successes among a string of defeats. Most recently, Manchester United had had their revenge just the day before the family meal, winning three goals to one.

"Tell me about it." Jahi, their father, said in a depressed voice. "We may have been European City of Sport in 2008, thanks to the City Council, but now our football team are getting as bad as the cricket team."

"I can't agree with that!" Mohal had laughed in return, "They would have to lose a lot more games to be that bad!"

"And to think Leicester once had really good teams." Jahi sighed, "I remember them. That's why they put up that statue in the town centre, in Gallowtree Gate. It looks a bit sad now. Another piece of history."

The family knew their father was referring to the 'sporting success' statue erected in 1998 in the middle of Leicester town centre, not far from the clock tower. A bronze set of figures, it celebrated the success of Leicestershire teams in 1996-7 when the cricket team had won the County Championship, the football team had won the League Cup and the rugby team had won the Pilkington Cup.

"So you'll be at the Town Hall for the inquest tomorrow?" Jahi changed the subject and asked his older son, who nodded. Everyone knew the Town Hall building, which, built in the Victorian era in an elegant Queen Anne style, occupied a central square in the middle of the town centre. As well as being an administrative centre for the City, and a venue for weddings, the family also knew it as a building which was always brightly lit and decorated for the annual Diwali festival.

"What kind of verdicts can an inquest give?" Jahi had asked Mohal next, just as their mother, Padma, peering over her brown designer frames, was spooning onto their plates a steaming liquid of split pea and vegetable curry.

Mohal, who was due to attend his first inquest, as part of his work experience with the Leicester Mercury, had mentioned this to his father earlier. Padma gave her eldest child a disapproving look over the pot of curry; she had been so pleased to have all her children under one roof for once, hence the carefully prepared food, and now they have to discuss this, was her irritated thought.

"And who is the dead person again?" this from Nayan, five years younger than Mohal and in his first year of sixth form. Padma rolled her eyes before moving round the table to fill up more plates. Rita smiled to herself. It was good to see her brothers incurring parental displeasure rather than herself for a change. In the summer, Rita had been attacked, and left unconscious, when chasing someone suspicious, and after that her parents had been anxious and over-protective of her, in her opinion. The phrase "Oh Rita!" expressed disapprovingly had seemed a common one whenever she told them her plans.

"It's that woman who fell at the cricket ground in the summer, you remember." Mohal told his brother, shaking his dark fringe out of his eyes as he spoke "The one who was found on the fire escape."

"Did she fall or was she pushed?" put in Nayan, not at all deterred by the subject from eating, and lifting a fork of rice and curry mixture to his mouth.

"Exactly." Mohal nodded wisely, tucking into his meal too. When he had finished a mouthful he turned to his father to answer his question.

"The Coroner hears evidence and then gives a conclusion- the verdict. There are various options. It might be natural causes, for example" he explained.

"Doesn't seem very likely in this case!" Nayan snorted, taking some naan to soak up the mixture on his plate.

"You don't know until people give evidence," Rita contributed, reasonably, "She might have had a weak heart or something."

Nayan stuck his tongue out at his sister at that point, but she chose to ignore him. Mohal pressed on as if there had been no interruptions.

"Or they could decide it was unlawful killing." he said.

"Now that's more interesting." Nayan observed, then lowered his head over his plate, catching reproving looks from around the table.

"Other possible results are accident, misadventure, self-neglect, lawful killing and, of course, suicide." Mohal listed the options for the benefit of the table.

"What's misadventure?" Nayan wanted to know, wrinkling up his nose as he pronounced the word.

Mohal had replied before Rita, who had opened her mouth to give the answer, could speak. "It's not much different from a verdict of accident but means the deceased took part in something that went wrong – like a drug overdose which they didn't mean to take."

"And does the Coroner say who did it. If they decide it's an unlawful killing?" Jahi asked, at the risk of annoying his wife further. Padma coughed in disapproval but said nothing.

"Oh no." Rita chimed in quickly this time; she had checked this out when she heard about Mohal's assignment. Mohal shot her a look of annoyance across the table. This was his area of expertise; he was the one starting to make his way in the world while she was just a first year student, he thought resentfully.

"No." Mohal repeated firmly. "The role of the Coroner is to find out who died, when, where and how i.e. the cause of death. They are not allowed to give an opinion as to who was responsible."

Rita nodded, she had read this on-line in the Coroners Inquest Rules, but she knew better than to antagonise her older brother further by saying so.

"What if the Coroner can't be sure why it happened?" Padma found herself drawn into the conversation despite her better instincts.

"The Coroner can give an open verdict." Mohal told them and, at the sight of their blank faces, he went on, "That means a narrative. It describes as much as is known but doesn't include a conclusion as to why. You remember that poor man who fell from the multi-storey car park?"

Jahi nodded. He had read about the case in the local paper, the Leicester Mercury, the paper for which Mohal hoped to work when he graduated in the summer, if his work experience went well.

"He had an argument with his girlfriend." Jahi said, recalling the case.

"Yes that's right." Mohal confirmed, "The Coroner didn't know whether he meant to fall from the car park – suicide- or if it was an accident. So the Coroner gave an open verdict."

"What is the dead woman's name again?" Rita had decided to indulge her brother by asking, even though she thought she recalled this fact from her research.

"Farah Ahmadi." he told the table.

"Mmmn" Rita said, pausing to finish the food on her plate, "Thanks, Mum, that was delicious!" she added, then, looking across at her older brother, "She was a physiotherapist wasn't she? I'm sure I met her."

"Oh Rita!" her mother's familiar phrase and tone appeared again. Padma was sensing that her daughter's interest in solving mysteries had been aroused.

"I'm just saying." Rita fought back, shrugging her shoulders to indicate her innocence. Her fingers were itching to check up on the woman on the internet, but phones and tablets had been banned from the family meal table since Mohal and Nayan had been caught playing a game while they ate.

"And she was found in the summer at the County Cricket Ground, at Grace Road?" Nayan spoke again, having also finished everything on his plate but hopeful that there might be more.

"Yeh," Mohal confirmed, "It looked like she had fallen down part of the fire escape steps at the cricket centre."

Nayan nodded. A keen cricket fan, he had spent many hours at the Grace Road ground, near Aylestone Road, watching Leicestershire play, and could envisage the site Mohal was talking about.

"The police have been investigating, so their evidence will be interesting, as well as the post-mortem findings which must have been suspicious." Mohal went on.

"Do we really have to talk about this at the table?" Padma finally voiced her displeasure. "Here we are all together for a nice family meal, which we can't do very often now your sister is at university." Padma looked accusingly at Rita as if this were something to be guilty about, "I think we can talk of better things than how that unfortunate woman died. And the subject is closed." Padma tried to regain control of the agenda.

"Now, has anybody seen how they are getting on with demolishing the indoor market? It will make the market area look quite different when they create the new square!" she said to change the subject. "I gather the traders are already in the replacement building and that it is much more pleasant."

Her children exchanged raised eyebrows with each other, but wisely said nothing.

Sunday 1st February 2015 9pm

After the meal was finished and they had stacked the dishwasher, with their customary differences of opinion over the best way to do this, Rita and Mohal were sitting companionably in the chairs at the end of the kitchen which looked out over Jahi's carefully tended garden, now settled in darkness. Both were scrolling through their phones. Rita usually spent her time on Buzzfeed and its quizzes- 'The hardest Harry Potter Film Quiz', 'The Ultimate 00s Trivia Quiz' etc. - but now she was scrolling through sites for local physiotherapy services. Suddenly she exclaimed, "Oh!" causing Mohal to look up from his screen.

"I thought I knew the name." said Rita, glad to be out of her parents' earshot, "Farah Ahmadi worked at the practice run by the Paynes."

Mohal looked puzzled. While his stomach was contentedly processing the lovely meal, he was struggling to understand. What was Rita talking about now? he wondered.

"The physiotherapist whose inquest you're going to." Rita went on.

"Covering." Mohal corrected in an annoyed tone, "I'm covering it. For the paper." he put Rita straight.

"Yeh, well, whatever." Rita waved her hand around dismissively, not wanting to show her brother she was in any way impressed, "Well she worked at the health clinic run by Mr and Mrs Payne, the one used by Priya's mum." Rita referred to her best friend from school, Priya Shah, well-known to Mohal, "She goes to see them for her back problem- she blames it on her business which she conducts on the lap top - and I've been to the Paynes' practice in Uppingham Road with her loads of times."

"Is it near the dental surgery?" Mohal asked, referring to the dental practice run by their parents.

"Yeh, it's not far from there." Rita was not giving her brother her full attention as she spoke; she was still swiping her phone for information.

"I'm sure I saw her a couple of times." Rita was searching for a photograph of the dead woman while trying to summon up a picture in her mind. "Yes! That's her." She had found an image on a professional website which tallied with her recollections. The face in the photo was of a woman, probably in her early forties, Rita thought, with a warm, kind, smile beneath brown eyes. The sort of face you would trust. She had wavy dark hair tied into the nape of her neck, making her look neat and professional. Rita remembered how she had a precise way of walking in the black Birkenstock sandals she wore with her white tunic and black trousers. When she went home at the end of the day, which Rita had seen her do as Mrs Shah often had late appointments with Mrs Payne, Farah Ahmadi had looked quite different, with her hair loose, her hook nose (which Rita had noticed as she was sensitive about her own snub shaped nose) less obvious as a result, wearing a print dress and high court shoes which altered the way she walked. Rita had thought it strange that a person who spent her time caring for the physical stresses and strains of patients would apparently risk her own well-being with those heels.

"What are you two doing?" Jahi, their father, had walked into the kitchen while Rita was recalling the deceased woman.

"Waiting for the dishwasher to finish" Mohal had said, not looking up from his screen.

"Oh, are you?" Jahi was standing with his hands on his hips. Neither child picked up the warning signs.

"And what about the table and the pans? You could be clearing everything away and washing the pans by hand!" Jahi spoke indignantly.

"Oh, OK" Rita pulled herself away from her screen to look at her father, "We'll do it in a minute."

"In a minute!" Jahi had moved from being indignant to being incensed. Did no one take any notice of him anymore? he thought.

"Do it now please. Your mother went to a lot of trouble to make the meal and the least you can do is tidy up for her." His tone was controlled and curt.

Mohal, finally alerted to his father's mood, looked sidelong at his sister. But Rita stood to challenge her parent.

"What about Nayan? Why doesn't he help?" she questioned.

"Never mind other people, young lady. When you are back from your fancy university I expect you to help out properly in the house, not put it all on your brothers!" her father boiled over, throwing his hands in the air before he turned on his heels and left the kitchen in a cloud of anger.

Rita sighed and went over to the sink.

"That was random!" observed Mohal.

"You clear the table." Rita replied over her shoulder, not wanting her brother to see she was upset.

Turning the taps on fast, she allowed her face to get splashed by the hot jetting water which disguised the tears she could feel stinging at the corners of her eyes.

She took a saucepan to soak in the soap-sudded water. The truth was, she was not all that happy at university. She was enjoying her history studies, but she had found to her surprise that she didn't like being on campus, surrounded by the other students, and she couldn't find many people with whom she had anything in common. The truth was that she found excuses to come home often; she missed its comfort and security. She liked to be in safe and familiar surroundings, and to have her parents make a fuss of her. She even missed her bickering brothers. A Classics student on her corridor had told her, "You're in limine." Which he had said meant 'on the threshold'. "You haven't really committed to university, you haven't let go of home."

Her father's outburst had made her realise that, although this was true, nothing was perfect. She slammed the clean vessel down so forcefully that, at the sudden noise, Mohal almost dropped the placemats.

Saturday 7th February 2015 12.30 pm

As the rumbling of the vehicle's engine finally ceased, Rita brought her mind back to the present and her current predicament. Reminding herself to call Mohal to find out more about the inquest verdict he had been so excited about – what did the police think? who gave evidence? she wanted to ask- Rita waited for permission to remove the blindfold which had been roughly applied to her head, ruffling up her brown curly hair.

Rita, with her friend Rohan, who she had known at school, together with other Warwick University students, were participating in 'Lost'. This was intended to raise money for charities and was similar to 'Jailbreak' which had taken place in their first term, but they hoped it would be slightly less challenging. 'Jailbreak' had been about how far away from uni the students could get without incurring any cost. 'Lost' was about how quickly they could return from a mystery destination, but also without spending any money. There were about 70 participants, forming 25 teams between them. Rita and Rohan had been promised £100 in sponsorship by family and friends.

Their phones had been taken as had all other electronic devices and watches – anything that might be used to work out their location. Loud music had blared into the coach, Royal Blood if Rita was not mistaken, belting out 'Figure it Out'; not her sort of music and some sort of joke, no doubt, the purpose of the music and the blindfolds to prevent them from 'figuring out' where they were being taken. As the coach had gained speed and executed a number of turns, Royal Blood, booming out their repertoire of garage music, had, to her frustration, prevented Rita from gathering clues by hearing sounds that might help to identify the route, as she had seen people do in TV crime dramas. Rita consoled herself that she had fashioned a large sign, currently folded in her confiscated backpack, so that the nature of their endeavour, and the good causes they were supporting, would be apparent to drivers if she and Rohan decided to try to hitch rides. Also, she was glad they had both elected to wear sensible clothes – jeans, hoodies, trainers and waterproof coats- in case they had to spend a long time outdoors. Others had been less cautious and were dressed in a variety of outfits, including two girls disguised as giraffes and three boys in false moustaches and large sombreros; Rita thought their outfits might be an encumbrance, or that they might be mistaken for hen or stag parties.

Permitted to see again and blinking in the light, Rita and

Rohan glanced nervously at each other, wondering if they had done the right thing to sign up for this. They would soon know.

Chapter

2

"In the game of cricket, a hero is a person who respects the game and does not corrupt the game. The one who doesn't or corrupts the game, they are the villain. They should be punished, and they have been punished in the past."
                    Virat Kholi, Indian international cricketer

Saturday 7th February 2015 12.30 pm

As the participants removed their blindfolds, clues about their destination began to filter through their ears and nostrils. The shrill piercing cry of seagulls could be heard, insistent and plaintive, and in such numbers as to suggest a coastal location. This was reinforced by a tantalising tang on the breeze which entered the coach as the passenger door was heard to swing open. The air had a salty twist to it. So they were at the seaside. But, they were all thinking, which coast and where?

Smiling at each other for reassurance, Rita and Rohan released their seat belts and rose to stretch limbs which had been cramped in the confined space of the coach seats for quite a time – exactly how long they did not know. Rita grinned as she saw beneath Rohan's unzipped hoodie a message written on his T-shirt – 'RESTLESS'- written upside down; very appropriate she thought as he flexed his arms and legs ready for action. Rohan was keen on sports and liked to be active.

They filed out of the vehicle with the others and queued to receive back their mobile equipment. Soon, to rival the seagulls' cries, the air was filled with the chorus of modern life as shrill ring tones, whistles, and musical phrases heralded the owners' reconnection with their networks and the internet. GPS was located swiftly by some, while others had phones they could talk to and shouted at them "Tell me where I am."

Rita looked around her. Near to where the bus was parked she could see a small boat repair business. Across the street and between the houses she could make out the masts of small boats. Quickly word got round.

"Exmouth!" was first whispered, and then openly exchanged among them. The talk among the participants continued-

"They've taken us to Exmouth!"
"Where is that?"
"Is it on a motorway?"
"Where do the trains go from?"
"Any shops?"
"I need to pee before we do anything else."
Then a shout went up –
"Let's find the sea!"

Rita and Rohan were carried along in the swirl of a group which rushed down an alleyway in the direction of the sound of crashing waves. As the alley opened out into a walkway they could see a silver-streaked bay on which several moored yachts were swaying like drunken dancers. The sun forced its way through the clouds from time to time with beams which shimmered on the undulating surface.

Brightly painted apartments overlooked this scene and the group followed the footpath which curled round the edge of the bay, before crossing a footbridge over the water linking the estuary to the marina. From this vantage point they could see a watery square where small boats were crowded together. Keen to get nearer to the sea, the group moved on, a few pausing to grab a drink from the Harbour View Café or to purchase provisions from the local shop. Ahead of them, they could now see the main road which skirted the beach and from which they would be able to descend to the sand. The whole coastline was opened out to their view; they could see the wide expanse of the blue-grey sea, and across the estuary to other inlets.

The teenagers formed into several groups, and laughed and joked as they jostled along the wide pavement, the rolling sea to their right, Regency-style hotels and holiday homes, across the road, to their left. Every so often, Rita could feel the warmth of the sun on her face, but between its appearances the wind was cutting and she was glad she had brought her green woolly hat to protect her ears.

She and Rohan were in no rush to begin the tedious task of waiting for someone to be generous enough to help them hitch their way back, so Rita smiled as Rohan joined the group that scrambled down from the road and across the rocks to plant their shoes on the sandy silt which sank beneath their feet as they walked. Rohan was distinguishable in the receding group with his well-developed chest and arm muscles emerging from his T-shirt. He had left his hoodie and rucksack with Rita. The tide had only recently turned, so the terrain was damp and the waves were near. Several of the group tore off their footwear and rolled up trouser bottoms to trot or gallop into the briny waters, yelling and squealing like children fifteen or more years their junior. The pleasure of the experience had disabled their inhibitions. Rita took up a viewing point, sitting among the slippery rocks, as the sea-obsessed group ran in and out of the waves which were crawling over the sand.

Recalling Mohal's message, Rita had decided to use the time to open her iPad and find the website for the Paynes' Alternative Health Clinic, where Farah Ahmadi worked. She studied more pictures of the physio, together with the smiling faces of Mr and Mrs Payne. She was thinking that she would be in Leicester in a couple of days for reading week- assuming they ever got back from Exmouth - and was planning when and how she could fit in a visit to the clinic. She became aware that the sea-seeking group were starting to return, breathlessly exchanging insights into the experience. Suddenly anxious, Rita saw Rohan stumble awkwardly. He must have put his foot on a stone or a rock she thought and she stood to see if he was alright. Rohan waved to their friends to indicate 'no harm done' and they scrambled over the rocks and continued, in smaller groups now, reconnecting with their teams, either moving along the promenade or taking the direct route to the town centre.

Rohan, alone on the sand, limped carefully towards Rita, looking abashed at his mishap.

"You OK?" Rita asked, concerned, and indicated they should try to rejoin the road via the sloping slipway rather than crawling over the rocks.

"I just twisted it a bit." Rohan's round face was twisted into a grimace.

"I'll be OK if I just rest it a while." Rohan went on.

Rita, looking at the pain reflected in her friend's face, doubted that.

"Let's see how you are on the pavement." she said encouragingly, trying to sound positive. Rita took Rohan's arm to help support his weight. She noted that underneath his thick black hair, which was curly like hers, but shorter, Rohan's forehead was damp- she thought with sweat not sea spray, though it was hard to tell- so he might be in more pain than he was admitting.

"Not so bad now." Rohan continued tried to put on a brave face but winced occasionally as he limped alongside Rita to a park called Manor Gardens which was on the opposite side of the road to the beach.

It was not long before Rohan indicated he would like to stop and the pair found themselves sitting on a bench overlooking a flower bed, the soil in which lay dormant save for a few snowdrops and signs of the imminent arrival of crocuses. Rohan's left ankle was more swollen, as Rita could see when he touched it gingerly and raised his leg to the level of the bench for a closer inspection.

"Ouch!" said Rita sympathetically, "That looks nasty!" She thought it was the sort of injury that, ironically, Mr and Mrs Payne would be able to help with at their clinic; but that thought was of no use as the clinic was hundreds of miles away.

"I'll be OK," Rohan tried to shrug it off.

"Let's find the train station and see if we can get a lift from someone?" he went on.

This had been their plan, reasoning that a driver dropping off passengers at a station might be willing to pick up new ones.

Rita and Rohan made halting progress across Manor Gardens to a zebra crossing which took them to the town centre. They hobbled down a passage-way with a pub on one side and a Church on the other. As the pair limped together through the pedestrianised shopping area, like a bad entry in a three-legged race, Rita spied a bakery and, on the corner, a Caffe Nero.

"Let's get a drink in there," she suggested to give Rohan another chance to have a break.

Settled at a table, with a mint tea for Rita and a hot chocolate for Rohan, plus Rita's favourite wafer biscuits, Rita picked up her phone, thinking there was someone she could call who might help with their predicament. After that, she planned to call Mohal, as she was anxious to get some answers to her questions about the inquest. Meanwhile, Rohan ruefully rubbed his ankle and swallowed some ibuprofen which Rita had presciently packed.

Rita saw she had missed a text message from Sammi -Sameer to give him his proper name- who Rita had met during Freshers' Week when she had joined the Asian

Society. Sammi was one of the small number of students with whom she had found she had something in common. He was studying law and, from what she heard from other students, was considered bright as well as hard working. Rita knew Sammi hoped eventually to work at his father's law firm in Birmingham. Sammi had two older sisters who had set out on successful careers, one as a pharmacist and the other a teacher. Sammi's text told Rita that a room in his student house was going to be free, unexpectedly, in a few weeks and asked, was she interested? Rita was excited, but first she and Rohan had to work out how to get back to uni.

Rita explained to Rohan that she might be able to organise a lift for them if they could get to Exeter. But he was stubbornly reluctant for her to try, insisting they could carry on as planned, unwilling to let Rita down, and saying "I'll be fine once the painkillers kick in."

Soon, the couple left the café and hobbled their way through the shopping street and the underpass to the train station. The station had an alarming air of being deserted, although a timetable on a TV screen assured them it was in use and that there were two trains an hour which went through Exeter.

The pair considered whether to risk boarding a train without a ticket - but they worried that a ticket inspector might not be sympathetic to their cause. Rita felt she couldn't get into any more trouble or her parents would never let her out of their sight. Rohan's ankle was clearly causing him trouble despite the pills, so they sat down together on a grassy area situated next to the station car park to discuss their options and keep any eye out for vehicles which might give them a lift. Across from their vantage point they could see the bay and the many colours of wind surfers' kites, which were being tossed in the air like manic butterflies. Bright reds, oranges, and greens streaked between the pale blue and white sky and the silvery sea. Rita unpacked her bag to find the fruit she had packed and offered an apple to Rohan while she peeled a tangerine for herself. The couple sat contentedly for a few minutes, forgetting their declared intention to look for vehicles suitable to hitch in.

"Oi. You two!" a loud voice hailed them and Rita and Rohan, startled, looked round to see where it was coming from.

In a corner of the car park was a green motor home. The side was emblazoned with the golden logo of 'Rosie's Road Runners'. Rita recognised the name. Her brother Nayan, a keen sports fan, had drawn her attention to the success of Rosie Hunter, a sportswoman from Leicester, and her success in running marathons, which she continued to do, but more as a celebrity entrant now, having won every women's marathon possible around the world. Now her name was synonymous with various ventures, including a team of runners who were also very successful, a sportswear range - for men as well as women - and a chain of gyms. Recently, Rita had read, Rosie Hunter had launched a selection of healthy option ready-meals.

The vehicle was quite large, almost the size of a small coach Rita thought. The voice was coming from the driver who had lowered his window.

"Want a lift?" was his next utterance as he pointed to the cardboard sign which Rita had made to advertise their endeavours to passing motorists and which, in her search for fruit, Rita had taken from her bag and left on the grass beside them. It read –

"HITCHING TO WARWICK UNI!!
RAISING MONEY 4 CHARITY!!"

"That would be great." Rita accepted quickly, nodding at Rohan to get his agreement.

"I can't take you to Warwick but I can take you to Exeter."

said the driver and Rita realised he was an American from the way he pronounced their university town as "War-Wick"

"Hop in." he added appropriately as Rohan struggled to his feet and limped towards the van. While he was climbing in, Rita decided to implement her plan, whatever Rohan might think, and made a quick call to ask for a lift from Exeter.

Rita and Rohan stepped up gratefully into the motor home and were greeted by another occupant. He was short and white and well-built, in contrast to the driver who was tall and lean and black. Both men looked like they worked out, Rita thought. The short man, who introduced himself as Peter, looked like a weightlifter, or maybe a wrestler, judging by his well-developed arm muscles which protruded from his green 'RRR' polo shirt. The driver, whose name they were told was Harry, looked as if he might be a runner.

The interior of the van had a table between two dark blue bench seats, from where there was a good view of a TV screen. At the front, a grey ladder led up to a bunk over the cab. Behind the seating area Rita could see there was a kitchen with brown doors and counters; she presumed there were also a shower and WC.

"What are you up to anyway?" Peter asked in soft tones with a Southern Irish accent. Despite the season, he was wearing shorts and had abandoned his green fleece on one of the bench seats.

Rita and Rohan explained about the university and the 'Lost' competition.

"I think we can help with that, can't we Harry?" Peter asked the driver.

"Sure can." Harry replied and Peter dug in his pocket and drew out a £20 note.

"There you go. Make sure it gets to a good cause." he said, handing it to Rita.

"Oh, cool, thanks, we will." Rita replied and put the note

away carefully.

"Where are you going anyway?" Rohan asked.

Harry started the engine and they belted themselves in as Peter explained.

"We've been doing a road race at Sidmouth. We just dropped off a couple of local runners who wanted to catch a train. Now we're off to a run in Bournemouth. But we can take you to Exeter, you're bound to get another lift there aren't you?"

"Yes," said Rita, "If you could take us to the station- " she checked her phone -"St David's station?" she asked.

"No problem." Harry confirmed.

"Now, what's the matter with your leg?" Peter asked Rohan, who exposed his swollen ankle for inspection while Rita looked out of the window of the motor home, taking in the coast, then, as they left the sea behind them, churches, shops and houses. When she turned her attention back to her companions she saw Rohan had his leg elevated on the table and Peter was examining the ankle.

"Yeh. I see. We get this kind of thing all the time. I'm sure I can help." and, while the vehicle waited at traffic lights, Peter went to the back of the motor home. Rita saw him lift a hatch-like cupboard door and for a brief moment she could see that inside was a cornucopia of medical equipment, not just a few pills and potions and the odd bandage but an array of devices, syringes and liquids in small bottles. Peter closed the cupboard door briskly and sat down again as the van moved off.

"RICE, isn't that what they say?" said Peter, pointing a cold spray at Rohan's leg,

"Rest, Ice, Compression, Elevation. I doubt it's broken, just a sprain." he gave his opinion, then "You can take the spray with you." he added.

"You're sure?" Rohan checked. "That's great of you."

"No bother. We've a lotta cans on board. Like I say, ankles

are a common problem for us. And the spray will help you kids get back home."

Rita, gazing out of the window again, saw they were passing by the Royal Marines' base at Lympstone, the wire fencing and austere exterior indicating the presence of the military. Beyond the fence, a clutch of men could be seen jogging and climbing over equipment in camouflage-coloured combat gear, weighed down by large backpacks.

"The things those guys do!" said Peter, "Still. You'd trust them to get you out of a fix now, wouldn't you?"

Round a bend in the road they saw a sign announcing 'Darts Farm' which seemed to be a food and shopping complex alongside an adventure playground where, like the Marines, children were enthusiastically running and climbing round an obstacle course. The road wound over the river and then they reached a level crossing in a town called Topsham. On leaving the centre of the town, the roads became busier and the density of housing increased as the outskirts of Exeter appeared.

"Feeling any better?" Rita asked Rohan.

"Yeh. Loads. That spray really did the trick." Rohan replied.

"Don't overdo it." Peter advised.

"Nearly at St David's" Harry told them.

Thanking their helpers profusely, the pair clambered from the motor home, taking their bags from Peter. "Good luck!" he called as he closed the door and the green van moved on.

Rita and Rohan found themselves outside a large white and stone edifice, a reflection of Victorian assurance, perhaps, or at least the certainty of Brunel who had designed the original station, although it was clear there had been many changes since that era, not least the introduction of a cash point in the wall and a WH Smith shop by the ticket office. The Great Western Hotel to their left also testified to the confident building of the Victorian age. Rita had read on her iPad, as they travelled, that St David's was the second busiest station in Devon, Plymouth being the first. It handled over 3 million entries, exits and interchanges a year. That day, though, all seemed peaceful. There were not many people about.

"What do we do next?" asked Rohan, feeling less confident now they were back to walking again. The two looked around the car park where all was stationary. Behind them they could hear an announcement of a train to Manchester, which stopped at Birmingham. To their right was a taxi rank. Both were tempting options.

"We'll be OK." said Rita confidently, sensing Rohan's anxiety "I've made arrangements."

As if on cue, a white Renault Clio appeared, driven by a blonde haired young woman whose good looks were striking. Beside her was a man in his early twenties with an appearance to match the driver's; he was also a blonde but his hair was cut short at the sides and full on the top of his head while the young woman's hair rippled down her neck and onto her shoulders.

Rohan gave Rita a puzzled look. How had she organised this? he wondered.

"Hi, Morwenna." greeted Rita. "So great of you to pick us up!" and she and Rohan climbed into the back of the Clio.

Chapter

3

"If the French noblesse had been capable of playing cricket with their peasants, their chateaux would never have been burnt."
                    GM Trevelyan, Historian, 1942

Saturday 7th February 2015 3pm

"I'm pleased to help after you helped me so much!" Morwenna Maitland had replied, pressing the accelerator on her automatic car and speeding up the hill towards the city centre.

Rita smiled to herself, looking at Rohan's look of surprise and Morwenna's air of nonchalance. Rita had been friendly with Morwenna's family for a few years, having helped out, with her friend Priya Shah, at the bed and breakfast run by Morwenna's mother. In the previous summer, Morwenna had got herself into a spot of bother with a boyfriend and Rita, while investigating an unexplained death at the Space Centre in Leicester, had helped Morwenna out of a fix.

"Giles and I" - Morwenna had made brief introductions as Rita and Rohan fastened their seat belts in the back of the car - "can run you back to Warwick, and then we'll visit my parents in Leicester. We don't need to be back at uni until Wednesday."

"If you're sure." said Rohan, relieved.

"That would be great." said Rita, gratefully.

"So you're raising money for charity?" Giles asked, removing the sunglasses which were perched on his golden hair and leaning forward to put them into the compartment in front of him.

"Yeh. We've got £120." Rita told him, recalling the additional contribution from Peter and Harry.

"Good for you!" said Morwenna, "I wish I'd done something like that." she said, sounding wistful; Rita was fairly sure that Morwenna was being fanciful and that the sort of discomfort they had suffered on the coach, followed by the prospect of hitching rides, would not have been attractive to her. Morwenna preferred shopping malls to country walks, Rita recalled.

As if on cue, Morwenna said over her shoulder, "Oh, did I tell you about the lock-in? It was awesome!"

"A lock-in?" Rohan queried.

"Yeh. Don't you have it?" Morwenna asked, "Well, anyway, last term, in the evening, the shopping centre in Exeter - it's called Princesshay - it's very smart. Well," Morwenna rattled on as she drove, "they closed it and then reopened just for students, with lots of discounts and special offers. It was sooo cool! I got loads of bargains. Just as well as I hadn't taken nearly enough clothes with me, don't you find that?" Morwenna looked in her rear view mirror at Rita.

"Oh no, I get by." Rita replied, "I wear the same sort of thing most of the time." she explained, looking down at her practical black trousers and top which contrasted with Morwenna's carefully chosen print shirt and tapered orange jeans.

"Oh, OK" Morwenna waved a hand as if to say 'it takes all sorts'.

Rita wondered where Morwenna's money came from, but she realised that her parents, Athena and Edward, wanting their only daughter to be happy at Exeter after a difficult summer, were probably willing to indulge her.

As they drove along a road which was called Southernhay, Rita could see Regency-style buildings on either side made of attractive orange brick with distinctive doorways decorated with white blocks.

"It's called Coade stone, after Eleanor Coade who invented it." Giles told her when she inquired.

Behind Southernhay, Rita could see, lay the shopping centre - Princesshay as Morwenna had said - and she also caught sight of the tops of the twin Norman towers of the Cathedral. On a corner of a lush grassed area, which carpeted the space between the rows of houses, they saw, incongruously, that a rugby post had been erected.

"Why is that there?" Rohan, a Leicester Tigers fan, was intrigued.

"It's because of the Rugby World Cup." Giles explained "Some of the matches are being played at the Exeter Chiefs' ground. Tonga, Italy and Georgia are among the teams who are coming in the autumn. But I'm more of a cricket man myself." he confessed.

"Oh really?" Rohan said, his voice rising with interest, "You play seriously?"

Before Giles could answer they had arrived at a modern block of student accommodation built in brown coloured brick; he opened the car door and dived out.

"Giles just needs to collect his stuff." Morwenna explained as Giles disappeared into the block.

"Anybody hungry?" Morwenna asked as they waited for Giles to reappear. "We can stop at a garage for provisions." she offered.

"I have some rolls." Rita remembered, undoing the brown straps on her black backpack and searching for the food, "We may as well eat them."

When Giles had returned, carrying an overnight bag, and Morwenna had started them on their journey, Rita and Rohan divided the rations among the four car occupants, Giles feeding Morwenna as she drove.

They discussed their courses. Morwenna was doing poems from the medieval period to the present day and had fallen in love with the Romantic poets. Giles turned out to be doing a PhD on Chaucer – the Sergeant at Law's Tale from the Canterbury Tales.

"I've never heard of that one." Rita said.

"I'm doing pretty well with it I think. It should be a good piece of work." Giles responded.

"What's it about?" Rita prompted, more interested in Chaucer's work than Giles's. "And what is a Sergeant at Law anyway?"

"He was a judge and wealthy landowner. Chaucer, who was writing at the end of the fourteenth century, during the time of the Hundred Years' War, says he had memorised all the laws of England since William the Conqueror and was an incredibly busy person. He was 'war and wys' that means clever and rather suspicious of everyone. His story is the fifth in the Canterbury Tales and reflects the attitudes of the time, but it has topical themes too, really." Giles said, "At the end of the day, it's about a woman, a princess, called Constance, who has a lot of bad luck. She marries a Syrian Sultan on condition that he converts to Christianity. His mother is so furious about his conversion that she plots to kill all the Christians in Syria, including the Sultan, and sets Constance adrift in a boat. Constance somehow makes it to Northumberland, then a pagan country, where she converts various natives. She ends up married to the King but, again, her mother-in-law interferes and Constance is adrift in a boat once more, this time with her baby son. She makes it to Rome and is finally reunited with the King when he goes there on pilgrimage."

"Marrying so high did the woman no good. Be careful what you wish for!" said Rohan when Giles had finished.

"Check out your mother- in- law!" laughed Giles, "I think that's the main lesson."

"Anyway," said Morwenna who had heard about Giles' PhD far too much, "Solved any more mysteries recently, Rita?" she asked, referring to Rita's knack for helping to solve murders.

"Not since the summer!" Rita smiled, "But I might look into an unsolved death. Mohal, my brother, went to an inquest last week. You remember the physiotherapist who was found dead at Grace Road, the cricket ground? Farah Ahmadi she was called?" she asked her fellow passengers.

"Farah Ahmadi." repeated Giles and Rohan together, both nodding in recognition, to Rita's surprise.

"Yeh. What do you two know about her?" Rita queried quickly.

"My father's the groundsman at the county cricket ground." Rohan explained, "Farah worked as a physio at the gym at the cricket centre there sometimes." he added.

"Yes, that's right," Giles confirmed. "She treated me there. I saw her death in the news in the summer, when it happened. Great loss." Giles was shaking his head. "Terrific physio. She was a great help to me with all my cricketing injuries."

"How do you mean?" Rita wanted to know.

As usual, Giles' explanation started with himself, "I started playing cricket at Oakham." he said, referring to a private school in Leicestershire known to the other car occupants.

Annoyingly for Rita, Rohan interrupted and said, "Fast bowler, I bet?"

Giles confirmed, "You got it, always preferred the ball to the bat. More of a challenge, you know? Mind games with batsmen. I'm left-arm fast."

The young men carried on talking while Rita waited for another chance to find out more about Farah.

Rohan asked, "Still play?"

Giles shook his head, "Not so much. I tried out for the County".

Rohan sat forward as much as the seat belt would allow, impressed,

"Really? Respect man! You must be good!" he said admiringly.

Giles shrugged modestly, "I guess pace bowlers don't come along so much these days."

Rohan nodded agreement, "No, England are short of good ones."

Giles snorted, "Tell me about it. And meanwhile Australia have been very successful in producing them - look at their team for the World Cup - Mitchell Johnson, Mitchell Starc, Josh Hazlewood, James Faulkner. Awesome pace and variation! And left and right arms! They've got the full package."

Rohan nodded enthusiastically in agreement, "You don't fancy our chances in the cricket World Cup then?" he asked Giles.

Giles scoffed, "No way!" he said, throwing his hands in the air in a gesture of despair, "It's ridic. Despite having lots of time to prepare, the team seems in disarray. The selection of players is hard to follow. I'm not surprised we lost to Australia in the first warm-up match. I don't see us winning many matches to be honest, not on those pitches. And I don't rate our chances in the Ashes series this summer either, if their bowlers are on form" was his pessimistic opinion.

"You go to Grace Road often?" Rohan asked the older student next. Rita waited for the answer.

Giles half turned to continue the conversation, "About 5 years ago I was there a lot. It tailed off when I wasn't selected."

"Any reason?" Rohan asked swiftly, earning a look of rebuke from Rita who wanted to know about the cricket ground, not about Giles and his cricketing career.

Giles answered easily enough. "I kept getting tendonitis in my leg. It was like my body literally didn't want to do it. I could do short spells, eight overs here and there, but a captain needs someone more reliable. I tried to build up my stamina in the gym. That's when Farah helped me.And more recently when my shoulder started to play up. We got to know each other quite well.Nice lady. But, even with the exercises, I couldn't keep match fit. I really admire the guys who can. When you see James Anderson and Stuart Broad turning in performance after performance for England you have to respect them."

Rohan agreed, "Yeh. They've stayed amazingly fit, although I know they've both had problems. So you don't play much now?" he checked.

Giles pursed his lips, "I still go to Grace Road occasionally. I have a pass to the gym there and I chat to the players."

"I'm surprised not to have seen you there." Rohan replied.

Giles waved his arms about airily, "Oh I was probably by the weights. I was told to bulk out a bit and I quite enjoy that part of exercising. Once I'm there I'm in the zone; I don't notice anyone."

Morwenna, who had only been half listening to the conversation, suddenly interjected, to Rita's frustration.

"Why is it called cricket anyway? It's an odd name?"

"Oh yeh," Giles replied, "It's probably from old English, like in the time of Chaucer? There's a word 'cryce' which means stick, and there was a game in the thirteenth century known as club-ball so it may have developed from that. It became popular in the 18th century when landowners wanted to test their skills against their tenants and workers. The first rules were set down in 1744."

"I didn't realise it was such an old game." Rita said to Giles, and then quickly turned to the topic she was interested in by addressing Rohan "Will you take me to Grace Road some time? Show me the ground and the gym? I'd like to see where Farah fell." She said the last bit quietly, realising it sounded in bad taste.

"OK" said Rohan reluctantly. He was not sure whether Rita's interest was a good idea.

"Borrow my gym pass," Giles offered, handing the card over to Rita. "I won't need it for a couple of months as I've put my shoulder out and I'm supposed to rest it."

"Cool!" said Rita, "Thanks a lot!" and she pocketed the laminated pass.

"So you say Farah was nice." Rita persisted while she had the chance. "What else can you say about her? You must have worked quite closely together while she was trying to get you fit?"

"We talked about this and that." Giles searched in his memory. "She was efficient, always on time, and she had a plan for me which she kept on her tablet and which she updated after every session. She knew her stuff." he added after a pause. "And she was keen on helping women to get on in the sporting world. She was a big supporter of Annie Zaidia?" as he said this he turned to look at Rohan for confirmation. Rita looked at Rohan,too,for an explanation.

"Oh yeh. She's a South Asian football coach. She coaches at Leicester City Football Club's Centre of Excellence. People used to think it odd to see her in her training kit with her headscarf – all five feet two of her - but everyone's got used to her now. She's got guts.Les Ferdinand is one of the people supporting her. She hopes to be the first South Asian female to get a UEFA B Licence." he told her.

"Wow! Impressive!" Rita wanted to check her out online at once, but didn't want to lose a chance to talk about Farah.

"Yeh, Farah used to talk about her a lot. How she would go far. I think with other opportunities, Farah might have been interested in becoming a coach." Giles offered.

Rita felt she was getting a good idea of Farah in her professional capacity, and it fitted with what she had observed at the Alternative Health Clinic, but what about her as a person?

"Did you talk about her personal life at all?" she ventured. Now it was Rohan's turn to send a warning look and he rolled his eyes at Rita.

"Not much." Giles sighed. "She is - was- in a civil partnership – I remember that – she told me the name of her girlfriend –partner- but I've forgotten."

"Female?" Rita confirmed.

"Yeh" Giles replied, "And when she was treating me for my leg they were thinking of having a baby. I didn't want to know the details, thank you very much, but they were deciding which of them would get pregnant and how they would bring the kid up. Farah was thinking of going part-time, fitting the baby round her work, or is it the other way round? I don't know how she was going to do it. She had lots of commitments."

"Mmmn?" Rita felt she was getting somewhere now. Photos of the burial on Facebook had included a woman with short fair hair and glasses and carrying a young child. Was this Farah's partner and child? Rita made a mental note to find out.

"She was quite busy then?" Rita had asked.

"Oh,yeh. There were other gyms where she gave advice, she had sessions at some care homes too, I think, and she worked at a practice somewhere. She was a hard working lady." Giles agreed.

The car was on the M5 now and Rita thought they would be back at uni in a couple of hours tops. Rohan had nodded off to sleep, she was pleased to note. A mixture of the soothing rhythm of the car and the painkillers was taking effect no doubt. His head was thrown back against the headrest, his face relaxed in sleep. His nap gave her time to think about Farah, what might have happened to her, and who else Rita could ask for information so she could find out more.

Chapter

4

"The last positive thing England did for cricket was to invent it."

Ian Chapell,
Australian international cricketer, 2002

Saturday 7*th* February 2015 8pm

They had arrived back on campus in the evening, Rohan reeling with the pain in his leg, Rita's mind spinning with her ideas about who to contact to talk about what happened to Farah Ahmadi.

"You made it in under 8 hours, that's pretty good considering. Do get your ankle checked out, won't you?" the organisers noticed that Rohan was limping. Their arrival time and the amount of sponsorship were recorded; the details of each team would be logged on the website. Rita and Rohan learnt that the first team back had returned almost three hours earlier, having hitched a lift in a fast sports car.

Rita checked with Rohan that he would be able to get to his room in his accommodation block unaided. He assured her he would be fine and apologised again "for being so feeble". Rita, with the cricket centre gym pass from Giles in her bag, thought it might all have turned out for the best.

"Don't worry about it." she said, "We got back OK didn't we? Quicker than a lot of people!" Judging by the list, the organisers had a long night of waiting ahead of them, fewer than half of the teams had made it back so far.

Rita sighed as she entered her room and sank down onto her bed, her shoulders and her spirits suddenly dipping. Now that they had returned, after a day which had had its alarms and concerns, the atmosphere of the campus and her room were bringing her mood down. She could not explain why this was. The buildings were convenient for everything she needed - lectures, shops and the library were within walking distance. The accommodation was modern, clean and well-arranged and there were areas of green on the campus where she could sit, with flowing water and fizzing fountains to calm the environment. Everything she needed was provided. Yet the unsettled feeling had persisted. She had never expected to feel like this. When she had seen the campus on the open day she had been enchanted. Other students didn't find it oppressive or depressing. What was wrong with her? she wondered.

"Give it time" her best friend from school, Priya Shah, had advised last term when she had confided her feelings. Time to call Priya again, she thought.

Shaking off the oppressed feeling which she could sense trying to take hold of her, Rita moved to the shared kitchen, slid one of her mother's vegetable bakes from the freezer and heated it up in the microwave. She took care to put on the fan to dispel the cooking smell as some students on her corridor had objected, although she had never voiced her own dislike of the odour of alcohol coming from the empty beer cans and wine bottles which were frequently left to decorate the kitchen and the corridor.

Rita carried the warm reminder of home back to her room and skyped Priya, who was a medical student at Oxford University. Priya's familiar oval face appeared on screen. She was sitting on her bed in her room.

"Like my onesie?" she asked and she stood so Rita could see the all-in-one black outfit with a hood which had cat-like ears.

"Awesome!" said Rita enthusiastically, taking up a fork of pasta bake as she admired her friend's outfit.

"How's your day been? How was 'Lost'? You're back quite

soon?" Priya asked.

"We went to the South West, to Exmouth!" Rita told her between mouthfuls of the pasta bake, "I would like to have spent longer in the area" Rita told her friend. "In the Wars of the Roses –"

Here we go thought Priya, pleased to see her friend's enthusiasm for historical events had not been dimmed by studying the subject at university.

"-the Earl of Warwick was a powerful figure. He started out supporting the Yorkist side, and then he fell out with them and sided with Lancaster."

"Oh, yeh" said Priya, thinking this interest of Rita's was no surprise. That period was a particular focus of her friend as it culminated in the death of Richard III at the Battle of Bosworth, or 'our Richard' as the young women liked to call him, since the discovery of his body in a Leicester car park.

"He went to France when he fell out with the Yorkist Edward IV. He came back by sea – effectively he invaded the country, with a force which the Lancastrians and their supporters helped him put together."

"And?" Priya was not sure she understood why Rita was telling her this.

"Well, his ships landed around Dartmouth and Plymouth on 13 September 1470 and then his men made their way through the South West." Rita went on, her face brightening with excitement.

"Oh!" Priya tried to sound interested.

"Warwick gathered support as he marched towards Exeter- just where we've been today! - and read out a declaration there claiming his invasion was authorised and that Edward was a usurper." Rita was in full flow.

"I guess that rebels always want to show they are on the right side." Priya observed.

"Everyone thinks they are fighting on the right side. That's what is so tragic about war and violence." Rita agreed.

"Just like the situation in Syria and Iraq?" Priya ventured. A close friend of Rita's family, Priya has been aware that Rita's brother, Mohal, had taken an interest in the conflict and followed his comments on twitter about the refugees who were being displaced in the fighting.

"Yeh, quite similar really. Whether people claim to be fighting for religion, or the rightful succession to the crown, it's all about power, and wealth" Rita summarised.

The friends paused a moment, recalling the terrible images coming on their screens daily of beheadings and the destruction of towns and ancient buildings, as well as the thousands of terrified people trying to flee and not knowing where to go to be safe from the frightening blackness of ISIS and their flag. Villagers in medieval times in England must have experienced fear, too, and wondered who would win as landowners gathered their forces on either side ready for the next bloody encounter, Rita thought.

"So how did you get back?" Priya wanted to know, "I'm guessing you didn't gather an army and march to Warwick uni?" she added, laughing. Sometimes it was hard to know what century Rita was living in.

Rita told her friend about the eventful day. Priya gasped when she heard about Rohan's accident and clapped when she heard that Morwenna and her boyfriend had come to Rita's aid.

"So it did you a favour, in a way," she reflected, shaking off the onesie hood and toying with the ends of her long black brown hair which was twisted into a large plait.

"You probably got back quicker than if you'd properly hitched." Priya added.

"I guess so." agreed Rita.

"It doesn't sound like Rohan has broken anything." Priya opined, with all her one and a half term's of medical training. "But he should get it X-rayed just in case. He sounds as accident prone as your brothers!" Priya, who had one, careful, older sister, had always been amazed at the number of times Rita's more boisterous brothers had ended up in A & E.

The comment reminded Rita of something, "And Mohal left me a voicemail." she said.

"Oh, yeh?" Priya leaned forward towards the screen at this news, interested to know what Rita's older brother had to say.

"The inquest he was covering – the death of the physiotherapist at the cricket ground - they've decided it was unlawful killing, but nobody knows who did it." Rita told her.

"Sounds like a case for you, Rita!" said Priya, thinking that an investigation might help to lift her friend's spirits.

"Well, yeh, I guess" said Rita, smiling slightly - as if she had not thought of this already.

"Tell me who the pathologist was. I might be able to help." offered Priya, who had attended a post-mortem in Leicester in the summer and knew the son of a Home Office pathologist. They had dated for a while but gone their separate ways when he went to study medicine at Cambridge. His name was Ben Cohen and his Facebook entry, Priya had recently discovered, said he was now seeing a student called Miriam.

"Now, what did Mohal tell me?" Rita tried to recall what her brother had said when they had talked briefly in the week about the inquest he was attending. "Oh yes, Gabriella Hopkins"

"Oh, OK." said Priya excitedly "Ben knows her."

She was gratified to see Rita look cheerful at this.

"Great! I've been trying to think how to get some information." Rita said.

"What else have you been up to? Any more historical finds?" Priya asked this to see if she could further lift Rita's mood, sensing her friend had been having a low moment.

"Well, yeh," Rita admitted "I went to St Mary's church in Warwick. I wanted to see the tomb of the thirteenth Earl of Warwick, the ancestor of the one in the Wars of the Roses."

"Really?" Priya decided to start to undo her plait as she settled more comfortably against a cushion.

"There's a Beauchamp chapel. That's spelt B-E-A-U by the way. The French word for beautiful?" Rita thought she had better explain, "Warwick's family liked to trace their origins back to the Beauchamps, an old aristocratic Norman family."

Priya nodded obligingly.

"It's an impressive tomb." Rita went on. "This Richard is dressed as a Knight and in gold-coloured metal which the guide says is an alloy called latten, similar to bronze. There are gold figures around the sides of the tomb, of people weeping. His head lies on a golden swan and at his feet are a golden griffin and a bear. Over the effigy is what they call a hearse."

"What's one those?" Priya was curious, "I thought it was a car."

"It is nowadays" Rita explained, "But back then it meant a frame which looks like a cage - his is of brass - which would have had a covering of material, called a pall, attached to it. There are only two other examples of hearses like this in England, I found out."

"Oh. When did he die?" Priya asked out of politeness really.

"1439" came the reply. "He died in Rouen but he left clear instructions about the construction of the chapel and that his tomb should be in the middle of it. The building of the chapel began in 1443 and took about twenty years. It has been described as the most lavish family burial chapel in England, except for Westminster. Warwick the Kingmaker, the one I told you about, who became the sixteenth Earl, is represented as one of the weepers, nearest to the altar on the south side of the tomb."

"And what happened to him after he came back to England like you said? The Kingmaker one?" Priya obligingly asked.

"He virtually ruled the country for a time as Lieutenant

for Henry VI." Rita told her, "When the Yorkist Edward came back to England he joined forces with his brother, Clarence, to fight against Warwick. The armies met at Barnet on Easter Sunday 1471. There was a lot of confusion, it was very foggy, but Edward won and Warwick was killed when he tried to flee."

"So that was that for him" Priya sighed, uncurling her legs from under her and turning to plump up the cushion she had been slumped against.

"Yes, he was buried at Bisham Priory near the Thames but nothing of that remains now. His daughter, Isabel, had married Clarence, Edward's brother. Of course, his other daughter, Anne, married Richard III." Rita replied.

"Oh, yeh, 'our Richard'" Priya looked like she remembered this.

"Were they in love? Did they have any children?" Priya wanted to know.

"It's rather sad" said Rita, stretching as she talked, she had got quite tense recalling all that history, "It was a marriage of convenience like they tended to be in those days. They had a son who died as a child and Anne died not long after. Our Richard knew a lot of sorrow."

"I s'pose so." Priya was reluctant to let their conversation end on a low note, given her friend's recent moods.

"When are they burying him? Richard III, I mean." Priya asked.

"Ooh it's going to be great!" as Priya had guessed, Rita was excited about some old bones being laid to rest in their home town.

"It's being called interment week," Rita told her, "It starts on Sunday 22nd March."

"Make sure you're back for that!" Priya replied "And we are meeting up for Holi before then, aren't we?"

The two friends made arrangements to rendezvous on 6th March at Spinney Hill Park in Leicester for the festival–

another excuse to go home, Rita thought. Then they said their farewells.

Saturday 7*th* February 2015 10pm

Rita washed up her bowl and returned to her room – reminding herself to reply to Sammi's message about the student house. Rita heard the ping of her iPad. She opened it to see what new message had arrived and was surprised to see that already Dr Hopkins had supplied a copy of her post-mortem evidence to the inquest on Farah Ahmadi. Attaching it, Priya said, "Ben asked Gabby, who said you can have this provided you keep it to yourself! Enjoy! xxx."

With excitement -she thought she would be tired after the events of the day but, instead, after her meal and the chat with Priya, she felt wound - up and ready to do more - Rita sat down to look at the document. The first part of the evidence listed the clothing and belongings of the deceased received by the pathologist service:

A white work tunic, size 10
One pair of black work trousers, size 10
Green stiletto shoes, size 5
White cotton bra
White cotton pants
Wrist watch with black leather strap.

No other belongings were recorded. Presumably her handbag and phone were taken by the police, Rita thought, making a note to check with Mohal.

The deceased was an IC 6 (meaning Arabic) female judged to be between 35 and 40 years of age and, setting aside her injuries, apparently in good health. Her body had been found at the bottom of the first part of a flight of fire escape steps. She appeared to have fallen down about 10 steps. The only mark visible on her at the scene was a head injury. There had been significant bleeding to the back of the skull. Time of death was estimated at between 2.30pm and 3pm in the afternoon of July 14th.

Rita read down, skipping over the details about the weight of her organs, noticing that she was not pregnant nor were there signs of sexual attack or of recent sexual activity. The interesting bit came at the end. Gabriella Hopkins had given evidence that the nature of any skull fracture could help to determine whether a person had genuinely fallen down a set of stairs or had been assaulted. Typically, in the case of a fall, the skull would have a fracture above what doctors call the 'brim line', roughly where a hat would sit on their head. If you were unlucky enough to sustain such a fracture you wouldn't survive but, otherwise, Gabriella had said, in the absence of other factors – like a crowd on the stairs leading to crushing -many people survived falls downstairs these days, despite the traumatic appearance of such an accident.

What about a broken neck? Rita thought. Isn't that what happens when you fall down a flight of steps? She saw Gabriella was specifically asked this by the Coroner.

No, the neck was not broken and there were no signs of strangulation either – the pathologist found no bruising on the neck for example, and the hyoid bone was intact. In any event, Dr Hopkins had said, it was another misconception that a fall of this kind would lead to a broken neck. In her experience this was rare.

However - oh good, thought Rita, here's the punchline- it was also unlikely, in Gabriella's opinion, that the head injury suffered by Farah Ahmadi, which was below the brim line, would have been caused by the fall down the fire escape. The pathologist had carefully examined the steps and the doorway leading to them to see if there was any point at which her head could have made contact with a hard surface. But she had found none. What was more, a minute examination by Scene of Crimes Officers had failed to find such a site either. Whatever it was that Farah's head came into contact with, Gabriella Hopkins' report concluded, it was not on those stairs. This was supported by the blood pattern which indicated that, although the wound was bleeding as the fall began, the bleeding was diminishing, indicating that her heart was barely beating, if at all, even as she fell.

So how had she died? A fair question from the Coroner, Rita thought.

In Gabriella's view, the likeliest explanation was a blow to the head by a blunt instrument. Possibly something made of metal, but that was speculation, she admitted. Anything organic or mineral – a wooden object or a rock for example- would be likely to leave traces, however small, in the wound, but there had been none.

Reading this, Rita thought the death of Farah Ahmadi was as puzzling as another death she had been reminded of when she had visited St Mary's church in Warwick to see the magnificent Beauchamp chapel. Against the wall and across from the golden figure of the thirteenth Earl of Warwick, who occupied pride of place in the chapel he had commissioned, lay two brightly coloured figures, side by side, in a highly decorated tomb. This was a later addition to the chapel. The figures were wearing Elizabethan dress; their hands were clasped together in Christian prayer. This was the tomb of Robert Dudley, Earl of Leicester. He lay beside his second wife, Lettice Knollys, who bore a strong resemblance to portraits of the young Queen Elizabeth I. But the tomb had reminded Rita of the death of the Earl's first wife, Amy Robsart, who had suffered a fatal fall down a flight of stairs, but whether by her own hand, or another's, had been the subject of speculation.

Rita emailed her thanks to Priya and asked her to pass this on to Gabby and Ben. Now she knew there were three questions to answer. Who hit Farah, why did they do it, and what did they use to do it?

Chapter 5

"Two things in India are religion - one is cricket, and one is movies - these are two things."

Preity Zinta,
Indian film actress who
became co-owner of an
IPL cricket team

Monday 9th February 2015 8pm

Rita could picture herself trapped in a dark room, unable to open the door or find any windows. As she struggled to escape, the darkness seemed to get worse, to close in on her until... Rita, jogging, on the running machine at the gym, shook herself out of the memory of the dream she kept having. It was like a bad film; it was all atmosphere and no plot. Back at home in Leicester, she had slept badly in her bedroom -the one she had swapped with Nayan in the autumn. Each time, just when the dream got too frightening to be bearable, she would wake with a jolt. What did it mean? Why did she keep having this dream? Had taking part in 'Lost' made it worse? How could she stop it? She had thought about this so much she was tired of thinking about it. Nothing she had tried had helped. Now, as she jogged steadily on the treadmill, her new plan was to ignore it.

Rohan had driven the two of them to Leicester – his ankle was sufficiently recovered to allow him to apply the clutch without wincing too much. The doctor at the campus surgery had agreed with Priya that a facture was unlikely but had not thought it necessary to go to the expense of an X-ray.

"It'll get better of its own accord. Keep using it but not too much. Come back if it gets worse." had been the advice. So the pair had returned to their home town for reading week.

Rita was finding the physical exercise at the gym provided some relief from the tension she was feeling following a difficult conversation she had just had with her parents-

"What do you mean you don't like the campus?" her mother was surprised.

"I thought it was lovely when we visited you." her father could not see the problem.

"Who is this Sammi? Who else would be in the house?" Padma was concerned with her daughter's safety.

"What about the cost? Haven't we paid for this year already?" Jahi was concerned with the practical implications.

"Won't you need another deposit? What if you don't like it at the house either?" her father had also said, showing his disappointment with this turn of events.

"How will you get to lectures?" her mother had questioned.

And on and on it went. Her mother, once Rita explained how she felt, had seemed to try to understand. Her father had seemed to find the idea of change difficult.

"Just when I thought you were safe!" he had said as she had left for the gym, giving them time to think it over. If they said she could not change her accommodation, she was not sure what she would do. Could she bear more months living in a place she disliked, sharing with people with whom she had nothing in common?

Mohal had come into the kitchen just when the discussion was getting intense. He had winked at his sister and left hastily, a glass of orange juice in his hand, but not before Jahi could exclaim to his back, "And I thought you were the difficult one!" Nayan, hearing the raised voices, had wisely kept to his bedroom.

The news item on the screen at the gym said that, following the inquest verdict, the Leicestershire Police seemed no further forward with solving the death of Farah

Ahmadi. They were questioning anyone who had been at the cricket ground that day. Rita thought, presumably they had little to go on and were hoping the person would give themselves away or that new evidence would emerge. Gabriella Hopkins, the pathologist, had not been able to speculate about whether the killer was tall or short, right or left handed. Farah's skull had been so thin at the point of impact that the wound was too deep for these factors to be clear, so the police could not narrow down the field that way.

As Rita was walking on the 'cool down' section of the regime she had chosen, the smiling face of Rosie Hunter appeared on the TV screen. The so-called news item was really a free advertisement for her new range of 'healthy meals' designed to suit every need – low carb, low fat and low calorie. The range was being marketed under the name 'Rosie's Diner' with a retro 1950s design on green and gold packs. You had to admire the woman's stamina and determination, Rita thought.

As the machine stopped and she stepped off, Rita tried to think how to describe her friend Sammi to her parents. She had promised to show them a picture. She felt that if they could see his Facebook entries they would approve. As well as being a hardworking and ambitious law student, Sammi was a happy go lucky sort of character, always looking on the bright side and finding something to laugh about. He wore mostly blue turbans, varying in shade from almost grey to the brightest of sky blues. His twinkling eyes looked out from black rimmed spectacles. He belonged to the University's fledgling Sikh Society and was helping to prepare a website for it. He had told her that Sikhs acknowledge one creator and believe in equality; they reject ideas about class or caste or gender.

He had a postcard in his room which said-
"Remember god, earn honestly, share with the needy."

Sammi was good company and altogether he was an honourable guy, she wanted to tell her concerned parents. He was genuine and respectful and mindful of his duties to his parents. All she had heard about him and seen of him was good. But would they understand that?

Rita planned to go for a swim next. She had already done a spell on an exercise bike and watched with amazement the speed and intensity of participants in a spinning class as they rode up and down imaginary inclines to music with a driving beat. She did not think that was for her. She had moved some weights on machines designed to improve the muscles in her legs, bottom, arms and shoulders. So, after the running, she spent some time dutifully stretching all the muscle groups she could think of to finish her routine, sprawling inelegantly on the mat, all the while thinking of a video she had seen designed to promote women in sport, and to encourage them not to be self-conscious about their appearance. Fortunately, other people at the gym seemed more interested in themselves, or else were distracted by what they could hear on their earphones, so they were unlikely to observe what she was doing.

Walking into the female changing room, Rita was quickly aware of half of a heated exchange which was taking place. A tall Asian woman stood, dripping from the pool, still in her swimming suit, a green one piece, with a phone balanced between her neck and her ear while she struggled to use her hands to extract her clothes from a locker.

"Really, Shakira, you shouldn't have done that!" she yelled, and then her towel and other possessions cascaded onto the damp floor, sending her temper up another notch.

"Huh!" the woman grunted in annoyance.

"No, let me tell you!" she was saying as she hauled her belongings onto a wooden bench and took the towel in one hand and the phone in the other, the better to berate the unfortunate Shakira, Rita thought.

"Don't make me have to come over there and sort it out! That's what I pay you to do!" the woman was saying.

Rita tried not to overhear and continued with her undressing, but, as the woman was shouting down the phone, the conversation – or, rather, her part of it - was unavoidable.

"I don't want excuses." the woman went on, putting Shakira on speakerphone while she dried herself. So now Rita could hear both sides of the row, or as much as the other person was allowed to say.

"We have an inspection..." Shakira began tentatively but was cut off by the woman's voice saying shrilly,

"Deal with it. I gave you instructions. Don't mess it up."

"But..." was all Shakira could get in next.

"I'll call you back." snapped the woman who angrily jabbed at her phone before putting it in her bag, then she towelled the rest of her body with angry strokes, hastily sprayed deodorant around the changing room and herself, and climbed into a green track suit, impatiently tying up her wet hair to stop it soaking her back. All the time she was sighing and muttering and Rita feared for Shakira when the call was resumed.

Rita had just put on her own swimming suit and was moving towards the showers before her swim when behind her she heard a loud 'bang' as the angry woman who had been on the phone slammed shut her locker door, then there was another crash as she exited the changing room, taking with her the fire of fury she had been stoking.

So much for a relaxing swim! thought Rita. She might as well make good use of the time to do some more thinking about what happened to Farah Ahmadi, she decided. As she propelled herself up and down the pool, alternating front crawl and breaststroke, Rita recalled the information she had gleaned from her brothers when she had spoken to them about the day when the physiotherapist died.

"So there was no cricket match?" was her first question

earlier that day as the three lounged together in the living room, like lion cubs after a meal.

"No." her younger brother answered. Mohal was checking the notes he had made at the inquest but Nayan was quicker. He had googled the cricket fixtures.

"Monday July 14th, Leicestershire were away at Worcestershire playing in the second day of a county championship match." Nayan elaborated.

"That's right." Mohal asserted himself as the eldest and the journalist.

"Did they win?" Rita had asked innocently.

Her brothers had laughed together conspiratorially. "Of course not. We haven't won a match since 2012!" Nayan let Rita in on the joke after a while. "Worcestershire won by 204 runs." he told her.

"Oh" said Rita not much wiser.

"The ground was being used for an archery course. By one of those summer schools." Mohal went on.

"Oh really?" Rita filed away the information. She had a feeling she might know how to find out more about that.

"Lucky no one was shot then!" Nayan had put in, standing up and then pretending to be hit in the chest by an arrow and collapsing back down on his chair.

"Ha,ha. You think you are so funny." Mohal, recalling his status as older brother, was not amused at this.

"So the team weren't there, the players?" Rita checked.

"No, unless there was anyone too injured to play who stayed behind to train; they might have been at the ground. The police witness said..." Mohal's information was cut off by his sister.

"Who gave evidence, out of interest?" Rita had asked.

"It was a female officer, Constable Gardner." Mohal told her, "But your friend Inspector Bridge was there too. That was the guy who helped me over that other business."

Brother and sister had nodded in understanding. When

Mohal had been accused of the murder of an MP, Inspector Jamie Bridge had liaised for him with the Metropolitan Police in London.

"The Constable said," Mohal looked at his summary, "She was first on the scene, with the ambulance. She secured the immediate area while the deceased was pronounced dead and the pathologist was called. At that time it looked like an accident, maybe one where there were implications for other public venues or fire escapes. It appeared as if she had fallen down one flight of steps. Constable Gardner's colleague, Constable Hann, found the top floor of the cricket centre, which housed the gym and a treatment room, empty, and got the ground staff to lock them up in case a forensic examination was needed. There were a few spectators in the stands, and a conference taking place in a meeting room. All their names were taken, as well as those of the people involved in the archery course- the pupils and their trainers, plus the ground staff of course."

"How many people altogether?" Rita had asked.

"Mmmn. Two security officers. Half a dozen ground staff, ten people at the conference, a dozen pupils, three archery trainers and about ten people in the stands. Plus catering staff for the conference and, I gathered, a couple of catering staff taking deliveries and stocking up. So around fifty people or so?" her older brother replied.

Rita thought about that as she ploughed up and down in the water. Fifty potential witnesses was quite a lot to interview, it seemed to her, but, on the plus side, they could all be identified; would any of them have seen anything, though? Presumably the pupils were unlikely to have been involved if they were in the middle shooting at targets? The same would go for their trainers. Likewise, anyone leaving the conference would have been noticed, surely? The ground staff sounded a more fruitful source of inquiry in Rita's opinion. They were usually strong men so they could quickly cover and uncover pitches and carry equipment to patch up surfaces or soak away sodden patches of turf; she had gathered all this from Rohan on their journey in his car to Leicester. But would any of them have had a motive? What about the catering staff who were taking deliveries? They could have had access to the gym area perhaps? Then there were the spectators. Who were they? Archery enthusiasts? Parents of the participants?

Pulling herself out of the water, Rita could see the police had a lot of work to do to uncover anyone with an opportunity and a motive, given the list of those present at the ground. Rita dried herself in the changing room in the company of two other young women who she had seen swimming in the pool, one tearing up and down at a furious pace, spray and arms flying, the other sedately scooping herself from one end to the other and back again in a slow breaststroke, as if she were practising mindfulness.

Rita watched herself in the mirror as she shook her brown hair while she applied the hair dryer to it, trying to tame her curls and coax them into a style. Eventually satisfied, she applied make-up to accentuate her cheeks and eyes which she thought were her better features; she hoped to draw attention away from her rather squat nose, which she disliked. As Rita was taking the rest of her things from her locker she recalled what Mohal had to say earlier that day about Farah's possessions.

"So what did she have with her that day? Did Constable Gardner say?" Rita had asked.

"Yeh." Mohal had given his younger brother a victorious glance, this was information he could not find on the internet!

"Let's see." Mohal had checked his notes again. "Nothing by the body. No phone or bag. So it wasn't as if she was planning to go anywhere, if you see what I mean. The Scene of Crime team combed the fire escape, the treatment room and the gym. They found her bag; they showed it at the inquest. It was a large sports bag, a blue one, with pouches for a water bottle, a purse and a phone."

"And was her phone there?" Rita was impatient to learn.

"Yeh. They checked that out. Nothing unusual on it. Some pictures of her partner and their baby. Her purse had a bit of money in it, and a few membership and credit cards. Apart from that, there were tissues, a dress she was presumably planning to change into, and some toiletries. Nothing odd."

As Rita finished getting dressed she felt something was missing from the list of Farah's possessions, but she couldn't quite put her finger on it.

"Nothing else?" she had checked with her brother.

"Nope" Mohal had shaken his head. "The door from the treatment room to the fire escape was open. Access to the gym itself is through a barrier which requires a swipe card. So it didn't seem that anyone unauthorised could have been there."

"But no one kept a record? There was no receptionist or anything like that at the gym?" Rita checked.

"We saw photos. It's not that kind of gym." Mohal told her. Rita thought it would be easier to imagine events when she had been to the Grace Road ground with Rohan, which she planned to do the next day.

"No CCTV?" Nayan had asked; having recovered from his arrow wound, he was playing Minecraft while he listened. "They always use that on Crimewatch now." he added.

"Not in that area of the ground." Mohal told them, "They only have it in places where the public have access."

"And that didn't tell the police anything?" Rita wanted to know.

"There was nothing untoward on the tapes for the day in question, no. And the security guards were keeping an eye on things. There were a few vehicles going in and out of the car park, visitors coming and going, nothing to arouse suspicion." Mohal replied.

Rita had sighed in frustration.

"The forensic people did check the gym and the treatment room for, I dunno, blood and fingerprints?" was Rita's next question.

"Blood, yeh. Once they knew she'd been hit they did a luminol thing - you know - even if a killer thinks they've cleaned up, this stuff can show where blood has been." Her brother confirmed.

All the siblings nodded. They had seen episodes of CSI where this proved an effective detection tool.

"How exactly does it work?" Rita thought one of her brothers would know. Sure enough, Nayan replied, "It's a powder which is mixed with a liquid containing hydrogen peroxide. The powder is made of nitrogen, hydrogen, oxygen and carbon."

Rita had pulled a face at this. How was this helping? she thought.

Nayan pressed on, "It reacts with the iron in haemoglobin. They spray the luminol in darkness..."

Rita had shuddered at this, reminded of her recurrent bad dream.

"And if there is blood, it glows, it's got a cool name, chemiluminescence!" Nayan ended triumphantly.

Rita filed this word away. It might come in useful one day, she thought.

"But there were no traces." Mohal said, bringing them down to earth.

Rita, as she walked out of the gym to the red Peugeot to drive home, pondered how Farah could suddenly have had a bleeding head wound at the top of the fire escape and not leave any traces of blood in the gym or treatment room? Did someone strike Farah at the top of the stairs in broad daylight, risking being seen - by the archery participants and their followers or the ground staff for instance? It seemed unlikely – it would be a huge risk and the forensic examination had not identified a place where blood had gathered in any quantity. Rita crossed the gym car park and, as she did so, she could see, sitting behind the wheel of a white Porsche, the angry woman from the changing room, still apparently engaged in an irate phone exchange with Shakira, unless she had moved onto another victim, of course. Rita hoped she wouldn't encounter the woman on the road. She was bound to be exhibiting road rage.

Thinking of loud arguments, Rita recalled another comment her brother had made.

"My money's on the brother." Mohal had said as the three had continued to ponder the events of 14th July the previous year.

"What makes you say that?" Rita had been surprised.

"I heard them having a heated discussion. In between sessions at the inquest." Mohal said.

"Heard who arguing?" Rita had asked, not following this.

"The brother, Rashid he's called, and Farah's partner. They were really going at it." he explained.

"What did they say?" Rita had questioned.

"It was hard to understand everything they were saying." Mohal consulted his memory, trying to reconstruct the scene in his head.

 "She said something like, 'You need to keep away from us. It's what she wanted!'

He said something like, 'You can't stop me, I'll do what I like.'"

As Rita drove back to Elm Drive, she was only half concentrating on the road; the rest of her mind was trying to decide what the conversation between Farah's brother and her partner might mean and whether it could have had any connection with Farah's death.

Chapter

6

"A cricket ground is a flat piece of earth with some buildings around it."

Richie Benaud,
Australian international cricketer
and commentator

Tuesday 10th February 2015 10 am

The next day, Rita had decided to follow her hunch about the archery course at the cricket ground. She remembered someone had mentioned it to her last summer.

"Hi Rita, lovely to hear from you, how's uni?" Rita's aunt Jaina's tones had been enthusiastic as Rita phoned her from her bedroom at Elm Drive.

Rita said her studies were going well (true) and that she was enjoying uni (not entirely true), then she steered the conversation to her cousins, Shona and Shreya.

"Is one of them around?" she tried to sound casual.

"You're in luck!" Jaina said; she was very proud of her daughters.

"They're both in at the moment. Shall I get them to call you on FaceTime? You can tell them all about uni. They'd love to visit you at Warwick."

"Yeh, that would be great." Rita tried to sound keen about a possible visit.

A few minutes later and she was looking on the screen at two seemingly identical faces; these were the almost immaculate features of her twin cousins, aged 15. They were 'mirror twins' according to Rita's mother, who had tried to explain. Each was a mirror of the other so that, for example,

Shreya was right handed and Shona was left handed. This was a bit disconcerting until you got used to it. It was literally as if they were not complete without the other one present, Rita thought, and she wondered how they would manage if they were ever separated. But that time was a way off.

For the present, two oval faces, surrounded by long, sleek, straight black hair, their mouths curled in smiles, cooed at Rita.

"Tell us about Warwick! Is it cool? What's the library like? What are you studying at the moment?" the dual bombardment lasted several minutes.

Rita did her best to sound upbeat and wracked her brain for aspects of uni life she thought the twins would find appealing, all the time wondering to herself whether she shouldn't be more honest. What if they bought her enthusiasm, went to uni, and then found it was not what they had expected? Oh well, they would probably go on open days and talk to lots of other people, Rita thought, to salve her conscience.

When the interrogation subsided, Rita managed to say,

"So, in the summer, you did some activities, huh? I think you told me about some?"

"You mean," began Shreya.

"The archery." finished Shona.

"We just knew you'd be interested! Are you going to solve that lady's murder?" Shreya sounded envious.

"I thought I'd see what I could find out," said Rita, trying to sound casual about it, "I did meet the woman who died. It makes me want to help if I can."

"What do you want to know?" Shona asked.

"So you were there when it happened?" Rita checked.

Her cousins nodded.

"Just tell me what went on that afternoon, from your perspective." Rita requested.

"OK, well it was the first day of the archery course.

Actually it never got finished. They cancelled the other day out of respect." Shona began.

"Who organised it? The course I mean" Rita was not sure why she asked this but she thought she might as well know.

"A holiday camp company – KidzAimHigh it's called. We've done courses with them before; abseiling and canoeing." Shreya explained.

Rita thought, 'respect'. She had no idea her well-behaved cousins were so adventurous.

"Mum drops us off so she can go to work, of course." Shona added by way of explanation, referring to her mother's job as the secretary at the private school which the twins attended.

"So we spent the morning having individual sessions to check we understood safety and how to shoot accurately. In the afternoon we were divided into two teams for a shooting competition." Shreya spoke.

"How many people were on the course?" Rita checked the information provided to the inquest.

"There were 10. Two teams of 5." Shona said and Shreya nodded agreement.

"And how many trainers?" Rita questioned.

"There were three coaches - Amy, Fred and Rashid" Shona replied.

Shreya took up the story again: "It was OK. The others on the course were quite fun. Holiday refugees like us. In fact, two of the boys were on the abseiling course the previous holiday."

Rita was really having her eyes opened now. It seemed her immaculate cousins, who were not even allowed a Facebook account, were encountering more than just challenging adventures on their holiday activities. But something they had said had set off an alarm in her head.

"Rashid?" Rita asked.

"Yes, well that's what was so tragic, and why they cancelled the course, I suppose." Shreya spoke again.

"What do you mean?" Rita was really interested now.

"Rashid, who was helping us with our target practice, was related to the woman who died, he was her brother! Fred told us!" Shona sounded upset as she told Rita this.

"Tell me more." Rita encouraged, thinking of lots of questions but deciding it was better to get the story in the twins' own words first.

"It was after lunch – we had made ourselves cucumber and chutney sandwiches, our favourite!" the girls shared conspiratorial smiles.

"We were in two teams, aiming to hit the blue ring on the target, that's worth 5 points you know." Shona told Rita. "The two targets were set up in front of the two scoreboards, so we were shooting in different directions. The scoreboards are on opposite sides of the ground."

"Oh" said Rita who knew less about scoring in archery than she did in cricket.

"My team became aware of some activity beyond the boundary. I mean where the cricket centre is. There were the flashing lights of an ambulance and a police car." Shona continued.

"My team didn't notice anything at first. Amy said to stop – she was cheering on Shona's team– and Fred, who was cheering on my team, said he'd go and check everything was all right. So we just sat on the grass for a bit." Shreya contributed.

"Where was Rashid?" Rita could not help prompting.

"Oh, he was around. He was the impartial judge of our scores." Shreya answered.

"So then what happened?" Rita asked them to go on.

"Amy came over and said a woman had had an accident. She'd fallen down some stairs. She was being taken away in the ambulance. She didn't tell us she was dead. Maybe she didn't know." Shona said.

Shreya nodded and took up the story, "Amy said a police

officer had asked if we could wait in the middle until some more officers could get there."

Shona interrupted her sister, "That made us all think there might be more to it than a fall."

Shreya took back the story, "About 15 minutes later a tall guy with red hair came over. He was wearing shorts I remember. Didn't look like a policeman at all."

"Inspector Bridge?" Rita asked, picturing the Inspector whom she had first met a couple of years ago when helping solve a murder in the lake at Abbey Park. He was not known for his smart attire.

Shreya nodded assent and continued, "He sat on the grass with us. He apologised for the disruption. He said unfortunately a woman had died."

"Mmmn" Shona spoke up as if she had just remembered something,

"Someone, I don't know who, said 'Who was she' but the police guy – the Inspector- said he couldn't tell us as the family were yet to be informed."

Shona looked at Shreya who continued, "Another police officer, a man in uniform, came to take our names and contact details. The Inspector said we could go once that was done and that the police officer would show us which exit to use. By that stage we could see a little white tent had been erected- you know, the kind you see on TV? - which suggested the police were covering the body while it was checked over. Grim!"

"We thought we'd go to a café with these boys we knew and call Mum from there!" said Shreya.

That was convenient, thought Rita.

"Just as we were giving our details, a phone rang. It belonged to Rashid who had come across the grass to sit with us. He sort of staggered up slowly while he was listening to the call. 'Oh my God!' he said and turned to look at the little white tent. He looked pretty shaken. The police guy - the

Inspector - seemed to realise something was wrong. He got up as well, saying 'Are you alright, sir?' and by the time we'd given our details the Inspector had whisked Rashid away." Shreya finished.

"We only found out later that he was the brother of the dead woman. Imagine!" Shona spoke and the twins shuddered together.

"And that was it?" Rita checked.

"Yes. The other two coaches were packing the equipment away when we left the ground. Mum got a refund for the cancellation I think." Shreya said.

"And we had to go to Dad's office instead!" Shona told Rita.

"Boring!" the girls said in unison.

"And you saw nothing suspicious?" Now Rita decided to ask her questions. It was not often she got to speak to someone who was at the scene of a murder, even if at a distance.

As if hearing her thoughts, Shreya said, "No, we were too far away."

"We did use the loo near that building." Shona reminded her sister.

"Oh, yeh," said Shreya, "I s'pose we did."

"All of you?" Rita was interested again, "The coaches as well?"

"Probably," said Shona, "I didn't notice."

"But you didn't see Farah when you were over there?" Rita wanted to be sure the group did not come into contact with the deceased physiotherapist.

"Not as far as I know." said Shona.

"And you didn't hear anything at the time she must have gone down the fire escape? No shout or cry?" Although the police had nothing to go on, Rita thought she might as well ask.

"No, although to be fair we were concentrating on doing the best for our teams. Using one of those bows isn't as easy as it looks!" Shreya replied.

Rita and her cousins said their goodbyes, Rita promising to invite them to Warwick. Maybe they would be more fun to entertain than she had thought.

After the call, Rita added the information to the notes on her iPad. Was it just a massive coincidence that Rashid was at the ground at the time his sister met her death? Rita saw her note about the row which Mohal overheard at the inquest between Rashid and Farah's partner. That was also suspicious. Could the twins be sure he was in the middle at the time the murder must have happened? Could their attention have been distracted by the archery competition, or by their obvious interest in these boys they had met perhaps? Yet the police must have ruled him out? Otherwise why would they tell the media that they were interviewing everyone who was at the ground? What were the rules of detection? she reminded herself-assume nothing, believe no one, check everything.

Tuesday 10th February 2015 11 am

Picking up Rohan from his parents' house in Braunstone, Rita noticed approvingly that he was wearing chinos and a pale green T-shirt today; on closer examination this turned out to have printed on it all the fielding positions in cricket. Where does he get his T-shirts from? she wondered. Rita told him what she had learnt so far. He grunted and nodded from time to time as he checked out his hair in the passenger mirror. Rita was not sure he was paying much attention.

Arriving at the cricket ground at the Curzon Road entrance, they used his father's pass to gain entry from the ground security staff.

"It's his day off so he doesn't need it." Rohan explained to Rita. As they parked, Rita saw there was CCTV in the car park. It was cloudy overhead, but not actually raining, so Rohan and Rita took the long route to the cricket centre, where the gym was, turning left and circumnavigating the ground. This gave Rita the chance to see the area from every angle and Rohan to point out the highlights before they took a tour of the scene where Farah had died. As her eyes travelled round the ground, Rita noticed the advertising boards for various local businesses: De Montfort University, Next, and the dairy, Kirby and West. There were a surprising number of buildings on the edge of the playing area, behind the seats. There was even a pub called 'The Cricketers'.

"The pitch is bigger than I imagined." said Rita.

Rohan groaned, "Not the pitch, the field. The pitch is the strip in the centre between the wickets, where they bat," he corrected, "and the space used for the pitches is called the square."

Whatever, Rita thought. To get a good view from the centre to anything happening in the buildings beyond the boundary you would need binoculars. It occurred to Rita that, if the emergency vehicles had not had their blue lights flashing, the archery participants might easily have failed to notice anything untoward had happened at the cricket centre.

The square - as Rita now knew it to be- lay under a purple tent on wheels.

"The covers", Rohan said, "it's being protected." Rita learnt that the covers for the pitches could be moved by hand, the covers for the field were put in place by the groundsmen using tractors. Rohan pointed out where these were kept, ready for action, proud of his father's organisation.

"That's one scoreboard." said Rohan "And there's the other."

He turned to point out the two constructions which were on opposite sides of the ground. The first was minimal and modern; the second looked more like a little house.

"It looks very complicated," said Rita looking at the spaces for numbers in different boxes. She had never been sure what her brothers, Nayan in particular, who was ultra-keen, saw in a game that could last for days and end in a draw.

"You have to understand it to appreciate it" all the male members of her family had told her when she tried to talk to them while they were watching highlights from the Indian Premier League, a shorter form of cricket which, it seemed to Rita, far from inducing somnolence like the long version, created excitement and mayhem in the Patel household.

"So are Leicestershire a good cricket team? Do they win cups and stuff?" Rita had not failed to notice that Rohan has been reticent about performances. If there were a trophy cabinet on the ground, that might be linked to the murder; what if someone had been stealing from it and got disturbed? she theorised in her mind.

Rohan shook his head regretfully, shooting down her fledgling theory and confirming what her brothers had told her.

"Sorry to disappoint you. The County are going through what is sometimes called a 'dry spell' I'm afraid. We haven't won anything for ages and we can't even win a single county match at the moment!" Rohan tried to make light of the situation. "We are in Division Two, of course. We managed a few draws last year – with Kent, Glamorgan, and Essex for example; but we lost several matches, including to Hampshire, Gloucestershire, and Surrey. Some were thumping losses, like 408 runs when we lost to Derbyshire, and an innings and 78 runs against Essex. We had a few wins in the limited overs competitions, but they were rare occasions."

"Oh dear." Rita sympathised.

"But there are signs of change. They have appointed Wasim Kahn as Chief Executive Officer and he seems to have some good ideas." Rohan found a basis for optimism.

"Is he good then?" Rita asked.

"He's the first British Asian to have that role. In fact he's the first non-white chief executive of a county cricket club. But that's not why he got the job. He has a good track record. He took on the Chance to Shine Scheme – that encourages youngsters from all backgrounds to give cricket a go. He's made it into an operation turning over £50m a year!"

"Was he a professional cricketer himself?" Rita wanted to know.

"Oh, yeh, he had first class games with several counties and scored nearly 3,000 runs at an average of 30.15." Rohan reeled off various facts.

Rita smiled, assuming these statistics were good.

"He's from Birmingham, but we won't hold that against him!" Rohan joked, "And he was the first British-born Muslim to play county cricket."

"Wow!" Rita was impressed at last.

"And now Moeen Ali plays for England and is on the front cover of Wisden..." Rohan paused, noting Rita's puzzled face.

"Wisden is a kind of guide to the cricket season. It has all the statistics for each County." he explained patiently.

Rita nodded appreciatively.

"So more Asians are getting involved at county and national level." he continued, warming to his topic, "Wasim wants to get the County into Division One, as well as increase membership and get the club more involved with the local community."

Rita gave Rohan another grateful look and thought she would ask later why there were no women chief executives of cricket clubs, like Karren Brady in the football world. Rita thought she knew the answer. Although women's cricket was taking off around the world, and the Women's Ashes would be played that summer at various county grounds, she knew that it was as recently as 1999 that the first women were admitted as members of the Marylebone Cricket Club at Lords. There was a lot of catching up to do, she thought.

"There are plans for the ground, too." Rohan went on as

they continued their circuit, past the pavilion which Rita saw contained various suites named after people – 'Charles Palmer', 'Illingworth and Cottesmore', 'David Gower'. It must be in one of these suites that the care conference was held on the day of Farah's death, Rita thought, making a note to check the evidence from the inquest.

"They want to build some apartments here - lots of grounds are doing that - and reinstate a proper facility for members. So I think things will get better." Rohan said cheerfully.

"At least cricket is a civilised game." Rita offered, "In a game which breaks for lunch and tea surely no one gets seriously hurt?"

"I'm afraid they do, but fortunately not very often." Rohan told her. "There can be nasty injuries in the field. And then there was that terrible accident in Australia last November. A batsman was killed."

"Killed?" Rita could hardly believe it, "How?"

"His name was Phillip Hughes. He was hit in the neck during a match in Sydney." Rohan spoke quietly, recalling the footage he had seen of the incident.

"How could that happen?" Rita wanted to know, "They wear helmets don't they?"

"They do, but this ball missed his helmet somehow. He was attempting a hook shot." Rohan mimed the action, which Rita thought looked a bit like a baseball stroke, "He was good, too; he played for Australia. All the players were very upset."

"It must have been a shock." Rita said.

"Batsmen probably get false security from wearing their helmet. I think they may look at the design to see if it can be improved." Rohan told her.

Rita shivered to think that someone could die playing a game on a field like this.

Arriving at the cricket centre building, the first thing

they saw was the fatal fire escape, its white steps shooting out from the side of the building. In fact, as Rita had looked around she had seen several flights of steps at the ground which looked fairly precipitate. Some were fire exits, others gave access to balconies. It occurred to her that if the killer had wanted to stage such an accident he or she had had a number of possible locations to choose from.

They took some time to look at the fire escape, which zigzagged to the ground, each flight made of about a dozen steps Rita guessed. They looked up to see the flat area between the first two flights, where Farah had been found, and the doorway at the top which led to the gym.

They walked together to the door to the cricket centre and entered via the ground floor, climbing the internal steps to the gym area. Rohan used his pass, and Rita used the pass which Giles had given her, to gain access. There was one person inside, shooting backwards and forwards rapidly on a rowing machine. He had earphones and did not acknowledge their presence. There was a large cricket bag near his rowing machine, so perhaps he was one of the team, Rita thought.

"That's his coffin." Rohan whispered to her, causing Rita to give him a startled look.

"That's what cricketers call their kit bags, because they are so big." he explained, grinning. "And kind of coffin shaped."

Rita looked disdainful at this and glanced round the range of exercise machines. The gym might be small, but it was well-stocked. At the far end, near an area where there were weights and mats, Rita could see the treatment room, the place where Farah would have helped gym members who needed the attention of a physio. At the windows, and the glazed door, there were brown blinds so that privacy could be given if needed. Through the slats of the blinds Rita could see a desk on one side of the room and a treatment table on the other. To the left of the desk was a white door which, she realised from their examination outside, led to the fire escape.

The idea that Farah threw herself down a flight of these steps seemed even more unlikely now they were here. The idea of her being struck and thrown down them was also abhorrent. Rita pictured the physiotherapist in the treatment room wearing her tunic, trousers and shoes. Then Rita stopped walking for a moment, hit by a thought which had been lurking ever since she saw the list of Farah's belongings. She made a mental note for later.

Smiling at the one occupant, who was too engrossed to smile back, Rita and Rohan left the gym. On the way back down the stairs Rita, recalling what her cousins had said, made a point of asking Rohan where the toilets were and he showed her their location, next to the cricket centre, as they had said, at ground level.

Rita was happy to have viewed the scene, but frustrated that it had yielded no clues, no further information, although what she had expected to find she could not say. They climbed into her red Peugeot and set off for Saffron Lane, passing a row of shops about 200 yards from the ground, with a parking bay situated outside it. Rita, propelled by an idea that had popped into her head, suddenly indicated and swooped in.

"Hey, where are we going now?" Rohan had seen the time and was ready for his lunch. Not another of Rita's wild goose chases, he was thinking. Gratefully he noticed the shops included a Greggs, so he thought he might use the opportunity to seek out a pasty while they were there.

"I just want to try an idea," said Rita, as she dived into a charity shop, one of two in the row, she had noticed. Rohan shrugged his shoulders in resignation, "See you at the car" he said as he headed for pastry at Greggs.

* * *

The first shop raised funds for an animal charity. As well as racks of second hand clothes, it stocked mugs, bookmarks, pens, and stationery on which the outlines of endangered animals were depicted. The elephant erasers were rather cute, Rita thought, as were the panda pencil cases and the rhino rulers. The person sitting behind the till was a young girl, probably no older than Nayan it seemed to Rita, presumably she was helping here for half term. She carried on looking down at her phone until Rita attracted her attention.

"Excuse me?" Rita interrupted her.

"How can I help?" the girl was attentive now and fixed her large brown eyes on Rita, tossing back her dark hair which had fallen over her face as she stared at her phone.

"Do you sell shoes?" asked Rita, "Only I can't see any."

"No, we don't stock them." the girl replied. "We don't have the space, not with all the animal stationery we stock." She indicated the table on which pictures of whales, woodpeckers and leopards lay.

"The hospice shop at the end takes shoes, if you want to leave any." and the girl went back to her close examination of her phone screen.

"Thanks." Rita said as she left the shop. Looking down the row of establishments, she spotted the shop for the hospice. It was next to Greggs, where she spied Rohan inside, handing over money in exchange for a paper bag with grease stains on the sides. Rita gave Rohan a cheery wave, which he acknowledged, as she passed by.

In the hospice shop, the assistant was a small balding man in a knitted waistcoat with spectacles hanging round his neck. He stood by the till which was in the middle at the back of the shop. To the right of the till was a tall shelf filled with books. A brown armchair sat invitingly in front of the books for anyone wanting to stay and browse. To the left of the till were clothes, the womenswear arranged by colour- whites and greys, blues and greens, oranges and reds. Rita's heart sped up when she saw, near the clothes, several rows of boots and winter shoes.

"Are these all the shoes you have?" she asked the man at the till "I was hoping for something more summery, some sandals perhaps?"

"We haven't put the spring stuff out yet," said the assistant, "We don't do that until March."

Rita's hopes faded. Then, "Follow me," said the man, "You can look in our shoe box if you like." and Rita was escorted to a door behind the till which led to the inner sanctum of the charity shop. On the threshold the man called out, "Jocelyn!" and a tall lady with long white hair in a ponytail appeared. She was wearing a grey dress over a white polo neck top and had a large badge with the logo of the hospice on it.

"Can you help this lady look through the summer shoes please" the man asked and left Rita in her care.

"Come in!" Jocelyn welcomed. "Sit yourself down there." She indicated a wooden stool under a work bench. "I'll get the box for you." and Jocelyn seemed to disappear behind a forest of plastic bags, to re-emerge with a container bearing the legend "summer shoes".

"See if there's anything there you like and I'll price them for you." Jocelyn offered.

"They are all paired up and we only keep the better ones. We don't put out the summer stuff until March." she told Rita, repeating what the man at the till had said.

"Thanks" said Rita and she set to, unearthing shoes which were kept in pairs by elastic bands. She found some sandals with gold thongs, white ones with silver trimmings, and..

"These are what I'm looking for," said Rita, cautiously extracting a pair of black Birkenstock sandals, size 5.

"Don't you want to try them on?" Jocelyn wanted to know.

"No, thanks," said Rita. "I'll give you £10 for them?"

"That's very generous! Come through and we'll give you a receipt. Do you want a bag?" Jocelyn was very solicitous.

But Rita had already put the shoes, as carefully as she could, into a plastic bag she kept in her pocket for just such emergencies, and she shook her head.

Back at the car, Rohan was leaning on the passenger door, most of his vegetable pasty demolished.

"Got what you wanted?" he asked Rita.

"Certainly did," she replied, grinning.

Chapter 7

"When I was pitted against Virat Kohli, I gave up."
India Women's Captain
Mithali Raj who was surprised
to beat Virat Kohli to the Padma Shri,
India's fourth-highest civilian award.

Tuesday 10th February 2015 3pm

Triumphant over her success at the charity shop, Rita had called "Thanks for the tour! See you Sunday!" as she dropped off Rohan; they would be travelling back to Warwick together at the weekend. Rita headed for Uppingham Road, thinking it was just as well that Mohal didn't want the car until that evening.

Meera, Priya's sister, had texted with their rendezvous time. Rita saw a parking place near the Alternative Health Clinic, her destination, and reversed into it, using the car's sensors and sending up a silent prayer of thanks to Mr Patel- "No relation!" as she and Mohal like to joke - who had taught her to drive and bestowed patient hours on her as she attempted to parallel park.

She was just in time. Across the road, and a few cars down, she could see Meera's silver Fiesta, which she had swapped for her beloved Mini when her baby had arrived. Meera emerged from the driver's side, opened the back door and took out her son, Theeran, still in his car seat. Rita watched as Meera clipped the car seat to the buggy frame she removed from the back of the car. Rita could tell that Theeran had filled out a lot since she had last seen him a few months ago.

Meera waved to Rita as she crossed the road to join the pair. They headed for the clinic which was run by Mr and Mrs Payne- appropriate name, Rita always thought. Rita had been there several times with Priya over the years. Priya's mother, Mrs Shah, said no one but Mrs Payne could sort out her back - "I'm a martyr to it", she would say. It was Theeran who had the appointment today. No one knew what he was a martyr to as he could not yet speak although a few sounds which might develop into words were starting to emerge from his seven month old lips. Theeran was here because everyone else was a martyr to his crying, every evening, six 'til ten.

"It's as if he can tell the time!" Meera said, exasperated.

"How is he?" Rita asked as they entered the calming atmosphere of the Alternative Health Clinic with its pale green walls and water cooler.

"He's not as bad as he was." Meera conceded, "But I think it's worth persisting with the cranial treatment. It seems to calm him down for a day or two."

Only a day or two! thought Rita, it must be a nightmare!

Mr Payne appeared, wearing a blue tunic over black trousers –similar work wear to Farah's thought Rita -and he invited Meera and her offspring into his treatment room, smiling in recognition of Rita, who reciprocated. As Rita had hoped, it was not long before Mrs Payne, who was short in stature but strong looking, with dark hair cropped close to her head, appeared from another treatment room and said farewell to a grateful patient.

"Rita!" said Mrs Payne, warmly. "How lovely to see you! How are you?" Rita offered well-rehearsed sentences about how much she was enjoying Warwick. A loud baby's shout was heard from the treatment room; there was nothing wrong with Theeran's lungs it seemed.

"Oh, of course! Priya's lovely nephew!" Mrs Payne said

kindly, recognising the cry.

"A sad business about Farah Ahmadi" Rita got to the point. She was not sure how long Mrs Payne would have to talk.

"Oh, I know, and such a shock when the inquest decided it wasn't an accident. I was so hoping she'd just fallen - you know what she was like for wearing her high heels - I just cannot bear to think that someone killed her - it's so cruel." and Mrs Payne threw her arms up in the air in a gesture of despair, giving a practical demonstration of the fact that she herself remained very flexible and not in need of the attentions of the Alternative Health Clinic.

"How much time did she spend here?" Rita wanted to know next, trying to build up her picture of the victim.

"She did a day and a half a week with us." Mrs Payne said, smoothing down the edge of her blue tunic with the palms of her hands. "She was very popular, especially with the sports injury clients. We had to replace her." Mrs Payne lowered her tone to a whisper and put her hand to her mouth to prevent the receptionist from listening. There was in fact little chance of that individual eavesdropping on them. A bespectacled young man with tawny hair, he was currently engrossed on something on his computer screen, hopefully the appointments calendar and not solitaire, Rita thought to herself.

"The replacement isn't nearly so good. Not the same rapport with clients. We've lost quite a few." Mrs Payne confided.

"And the rest of her time? Where else did she practise?" Rita wanted to check what Giles and Rohan told her. Mrs Payne looked puzzled for a moment, then shook her head and tried to remember.

"Well, she advised at a couple of gyms. One at the cricket ground, of course, where she died..." she paused, "The other was at a leisure centre used by a lot of runners, I believe.

She'd tell me about the costumes some of them wore to raise money for charity. People are so crazy!" Mrs Payne smiled at the memory.

"Anywhere else?" Rita prompted.

"A couple of care homes, just an afternoon now and again, helping the residents to stay flexible and sorting out aches and pains." Mrs Payne's eyes were raised as she tried to remember.

Another cry could be heard from the treatment room, followed by Meera's soothing tones.

"We certainly deal with all age groups!" Mrs Payne rose to go.

"And she had a baby?" Rita was determined to find out what she could.

"Yes, that's right. A little poppet called Lucy. It's probably about a year since she was born." Mrs Payne confirmed.

"Farah took time off?" Rita checked.

"Yes, well just a couple of weeks." Mrs Payne confirmed.

Rita looked confused.

"Farah wasn't the birth mother." Mrs Payne said, seeing Rita's confusion. "Her partner, Maria, was the one who carried the baby. But once Lucy was born they both looked after her. I think Farah was thinking of cutting out one of the gyms to have more time with the child."

"And you returned any belongings she left here to Maria I suppose?" Rita asked.

"We did, yes," Mrs Payne spoke slowly. "It was a bit awkward. We didn't want to upset her, so we asked the brother what we should do, but he was a bit short to be honest, well rude I'd call it, so in the end we had to bite the bullet and arrange to go and see Maria. It was a difficult time I suppose, but there we are..." Mrs Payne's voice tailed off as her husband called out to her. Rita thought she had drawn a blank; there was nothing more to find here.

"Just a moment." Mrs Payne said, "I almost forgot!" she

turned back to Rita, replying to her husband, "I'll be there in a minute."

"Yesterday, we were clearing out the desk in the second treatment room – Farah and I shared it – when we came across her diary. It must have been a personal one, the police had her professional one I'm sure." as she spoke, Mrs Payne hurried into the second treatment room and emerged soon afterwards with a slim volume in a purple leather effect cover.

"I was going to get round to giving it to Maria." said Mrs Payne.

"I'm seeing Maria this week, to offer my condolences over the inquest and so on." Rita said, quickly making up her mind to do so.

"Oh, OK then. Take it with you if you would." Mrs Payne said, clearly happy to avoid another awkward meeting with Farah's partner.

"Lovely to see you." Mrs Payne said as she moved towards the first treatment room.

While she waited for Meera, Rita flicked through the diary. She turned to the week of Farah's death and could not help emitting a low whistle. There was only one entry. On 14th July it said simply 'R.2.30'.

How strange that the letter 'R', which marked the spot in the car park where the Plantagenet King had lain, might now provide a clue as to who killed Farah, thought Rita.

Tuesday 10th February 2015 6pm

"Have you registered to vote?" Rita was sitting on her bed in her room at Elm Drive, skyping Priya. They were talking about the general election due to take place later that year.

"Not yet, have you?" Priya replied.

"Of course, and so should you!" Rita was indignant. "We have a voice; we should make the most of the chance to use it! It is so easy, you can do it on-line."

"OK Mrs Pankhurst!" Priya laughed, "I will register."

"Seriously, from trolls to the Taliban men are trying to keep women quiet. We need to show we won't be silenced!" Rita was vehement.

"Yeh, I know. There's a lot of talk in college about women being attacked at night, or getting wolf whistles and abuse in the street. Some men seem to think they can get away with anything. We need to find ways to show that they can't!" Priya was sympathetic.

"You should hear how some of the students talk – the men about the women I mean – it's so patronising." Rita warmed to her theme. She had heard these comments from male students on her corridor. It was another reason she wanted to live elsewhere.

"Men must feel threatened. You only attack if you feel you need to defend yourself." Priya opined.

"But threatened by us? Honestly!" Rita was sceptical.

"Well maybe not just women, but the power we have over them? Their feelings towards us? Women are a threat and must be silenced. Why else do some Muslim communities put women in veils and cover their mouths? Even their hands and eyes, like ISIS do? What more of a symbol do you need?"

"But Islam believes in equality" Rita retorted, recalling something that a friend of Mohal's had told her.

"Well it's not doing it very well if you ask me." Priya was indignant. "In our training we have to learn about cultural sensitivities. Women who need to be examined only by women is one. Do you know what happens in Saudi Arabia? Male guardians have to agree before a woman can visit a doctor and sex segregation is enforced in the workplace. Women have no legal rights and need the permission of their guardian to bring proceedings, even if their complaint is against that guardian!"

"We are lucky to be living here and now." Rita said.

"You bet. But then look at those girls going out to Syria

to be jihadi brides. Can they really understand what is involved? However promiscuously some people in the UK behave, it cannot be worth giving up your freedoms for that kind of slavery, can it?" Priya was incredulous.

"No, I think you're right, of course" Rita said recalling newspaper articles about school girls who had left for Syria. "I gather if the husband dies the girl gets given to another fighter. I don't think she has any choice. But if you look at the websites…"Rita had been on the internet to see what sort of propaganda was influencing girls from relatively comfortable backgrounds to leave the safety and security of home in England for the uncertainty of a battle-torn land thousands of miles away.

"What do they say?" Priya asked.

"It makes it sound like they can have it all. Big houses, strong husbands. They tell them lots of well-known brands are available – food, cosmetics and toiletries. The most telling phrase I think is 'the Caliphate has been established' as if it is a settled thing, and as if it would almost be a sin not to go there ." Rita told her.

"Terrible propaganda!" said Priya.

"It's very clever and plausible." Rita told her. "It's like grooming. A woman who went over there provides a list of what the girls should bring with them. And they travel to countries like Turkey before they cross into Syria. It makes it hard for their families and the authorities to stop them."

"And even if the Qur'an supports equality, how does that explain segregation – separating men and women at meetings and those schools where they have tried to introduce segregation?" Priya pressed on. "Now I hear they are planning to have a separate mosque for women in Bradford because the men say there is no room for the women in the current mosque – that's not an excuse!."

"I don't know when we will treat people equally" Rita sighed, "Look at the caste system, after all. And lots of religions and institutions have practised some sort of separation. Look at your Oxford colleges, first women couldn't get degrees at all, then the colleges were single sex; it's only relatively recently that they have been open to men and women."

"Yes, I know," Priya answered her, "Many societies have tended to favour boys, haven't they? Look at India where female literacy and education lag behind even though there has been a massive growth in female employment and business ownership."

"Yes," agreed Rita, "We have got a long way to go. All the more reason to vote, and not listen to the extremists." Rita asserted.

"Anyway, how's reading week going?" Priya decided it was time to change to another subject.

"Not getting much work done!" Rita admitted, "But I am making progress with the death of Farah Ahmadi" and she told her friend about her finds.

"Do you think the shoes might have traces of blood on them? Or fingerprints, or DNA?" Priya was intrigued.

"Hard to tell." Rita conceded. "There are some marks and you never know what forensics might turn up."

"And the diary?" Priya prompted. "Who do you think the mysterious 'R' might be?"

"Obviously I think it's Rashid, her brother. He was there at the cricket ground and he had an argument with Maria, Farah's partner, at the inquest." Rita told her friend. "I think the police should look at him again and I intend to tell Inspector Bridge when I hand the items to him!" she said enthusiastically.

Chapter

8

"The bat is not a toy. It's a weapon. It gives me everything in life. Which helps me to do everything on the field."

Virat Kohli Indian,
international cricketer.

Wednesday 11th February 2015 11am

"What do you mean he's busy?"

The next day, still fired by her enthusiasm for her theory, and armed with her 'evidence', Rita had gone to Mansfield Street police station in the town centre. She tried to have a conversation with a civilian police clerk through a Perspex screen.

"I wanted to show him something, something that might be relevant to an inquiry." Rita explained.

"I'm sorry, Madam, Inspector Bridge is tied up today. I can ask someone else on his team if they can spare the time?"

The clerical assistant, in her forties, a one-woman ecological disaster zone, with hair and skin whose colour- bright red and bronze respectively - could only have derived from chemical application, looked sceptically at Rita.

"Or you could leave it with me and I'll pass it on." she offered.

"No, no" said Rita quickly. "I need to explain. It won't make sense otherwise."

The assistant looked doubtful again, as if she thought it unlikely that anything Rita had to say would make sense.

"I'll try Constable Gardner." the clerk said reluctantly and she turned her back to Rita to make the call. Rita did not move. She was not to be deflected.

The assistant turned to face Rita again. "If you would just sit over there?" she waved at a row of plastic seats which were folded against the wall on the side opposite the counter; their appearance was like that of seating in a bus station. The apparent intention was to prevent visitors from making themselves comfortable here, Rita thought.

"OK." Rita said slowly and she took herself and her possessions to the indicated area.

To pass the time, Rita read the posters on the walls; these advertised numbers to ring to report a crime or get victim support. There was also one for the Samaritans and one for a rape crisis centre. This must be the 'Big Society' thought Rita. The police were so under-resourced that they needed to point you in any direction but themselves. This fitted with her experience at the police station nearest to her home. Ostensibly 'open', it had no front door and invited those wishing to use its services to call a number and leave a message so they could be called back, or to contact them on-line. Rita had wanted to see a real person to hand over her treasures; the clerk behind the desk might be the nearest thing, she supposed, if no officer could be summoned.

The walls reminded Rita of her first term at uni, when there seemed to be a poster for every society and activity, as well as reminders of things that needed to be done -'Don't be a blockhead, be a sochead!' 'Have you enrolled on your course?' 'The SU needs you!' She had enthusiastically done all that was recommended before she went to Warwick, including on-line enrolment, using a photo she had uploaded, paying fees and sorting out her accommodation, and registering for access to all relevant IT accounts. There had been information required by the health centre and an 'Eating at Warwick' account which would make it easier for her to eat around the campus. Rita had also joined Warwick Sport so she could do a gym workout and some jogging at the sports field.

After her parents had left her in her accommodation that first day – saying with false cheer "You'll be fine" and "See you soon!"- she had been surprised how difficult she had found that first evening. Everyone who, like Rita, had arrived on Friday-her parents needed to be at their dental surgery for the private patients on Saturday- had gathered in the kitchen and exchanged names, studying the many posters in the kitchen concerning food hygiene and various uni organisations and helplines. Freshers' week activities would start the next day, so they were free to familiarise themselves with the campus.

Rita had chosen to eat with a group of Chinese students from another corridor; they had seemed less intimidating than some of the others who appeared to Rita full of confidence and sure of themselves. From the stories which had been swapped in the kitchen she had learnt that their ages varied from between 18 and 21. A few of the students had taken gap years before starting uni; others had come to Warwick having tried out another uni and not been happy. Two of the girls seemed to be there with their boyfriends, some were already eyeing up other students with a view to pairing up. Drink was a big topic of conversation. That was when Rita started to feel she had little in common with them, she thought.

Things had improved the next day at the Freshers' Fair in the SU Atrium. Rita had filled her pink satchel bag, which she had brought to uni in preference to her red Cath Kidston bag, with leaflets and freebies. It was in discovering there was an Asian Society that she had first met Sammi, who had been at their display with friends from his shared house. In the evening she had gone with Sammi and his companions to the Club MTV Welcome Party, but they quickly decided it was not for them and had bought Indian snacks and sweets from the campus shop and taken them back to Rita's room to eat.

Sammi and Krishna had rearranged her room, swapping her desk and bed around, and Daz and Siva had made decorating suggestions - get some cushions! Get some posters! Check out Pinterest for ideas!

On Monday, she and Sammi's crowd had gone to the indoor market. Together they bought items from a vintage stall and found some turquoise elephant cushions and a matching bedspread for Rita's room. She was pleased with these; they complemented the china elephants she had brought from home which doubled as candle holders. She had spent some of Monday afternoon at the house shared by Sammi, Krishna, Daz and Siva before she returned to her accommodation. She had fallen asleep watching YouTube clips and woke in the early hours. Going to the kitchen to make a sandwich, she had found some of her fellow inmates the worse for wear after over-enthusiasm at a paint party. They kept giggling about how they had glowed in the dark because of the water-based fluorescent uv paint which was splashed about.

Most of her hall mates had been too ill the next day to go to the Sports Fair, but Rita went and that was when she saw for the first time the video about to be launched called "This Girl Can", a film to encourage women to take part in sport and not worry about their appearance when doing so. Rita thought it was pretty good, but she would have liked to have seen a wider range of women represented, such as the hijab-wearing girls at school who played netball and the modest costumes now available to help girls of certain backgrounds not to feel awkward about swimming.

On Wednesday, all the Societies made their pitches for new members and Rita found herself torn between so many it was hard to choose. Thursday was the Democracy Fair. As her older brother was interested in politics, Rita found this interesting and some lively debates had ensued about whether it was worth voting. "Look how the Liberal

Democrats lied about tuition fees!" one young man said. "Russell Brand says it's a waste of time to vote." another had shouted. Rita had retorted "Suffragettes died for our right to vote!" and followed this remark up with "And there are so many countries where voting isn't allowed! We are the lucky ones!" This earned her a round of applause.

The next day was the Volunteering Fair and Rita had signed up to help do some canal path clearing with a local environmental group. In between times, she had checked out the Library and the online undergraduate skills programme, which she planned to benefit from, and registered her modules for the year. By the weekend she had been impatient to get down to some history studies at last.

As Rita waited for Constable Gardner to turn up, her memories of her first term were disturbed by the sound of her phone; it was a Bollywood ringtone, Zuby Zuby, which made her want to dance whenever her phone rang.

"Miss Patel?" a male voice said in a clipped Scottish accent.

Oh dear, another cold caller, Rita thought; no she hasn't had an accident that wasn't her fault and she didn't have PPI, she rehearsed in her head.

"I'm Andrew Brown from Leighton's," he named a large firm of solicitors in Leicester. What could they want with me? Rita wondered. Surely they didn't know she was at the police station?

"I am calling you about Richard Gregson." Now Rita was surprised. Mr Gregson was an old friend, in every sense. Her uncle, Bandhu, had introduced them when Rita had needed help with a history project. But Mr Gregson had also once lived in the house next door to Rita's parents', in Elm Drive, and had helped cast some light on a death which Rita had investigated. He was a kindly man who lived in a residential home. Rita felt guilty, suddenly; she had not seen him since the summer, when she had helped him over the disappearance of one of the residents. Why was this solicitor calling her about him now? she wondered, fear starting to tighten her stomach.

"I'm sorry to have to tell you that he has passed away." the man continued as if using a euphemism would dampen the effect of the news.

"Oh dear," said Rita, "When did it happen?" she asked, feeling bad that she had not made more effort to visit Mr Gregson.

"A couple of weeks ago." the man told her, and Rita felt a sinking feeling. Mr Gregson had set off on his next journey and she did not know.

"Was there a funeral?" she asked next, not sure if the legal adviser would know.

"Oh yes, Mr Gregson had put arrangements in train with us." he assured her, as if this was just another legal transaction. "We attended, together with some staff from the care home." Oh dear, Rita felt sadder now and started to slump down against the wall which was behind the plastic seat at the police station. She recalled that Mr Gregson had no children and his wife had died a few years before. The only relative she could remember him speaking of was a nephew in New Zealand.

As if reading her thoughts, the solicitor said, "We are liaising with his nephew in New Zealand about the estate. That's why I'm ringing." Rita was puzzled.

"There are some photographs he put aside which he wanted you to have," Andrew Brown explained in his Scottish accent "If it's alright with you, you could collect them from the nursing home, and it will save them from getting damaged in the post."

Rita thought she might as well, since she was in Leicester anyway, so " OK" she said and the call ended as she added this to her list of things to do, her chances of getting any actual reading done in reading week receding. Poor Mr

Gregson, having no family to arrange his funeral and wish him a safe passage. She would light candles for him she thought, adding this to her ever-expanding list of distractions.

Rita was still remembering Mr Gregson when Constable Gardner appeared to disturb her thoughts and buzzed herself through to where Rita was sitting.

"Miss Patel?" Rita looked up to see a round-faced black woman beaming at her, her hands clasped together in front of her substantial frame, her thick dark hair tamed with a large plastic band across the top of her head. She wore black trousers under a long white shirt which had a black edge around the collar. The police officer no doubt aimed to look smart and efficient but, possibly because of the call she had just taken, the effect she had achieved was closer to that of a funeral director, Rita thought.

As she looked at the officer some more, Rita was fairly sure they had met before. When Mohal was accused of murder, she was one of the officers who had searched their house at 10 Elm Drive.

"You have something to give us?" the Constable said hopefully, still smiling.

"Yes," said Rita, "I think I should explain."

"You'd better come through then." said the older woman still smiling and she took Rita through the grey security door, turning them left into a corridor of grey doors, reminding Rita of her old school, and she opened one of the doors, marked 'Interview Room 3', changing the sign on the outside from 'Vacant' to 'Interview in Progress'.

"Lucky there's a room free or we'd be doing this in the corridor." the Constable half joked as she indicated a plastic chair for Rita to sit in and drew up another so she was sitting facing her.

"Now, how can I help you?" Constable Gardner still wore her smile. Rita wondered if she ever stopped.

"It's about the death of Farah Ahmadi." Rita started.

"Oh yes?" the smile continued.

"I heard about the inquest verdict." Rita pressed on.

"Did you now?" Constable Gardner nodded.

"I heard you were interviewing people again." Rita was finding this harder than she thought.

"Were you there? At the ground? On that day? I don't remember you from the lists." the Constable was still smiling but she had raised one eyebrow.

"Well, no, but…" Rita hesitated, searching for how to explain her interest.

"Then how can you help us? We have a lot to do you know." the officer's smile did not waiver despite her words.

"Well, I've found a couple of things." Rita tried again.

"Found? What things?" There was nothing wrong with Constable Gardner's listening skills it seemed. She looked down at Rita's satchel bag.

"Well, my brother was at the inquest." Rita tried another way in.

"Was he? Why?" the officer asked in even tones.

"He's a journalist, or he's going to be, it was an assignment." Rita paused, not sure why she was talking about Mohal.

"Do go on" Constable Gardner prompted, looking at her watch. She was still making no attempt to take any notes, Rita saw. She was unsure that the police officer was taking her seriously.

"So I knew Farah" Rita tried another tack.

"Did you? How?" again, Constable Gardner spoke smoothly; Rita felt as if she was not being believed. It was as if she could see her words sliding down the side of a steep hill every time she spoke.

"I met her a couple of times" she explained.

"So you didn't 'know' her." Rita could hear the quotation marks as the police officer spoke.

"Not exactly. She worked at a Health Clinic. I used to go there to keep my friend company while…" Rita was losing her grip on her words.

Constable Gardner was nodding but she looked up at the clock on the wall.

Rita took the hint and got to her conclusion.

"Well, that's not important. Anyway, when I saw her at work, in her uniform, she wore black Birkenstocks on her feet. She only put on her stilettos when she left at the end of the day."

"And?" the smile was looking a little frozen now. The officer's eyes had stopped twinkling.

"And I knew you only found the stilettos." Rita continued "So I tried the charity shops."

"You tried the charity shops," repeated the officer, as if Rita needed to be humoured.

"Mmmn. The ones near the cricket ground, on Saffron Lane." Rita confirmed.

"You've been to the cricket ground? At Grace Road?" the Constable leant forward.

"Yes, I went to have a look…" Rita hesitated, thinking this made her sound bad, and went on "but anyway, the point is…"

"The point is?" Constable Gardner echoed.

"I asked at the second one, the first didn't have any, and I found these…"

Rita reached down to her satchel bag and produced the plastic bag with the size 5 Birkenstocks in it, opening the top for the officer to look in.

She offered the bag to Constable Gardner who seemed reluctant to touch it at first. The officer looked from bag to Rita and back again for a few moments.

"What do you want me to do with this?" the Constable asked, the smile finally melting from her mouth.

"Well, test them!" Rita said indignantly "There's a mark that might have been blood…"

"You've checked them over already?" still the officer

refused to take the bag.

"I was as careful as I could be. I put them in the bag as soon as I found them. I touched them as little as possible." Rita's tone was pleading, "Please, I really think this is important."

Constable Gardner sighed. "Oh, very well, I'll take them, but I can't promise to do anything with them. We haven't the resources to check every pair of shoes that walks in here." she said.

"Thank you," said Rita, then, as it looked as though the Constable wanted to leave the room, "There's something else." she added.

"Something else." the police officer, who had half risen, sat down again, placing the bag of shoes on the floor and clasping her hands together, either to indicate she was listening, or in prayer, Rita could not be sure.

"Yes. I went to the Alternative Health Clinic, where Farah worked." Rita explained.

"We are aware of her workplaces." the Constable had stopped repeating Rita's words and started to sound defensive.

"Well, I spoke to Mrs Payne, who owns the clinic with her husband." Rita felt she was not explaining this at all well either.

"Yes?" Constable Gardner sounded like she wanted Rita to hurry up.

"And she said she'd just found this diary. It belonged to Farah. It was in a drawer in a desk which…" Rita caught the disapproving look in the Constable's face.

"Well it doesn't matter now. There it is." Rita took the diary from her satchel bag.

"And you've touched it?" the Constable said as she stood to put on disposable gloves which she took from a box on a wall of the interview room.

"I said I would take it to Farah's partner." Rita found herself saying.

"To save Mrs Payne the trouble. But then I saw the entry

on July 14th, the day Farah died, and I thought you'd be interested." Rita summoned up an enthusiastic tone in the hope it might be catching. It wasn't.

Constable Gardner looked sceptically at Rita, then took the diary with her gloved hands, turned to the relevant page and read the appointment.

"'R', you see?" Rita pressed home her point, "Well, it could be her brother, Rashid, couldn't it? He was at the ground that day and…"

"Well, thank you Miss Patel." the police officer stood up firmly this time to indicate the interview was over.

"We may need a statement from you in due course." the Constable ushered Rita from the room, carrying the 'evidence' with her.

"I think you've had contact with us before," Constance Gardner said.

As if I am a criminal or something, Rita thought.

"So if we need you, I daresay we have your contact details?" the police officer checked.

Rita nodded.

As they reached the door, the Constable finished, "And can I suggest that you leave the detective work up to us? We're trained for it, you know!" the smile returned to the Constable's lips, but her eyes were not smiling.

"OK, thanks." Rita said and left the police station, her satchel bag lighter, and her heart heavier. Would the police take any notice of her suspicions, and test the shoes? She could not be sure.

Chapter 9

"I want to give my six hours of serious cricket on the ground and then take whatever the result."
Sachin Tendulkar,
Indian international cricketer

Thursday 12th February 2015 2pm

The next day, with a heavy heart, Rita had driven to Oak Trees Care Home. She realised this was probably the last visit she would make. It all felt very sad. Mr Gregson, with his large grey moustache and twinkling eyes, had been a good friend. Rita parked her car at the care home in Thurmaston, used the new entry phone – it was not there last time she called- to get inside Oak Trees and asked at the reception desk about the photographs which Richard Gregson had left for her. A care worker, wearing a brown tabard over a black top and trousers, ushered her into an office which was located behind the desk, then disappeared to find the photographs.

Rita noticed the tabards, which all the care workers were dressed in, were brown, a different colour to those worn when she had been there last. There was a new banner in brown by the desk too. This declared that the home was under new ownership and was now in the Acorn Homes chain.

While she sat tucked away in the office, two other care workers came to the reception desk, absorbed in a conversation which Rita could not avoid hearing.

"Mrs Massood does not want any questions asked. Just do your job and go home, that's my advice, if you want to keep your job. She was hopping mad when Farah said she'd tell the inspectors what she'd seen. Well they should have been more careful in front of her, of course." Voice 1 was a woman with a local accent.

"Farah? I don't think I know who she is?" asked Voice 2, a man's voice with a soft tone and a foreign accent, maybe Spanish or Italian, Rita thought.

"You wouldn't know her. She used to be a physio here, but she's not here now. Anthony does her visits and he keeps himself to himself." Voice 1 said with authority.

Rita was sitting very still now, hoping to hear more. They could only be talking about Farah Ahmadi. What was it that she had threatened to disclose? The talking stopped abruptly as Rita heard the footsteps of the care worker returning with her photographs.

"There we are!" he said brightly and handed over a large brown envelope. Rita thanked him and took the package to the car to examine in privacy, pausing to look back once more at the Home and to recall the help and kindness which Mr Gregson had shown her in the past.

Back in the car, Rita could wait no longer and slid her fingers under the sealed flap to open the envelope. Inside were photographs and a memory stick; presumably there were copies of the pictures on the stick, Rita thought. The photos were black and white pictures taken by newspaper photographers and depicted the arrival in Leicester in the 1970s of Asian families from East Africa. Mr Gregson had been on the Council at the time and must have come by the photographs in that capacity, Rita guessed as she studied them. This was part of her parents' history. She had to show them. It would bring back memories.

Before leaving the car park, Rita looked up 'Mrs Massood' on her phone, having picked up the name mentioned in the care workers' conversation she had overheard. What could Farah have witnessed which so alarmed her? Rita wondered. She found that Ramlah Massood was in her mid-forties and an influential businesswoman in the East Midlands. Apparently, she owned the Acorn Chain of half a dozen care homes and had shares in a couple of gyms as well. There was a picture of her receiving a business award the previous year. Rita was surprised to see that she recognised the woman; she was the person who had been having the animated phone conversation with "Shakira" at the gym the other day. It seemed she never rested from her business concerns, Rita was thinking, as her phone started to ring - 'Zuby, Zuby'.

She saw it was her mother's mobile number, a rare event; Padma usually waited until she got home from the surgery to make family calls and used the phone in the house. Rita went through a check-list in her head as she started to answer the call; was she late? no; was there something she was supposed to have done? no. Rita could only guess; perhaps her younger brother, Nayan, who was about to start driving lessons with Mr Patel needed a lift somewhere and wouldn't ask her himself?

"Oh Rita, when are you coming home? Are you on your way?" her mother sounded agitated.

"Coming, Mum" she tried to sound reassuring. "I'm just at Thurmaston, about to leave."

"You're not driving? I don't want to talk to you if you're driving." her mother asked anxiously.

"No, Mum, I haven't started yet. What's the matter?" Rita decided to ask, since it was clear from her mother's tone that there was something wrong.

"It's your father, Rita; he's been taken ill at the surgery." Padma sounded flustered.

"What kind of ill? And where is he now?" Rita asked two questions at once.

"We're at the Infirmary. He's having some tests. They think.." her mother paused before she said the words, "They think he may have had a heart attack!"

"Oh no," said Rita, stunned into dropping her car keys, the

envelope and its contents, into the well beneath the pedals of the car. "How is he? What happened?" in her shock she couldn't stop asking multiple questions.

"He had pains in his arm, and then he collapsed. I wasn't there. Aisha saw it happen." her mother named one of the dental nurses at the practice. "She got him to sit in a chair and called an ambulance. I came with him to the Infirmary of course. But I wanted to ask you to go home and bring Nayan over here." her mother's voice was insistent, as if Rita was going to argue!

"You think we should come?" Rita was frightened now. Her mother must be worried if she wanted Rita and her brothers there. In most crises she usually managed on her own and told them about it afterwards. "Yes I do." Padma was firm. "Mohal is already in town, at the library, he's getting a taxi here."

Now Rita knew this was an emergency. When had her older brother ever taken a taxi?

"OK, Mum, you hang in there and give Dad my love. I'll get there with Nayan as soon as I can." Rita replied.

"Drive carefully" her mother remembered to say before she ran off.

Rita felt around in the foot well until she located the photos and her keys. As she picked them up she saw her hands were shaking. She took a deep intake of breath and exhaled it slowly through puffed-out cheeks before she put the key in the ignition and set off for Elm Drive.

Thursday 12th February 2015 3pm

As she drove along, Rita realised she had forgotten to ask her mother if she had called Nayan. She assumed she had and that he would be as anxious as she now felt. What was happening to her father? Would he be alright? How had this happened? There seemed to have been no warning. As well as her anxiety about her father, Rita was concerned for her mother. She would be worrying so much! If either of them were going to have a heart attack she would have thought it would be her mother, who was always fussing and had to have things 'just so'. Her father was usually more laid-back and easy-going.

Rita hardly noticed the journey or the other cars on the road but she must have travelled safely on 'automatic pilot' as there were no incidents and as she steered into Elm Drive she could see her younger brother standing outside the glazed front door of their house, anxiously checking each car that turned into the road. He ran down their drive when he saw the red Peugeot, raced to the passenger side and jumped in, as if his speed would somehow assist his father's recovery.

"Mum rang you then?" Rita asked as she pulled away and headed for Leicester Royal Infirmary.

"What do think happened? Was he overdoing it, do you think? He's been in a bit of a bad mood recently, do you think that has anything to do with it?" in his fear Nayan spoke in a stream of consciousness.

"Mum said he was in the surgery, so it sounds like he was just doing his normal thing. We'll find out more when we get there." Rita was matter-of-fact, trying not to speculate, "He'll be fine, you know." she looked across at her brother, trying to convey a reassurance she did not feel herself.

"Mohal will be with Mum by the time we get there." Rita added after a while as they waited at a set of traffic lights; she was trying not to feel impatient with the other cars, but, now she was more aware of them, she was finding them annoying. Take the car immediately in front of them, for instance, which decided to wait for a parking space and blocked the road. Didn't they realise she was on an emergency? At last Havelock Street and the car park appeared and Rita began the search for a free space.

"There!" Nayan was a useful scout and spotted one not

too far from the entrance. Parking quickly, the siblings raced to the building and A & E, anxiously seeking out the faces of their mother and brother.

"Hi" Mohal was there, looking uncomfortable on a blue plastic chair, his body leaning forward, his hands together as if in supplication. Mohal's long dark fringe had been ruffled by his fingers and bits of it were sticking up, making him appear alarmed. He looked up at Rita and Nayan,

"Mum's with him now. He's in one of those cubicles. You should wait here with me." Mohal's voice was unusually strained. The fear and worry had communicated themselves to him, too, Rita saw.

Rita and Nayan sat in chairs either side of their older brother.

"How is he?" Rita asked.

"Mum said he was in pain." Nayan put in.

"Yeh, he started complaining about his arm. Aisha realised something was going on. By the time the ambulance got there he was saying there was pressure in his chest and his jaw was tight, Mum said. The paramedics were great apparently;they slapped an oxygen mask on him, and gave him aspirin. Now he's attached to a load of monitors and they've given him nitro-glycerine."

"Nitro-glycerine! That's an explosive isn't it?" Nayan was fascinated.

"It thins the blood or something, helps it flow more easily, and saves the heart some work." Mohal tried to remember what the doctor had said when she spoke to his mother.

"Oh,OK." Nayan tried to grasp what Mohal meant.

"Will he need an operation do you think?" Rita asked, thinking she would speak to Priya later and get the benefit of her medical advice.

"They don't know yet. They might do a procedure that opens up an artery or they may use clot-busting drugs." Mohal shook his head slowly; this was all too much to take in.

"Do you want some water?" Nayan stood up to go to the water cooler, anything to keep busy, to keep moving; he could not bear to sit still and wait for bad news to emerge from behind the curtain. His siblings nodded, so Nayan ferried plastic cups to their seats until all three had water to sip.

Their mother appeared, weighed down by her own jacket and that of their father. Mohal relieved her of these while Rita found her a chair and Nayan went for another cup of water.

"Thank you, thank you." Padma gasped.

"How is he?" Rita asked anxiously.

"Oh, you know your father! He's trying to laugh it off but he's worried, really, I can tell. They are doing some more tests now. They've given him some pain relief but it doesn't seem to be helping. I don't know..." Padma's voice failed her as her words ran out and she wiped tears from behind her brown designer frame glasses. Rita had never seen her mother so helpless. She put her arm round her.

"I'll be alright." Their mother shook her head of curly brown hair and adjusted the frames on her squat nose, setting her shoulders back and taking some sips of the water. "You should go to see him soon. He'd like that." she told her children.

As they waited impatiently for the doctors to finish their tests, the four became aware of a commotion rippling its way through A & E and heading for them, like an earth tremor. The noise was generated by the group around a figure clad in her trademark green tracksuit. It was the runner Rosie Hunter making a surprise visit to the hospital. She paused to speak to everyone, visitors and patients alike, extending her sympathy and best wishes as she went. Her entourage of helpers also shook hands and offered help in the form of hot drink vouchers. There were many pauses so that selfies could be taken with the celebrity athlete. When she reached the Patel family she seemed to sense that things were tense around them. "I hope you get some good news soon." was all she said, briefly shining the beam of her smile on them, and then she swept on, exiting by a door which Rita had not noticed before, presumably the group were on their way to a ward.

Just as they had passed through the door, a doctor appeared and told them that Jahi could have visitors again, "But don't excite him. Keep it calm in there." was her instruction as she moved on to treat another patient.

Rita walked slowly towards her father's cubicle, wanting to see how he was but feeling apprehensive; she was dreading that he would look very ill and weak. She found him, to her relief, in good spirits - or pretending to be.

"Come in! Come in!" he welcomed them, "All my children together! It must be my birthday!" The siblings grinned at this, a typical comment.

"How are you all?" he asked, "I am sorry to drag you down here." Then he winced and paused for breath. Rita realised his breathing was not even; it was coming in short bursts.

Rita sat on a chair by the bed and took her father's hand.

"Don't tire yourself." she said comfortingly, "We're here to make sure you get better, and to look after Mum."

Jahi gave his daughter's hand a squeeze.

"I'll be right as rain soon." he said and lay back on his pillow to catch his breath again.

Rita looked at the monitors which were checking her father's heart rate and blood pressure. Numbers were flashing and lines were wiggling across the screens. As long as none of the alarms goes off, she thought; the shock would be enough to finish anyone off, never mind her father in his weakened state.

"Have they given you a scan?" Rita had messaged Priya and this had been one of the things she had mentioned.

"Oh yes," Jahi said, "They have these clever machines now.

They can scan you while you lie here. It's like scanning goods in a shop." Rita was surprised to learn the procedure was so easily done, but pleased to know the doctors had done what Priya mentioned.

"They think they can fix me with medication. I can go home soon." their father said.

Go home? Rita was horrified. What if her father had another heart attack? Surely this was the best place for him to be?

The doctor returned and the siblings removed themselves to the waiting area, sending in their mother to hear the latest news. Rita thought about the photographs waiting in her car. She hoped her father would soon be well enough to look at them. A trip down memory lane might be just what he needed to cheer him up. He was her priority now; she would leave the case of Farah Ahmadi to the police, she resolved.

Chapter 10

"Cricket- a game which the English, not being a spiritual people, have invented in order to give themselves some conception of eternity."

Lord Moncroft 1979

Friday 13th February 2015 3pm

Rita's resolution to concentrate on her father's condition lasted almost a day. Life became difficult as soon as Jahi came home and her mother was standing guard. The atmosphere at home was so intense that Rita decided she needed to escape to see Priya. She wanted to talk face to face about her father's condition, and she couldn't wait until Holi the next month; in any case she doubted her friend's resolve to turn up for the celebrations since Priya had been back to Leicester so little after she had started at Oxford. Rita worried that her friend was working too hard – another excuse to go and see her.

Priya was studying medicine at Merton college- "It's really called the Pre-Clinical course", Priya always corrected Rita. Whatever it was called, Rita thought it seemed to be all-consuming. Her friend barely came home during the Christmas holidays-"I have so much reading to do!" was her excuse- and she had not been back this week even though most of their friends were at home. Priya said when challenged "I need to make the most of this opportunity. I must work to qualify. I can't afford to get behind. You can't imagine how much there is to learn!"

So Rita found herself on the platform at Leicester station, just twenty four hours after her father had been in hospital, grimacing as she recalled the way her mother had organised everything following her father's discharge. She had allocated him a chair in the kitchen from which he could see his garden, operate the television, and talk to her while she prepared his meals. Padma had downloaded a number of recipes containing the sort of ingredients which were advocated on one of the many information leaflets Rita's father had brought home from the Infirmary. With the leaflets, the discharge paperwork, and the drugs, it was as well that there had been four of them to help him when the time came for him to leave the Medical Assessment Unit, Rita had thought.

"As we are not operating, we won't admit him to cardiology, we would only watch and wait, which he can do more comfortably at home." the doctor had said, adding that they would make an appointment for him to be seen at Glenfield, the cardiac treatment centre, "for monitoring purposes".

Rita was unsure about the use of 'comfortably'. While Jahi tried to adjust to the idea that he had had a heart attack, the rest of the family were anxious not to precipitate another. Her brothers were being unusually kind and helpful and observing a self-imposed ceasefire in their fraternal hostilities and banter. Padma was intending to steer all news of the dental surgery, its finances, patients and day to day concerns, away from Jahi, which meant that she was flustered – torn between the need to give Jahi her attention, the meals she wanted to cook for him, and the business decisions which needed to be made. Rita was avoiding further discussion of her unhappiness with her university accommodation and had not broached again the opportunity offered by Sammi. The heart medication was on a tray on the grey counter, together with all the emergency numbers they needed in case Jahi took a turn for the worse, so no one could forget for an instant what had happened. While Jahi was 'comfortable' his family members were walking on egg shells.

"You are not to sit around all day." Padma had lectured her husband. "Gentle exercise is required, a short walk at least once an hour." She had set an alarm on his phone to remind him to take this step, and every half an hour the alarm rang out loudly, putting everyone's nerves on edge.

The train to Birmingham pulled in. It was a short, three coach, affair, stopping at Nuneaton and Coleshill Parkway according to the electronic information scurrying along the board; it looked more like a bus than a train, but Rita would be on it only for about 50 minutes before she changed for Oxford. An announcement regretted the lack of 'at seat refreshments' by which the operator meant the trolley of hot drinks, plastic-covered sandwiches, crisps and chocolate bars which were often peddled between the carriages. The failure was 'due to earlier staff shortages' apparently. Rita missed having Priya by her side. She would have giggled with her at this announcement.

Rita waited for several passengers, or 'customers' as the train companies like to call them, to get off the train – a buggy, a walking stick and a man carrying an old fashioned camera tripod. Hadn't he heard of the selfie stick? Rita wondered.

She had just got on the train, or 'boarded' as the announcements say, and was sitting by a window, when a group of figures standing on the platform outside the Pumpkin Café caught her eye. Beneath the steady gaze of a poster of Rosie Hunter advocating "Race for your life with Rosie's Roadrunners!" were a couple and a small child. It appeared the woman and child were due to get the train, and that the man was there to wave them off. As they lingered, saying their 'goodbyes', Rita feared they would leave it too late and that the shrill beeping of closing doors would begin.

The couple finally unlocked their lips, the toddler being held fast by the woman while she managed to snog, an impressive feat, Rita considered. The mother, who she had been admiring, came aboard, whispering to the child, possibly a girl but it was hard to tell at that age, in Rita's view, which she carried on one hip.

"Wave bye bye to Daddy!" and the child duly did.

Rita's eyes moved from the woman and child to the man and back again, and then returned to the waving figure on the platform. It was Farah Ahmadi's brother, Rashid, distinguishable by his high cheek bones and hook nose, which were similar to his sister's and gave his face the same lean look.

As the train set off for Birmingham, Rita barely noticed the urban scenery of the smart Welford Road Rugby ground, standing proud on an island between a confluence of roads, and the housing of the inner city which had taken a battering from the Luftwaffe in the Second World War and been rebuilt piecemeal. She was thinking back to her skyped conversation with Priya about the way Constable Gardner had seemed to dismiss her suspicions concerning Rashid.

"They are bound to be sceptical" Priya had pointed out, "Anyway, I thought the police had checked him out, that eye witnesses say he never left the archery?"

"Yes, I know, but it all fits! The diary, the argument! And eye witness evidence is notoriously unreliable, you know. People remember what they think they saw." Rita had been enthusiastic for her theory. As they had been talking, Rita could see that Priya was absent-mindedly plaiting and unplaiting her brown black locks.

As she thought back to this discussion, Rita was scrolling through her phone to find the photos of Farah's funeral. There was her partner Maria, with short blonde hair and glasses, wearing a slightly bewildered expression, as if she were lost. She was standing with their baby, Lucy, in her arms. There, next to them, was a man in a dark suit with his arm round a slim woman with long blonde hair, her body sheathed in an elegant black dress. Rita stared at the picture, moving her head closer to the screen to be sure. This was

Rashid. There was his fine, lean face. The woman he was with at the graveside must be a partner or a wife, she thought. They were standing very close, closer than you would stand even in grief, they were holding hands, and their heads were near each other.

The only problem was that the woman who Rashid had just put on the train, with a child who called him 'Daddy', was a brunette with her hair cut in a short bob and more of an hourglass figure than the pencil-straight thinness of the blonde in the picture. Even if she had changed her hair colour and style since the photograph, she could not have changed her body shape so dramatically, Rita thought. So who were these two women in Rashid's life?

Rita had asked Mohal to check out Farah's family as far as possible. Her parents had died in a car crash in Iran, there were no other siblings, and there were some cousins in Germany, was what he had told her. So that was why the funeral party was small. As Rita glanced out of the train window she could see they were moving into the heart of England, which was scarred at frequent intervals by low, grey, anonymous, distribution warehouses which looked like stunted pyramids erected to the gods of logistics. To emphasise the strategic importance of the countryside, many fields were populated with pylons which seemed to stride like silver giants across the country, their wires like the product of giant spiders. Clumps of houses could occasionally be seen, ribbons of development which flowed into villages and out again, interspersed with the occasional school building or church.

Rita had already tried social media – Facebook, Twitter etc. – for information about Rashid, but with no success. Maybe Rashid had joined the ranks of those who had opted for privacy over sharing their successes, Rita pondered. Even his Linked-in entry did not have a picture. Something else to discuss with Priya, as well as her historical research, she resolved. Rita recalled how Priya had tactfully inquired about her projects, even though she found Rita's enthusiasm hard to understand.

"So tell me what history you've been looking into," Priya had prompted her friend.

"You know they've moved the ledger stone?" Rita had replied.

"The legend what?" said Priya.

"No, ledger, it's a stone slab that the Richard III society loaned to Leicester Cathedral in 1982." Rita explained. "It was in the choir area – the bit near the altar. It says on it –RICHARD III,KING OF ENGLAND, KILLED AT BOSWORTH FIELD, IN THIS COUNTY, 22nd AUGUST 1485. Buried in the Church of The Grey Friars."

"So they put that stone in before they found his body you mean?" Priya was amazed at these people's tenacity.

"Yes. Way before. They never believed the stories that his body was thrown in the river. They just knew he was in Leicester somewhere." Rita confirmed.

"But not that he was under a car park!" Priya laughed. "And under the letter 'R'!"

"That's right. Well, anyway, once the legal challenge by the Plantagenets failed, and it was clear that he was definitely going to be buried in the Cathedral, they moved the stone to the new visitor centre."

"And they'll give him a proper tomb instead?" Priya asked.

"Yes." Rita was pleased her friend understood what she was telling her.

"You'll have to go and see it!" Priya tried to share her friend's enthusiasm.

"Of course I will. In the meantime, I found another interesting tomb." Rita replied.

"Go on" Priya had encouraged.

So Rita had described the brightly coloured and highly decorated tomb of the Earl of Leicester and his second wife, in the Beauchamp Chapel of St Mary's church in Warwick.

"Who was he exactly?" Priya obliged by asking.

"Robert Dudley. He was a favourite of Elizabeth the First. She made him Earl of Leicester." Rita told her.

"Oooh! Did they like each other a lot? Were they in love?" Priya wanted to know.

"She was very fond of him. She liked to keep him close by her. She called him her 'Bonny sweet Robin' and 'My eyes'" Rita replied.

"Sounds like she was keen, then. But they didn't marry? She was the 'virgin queen' wasn't she?" Priya could recall that much from her history studies.

"Yes, if she loved anyone it was him, I think." Rita agreed, "They knew each other as children; they shared fear and anxiety as Protestants during her sister Mary's reign. They were both held in the tower when the plot to put Lady Jane Grey on the throne fell apart. And Dudley was there at Hatfield House when the courtiers rode to tell Elizabeth that Edward was dead and to surrender the Great Seal to her as their Queen. He was one of the few people she knew she could really trust."

"But not enough to marry him?" Priya was curious.

"Well, to begin with he wasn't free to marry. He first married when he was young, and then there was a scandal about his first wife's death which made it difficult for him and the Queen to ever get together. He did try though. He put on a fortnight of entertainment for her in 1575, when the scandal might have been forgotten, at Kenilworth Castle, which he had spent a fortune restoring. He built a huge lake from which actors declaimed as the Queen arrived;there were fireworks, acrobats and plays and specially constructed gardens,plus,of course, lots of opportunities for hunting, which the Queen liked."

"It's so romantic!" Priya was enchanted by the idea. "And did he pop the question?"

"It seems he didn't. It's possible the Queen evaded him. She might have got wind of his affair with one of her ladies in waiting, Lettice Knollys. Towards the end of the visit, when he might have been planning to propose, the weather turned and the Queen went home in the rain." Rita answered.

"Shame!" Priya said, "Typical of this country! Rain always spoils things!"

"Robert Dudley married Lettice – she was Elizabeth's cousin and looked awfully like her - the Queen was furious when she found out. Lettice was banned from court." Rita told her friend,

"That's the one he's buried with in the tomb I saw." Rita went on, "But Elizabeth still relied on Dudley and never forgot him. He died suddenly at Cornbury Park near Oxford, possibly of malaria, no one knows exactly. When she died 15 years later they found in the Queen's treasured possessions a letter from him written just a few days before his death. On the outside she had written 'His last letter.'"

"Aaah" Priya sighed.

"He was good-looking. I've seen his portrait in the National Gallery." Rita paused to rummage through some postcards.

"See!" she had held up to the screen a picture of the Earl. He was shown in a russet outfit with lace ruff and cuffs, the seal of the Privy Council in the top left hand side of the picture, a green velvet curtain to the right, behind him. His left hand rested on his hip, his right hand on the arm of a chair. He wore a sword at his side. The overall effect was of nonchalant charm, a man sure of himself, which no doubt he was in 1575 when it was painted, Rita had thought. The portrait was a cut-down version of a full length portrait he had commissioned for the revels he had laid on to entertain the Queen at Kenilworth Castle.

"So sad they couldn't be happy together" said Priya.

"Elizabeth appreciated his loyalty." She said "I only show

him favour because of his goodness to me when I was in trouble during the reign of my sister. At that time he never ceased his former kindness and service, and even sold his possessions to provide me with funds; and on this account it seems to me that I should give him some reward for his fidelity and constancy." Rita paused for breath.

"That's nice." Priya observed quickly. "And is there still an Earl of Leicester? Did Dudley have children?" Priya wanted to know next.

"No, the title began in the twelfth century and there have been various interruptions. Robert Dudley died without a legitimate heir. His wife Lettice miscarried one child." Rita told her, "She had another, a boy, but he died when he was only little. There's a sweet memorial to him – the noble impe they called him- in the chapel at the church in Warwick."

"So no kids?" Priya wondered how a man who, from the picture Rita had shown her, was so attractive, at least for his time, and confident looking could end up with no offspring.

"No legitimate ones." Rita told her. "But he had an illegitimate son from an affair with Lady Dudley Sheffield." Rita continued.

"Naughty boy!" said Priya.

Rita nodded,"Hmmn. He wouldn't be the first man to have more than one woman on the go, and he certainly wasn't the last!" she said.

"So no one legitimate to inherit the title then?" Priya checked.

"No. But the title was revived. The last time was in 1837. The family live at Holkham Hall in Norfolk. You might have heard of it?" Rita went on.

"Don't think so?" Priya was doubtful.

"Well, remember that film, Shakespeare in Love? The one which that English teacher made us watch? Gwyneth Paltrow dressed up as a man?" Rita reminded her friend.

"Oh, yeh, that one!" light dawned in Priya's memory.

"Well the scene at the end, when she walks in the sand, that was Holkham beach, next to the House." Rita said.

"Oh, amazing!" now Priya could picture it.

Thinking that there was a place in Oxford she could visit that was connected to Robert Dudley, Rita looked out from the train to see a large edifice which was the Crown Records Depot; this was followed by Birmingham University, where there were several cranes busy at redevelopment work. Rita recognised the first part of her journey was ending. Sure enough, a man in a uniform had entered the carriage and begun to clear up the detritus of the trip into a clear plastic bag in preparation for the new passengers waiting to board at New Street. As she stood to leave, the train was crawling past containers which were piled like coloured parcels with names from all over the world written on them – HAMBURG, HAPA-LLOYD COSCO, CHINA SHIPPING. Travel across the world was just taking off during Elizabeth's reign, Rita thought; Sir Walter Raleigh and Sir Francis Drake, for whose adventures Robert Dudley had provided financial backing, were exploring new worlds and bringing back new products, and his own illegitimate son had been an explorer. Now see where it had taken us!

Rita shook herself into the present. She needed to find her connection to Oxford. She noticed the mother and child who had waved to Rashid were at the train door ahead of her. Stepping down and walking along the platform, Rita found herself on an escalator standing just behind them. After that, she lost them in the underground cavern which was Birmingham New Street station, where workmen in orange boiler suits carrying out improvement works mingled with passengers attempting to navigate their way to their trains. Rita thought she saw the pair quitting the station altogether. Was that because they lived here? Or were they were visiting someone? Abandoning her decision to leave the case of Farah Ahmadi to the police, Rita speculated as she walked to the platform for the train to her destination, thinking that she must discuss Rashid's dodgy behaviour with Priya when she saw her.

Chapter 11

"Cricket is my life. Before the cancer, I was happy-go-lucky. I used to think about my career and worry about the future. But post it, my thinking has completely changed. I'm happy to eat and breathe normally. I'm happy to have my life back."

Yuvraj Singh,
Indian international cricketer

Friday 13th February 2015 5.45pm

"So excited!" said Rita.

"This is going to be awesome!" Priya replied.

Rita had caught sight of Priya who was waiting by the ticket barrier at Oxford station. Her friend had her hair loose today, Rita had noticed, and it floated around the fur hood of her green parka coat which she wore over skinny black jeans and laced black boots. As soon as she saw Rita, Priya jumped up and down, causing her hair to fly in the air with a short time lapse before it landed again on her shoulders.

The two young women embraced and laughed, glad to have physical contact after their screen conversations, exchanging their joy.

Priya led Rita to a bus stop which seemed to be a temporary one.

"There are so many roadworks!" Priya explained.

"This one's supposed to improve the traffic, but at the moment all they've done is switch off the traffic lights, which actually makes it flow better!" Priya continued.

The bus took them past an ancient castle which seemed in good condition from what Rita could see and around the site of a twentieth century concrete multi storey car park which had been half demolished.

"More roadworks to come!" Priya told her. "They are redeveloping a shopping centre. They say John Lewis may open here! Hope they do!"

The bus wound along the High Street and Rita caught sight of the church of St Mary the Virgin. "I want to go in there if we can." she told Priya, who looked surprised, but shrugged; no doubt one of Rita's history projects was involved, she thought.

There were more roadworks which Rita could see as they reached the end of the High Street, passing Magdalen College, which the young women had visited when in the sixth form, and then the bus turned along Cowley Road. Soon Rita could see several Asian supermarkets and restaurants and the road seemed to be teeming with life, reminding her of parts of Belgrave Road in her home town of Leicester. "Next stop!" Priya told her and the two alighted, crossing Cowley Road to reach Howard Street, where Priya was sharing a house with three female students. The house was about half way along the road. It had a bay window and a blue front door at ground level and two long thin windows above on the first floor, which looked like eyes squinting at the street. The clue to student occupation was that, as well as two wheelie bins, one blue, one green, the front garden was decorated with four bicycles.

"Come in". Priya showed Rita into a narrow hallway with a wood effect floor. "Katrin's room is here" Priya pointed to the door on their right, "and this is Lauren's" she said as they passed another door. Ahead of them was a kitchen area, the floor stacked like a supermarket with dry goods – cereals, pasta and tins of tomatoes, beans and vegetable soup.

"We find if we buy in large quantities we can save." Priya explained, "We get a big shop delivered once a month." Rita was impressed with the organisation of the occupants of the house.

The kitchen area led into a conservatory where light flooded through the glass roof. A wooden table and chairs sat in the centre and around the edge were window seats piled with red cushions to sit on but also doubling as storage space. A young woman with short ginger hair, wearing an overlarge rugby shirt and white leggings, was perched on the window seat, her legs curled under her. She was gazing intently at the screen of her iPad. "Hi" she removed her earphones to greet Rita as Priya made the introductions.

"This is Lauren".

"Katrin's out." Lauren told them, replacing her earphones.

Priya led the way upstairs to show Rita her room on the first floor, which Rita would be sharing. The room looked out over the street through white net curtains. It seemed a pleasant road, with Victorian terraces on either side, occasionally broken up by more modern constructions. Judging by the number of bikes she could see, a lot of the houses were occupied by students, Rita thought. She wondered how noisy it got, especially at night, thinking of the students on the corridor in her accommodation block on the campus at Warwick and their constant parties.

Priya had draped Indian materials over the room; there were black curly designs on purple cloth, and blue and silver patterns on deep yellow and green material. "I get them from the covered market, there's a great shop there." Priya told her. The fabrics gave the room the appearance of an eastern tent, Rita thought. She noticed the heavy medical text books piled up on the desk and the bowl of fruit which Priya kept by them. This seemed to be a place where her friend spent a lot of her time.

"Ayeesha's next door." Priya indicated the other bedroom as she gestured to Rita to leave her backpack – she had brought her favourite black one with the brown leather straps- in the room. "Let's go to a café before dinner. We'll take a walk tomorrow; I have something to show you!" Priya said mysteriously.

Friday 13th February 2015 9pm

The evening was spent getting to know one another, first in a café on Cowley Road, and then through the creation and consumption at the house of a meal of quiche, couscous and Greek salad from a local deli. The five young women talked amiably as they drank together, prepared food and ate it.

"So where's the temple in Oxford?" Rita asked innocently, thinking she had not seen any sign to it, although she had seen a mosque from Cowley Road.

"There isn't one!" Priya said to her surprise. "There's a campaign to raise funds. There are 10,000 Hindus in the county and they manage to organise an annual Mela; it raised £4,500 last year and the temple project has raised £110,000. But they reckon they need £500,000. Meanwhile, people get together in Community Halls."

"Oh" Rita was taken aback, thinking of the numerous temples in and around her home town. She told Priya about the Shree Krishna temple in Leamington Spa which she had visited with her friends from the Asian Society. They held lots of events and raised money to help others.

"And there is another temple in Coventry." Rita added, "We aren't short of them!"

"There's a temple in Reading." Ayeesha told her. "That's probably the nearest."

"Yeh." said Priya, "It's on Facebook. I'll show you!"

"Friday 13th today! Lucky nothing bad happened!" Katrin observed when they had looked at the page on Priya's phone.

"How many times do you think that date occurs? It seems pretty rare?" Priya asked.

"It's more common than you might think. There is always at least one according to this." said Lauren, looking it up on her phone. "Three is the most. There was one in 2010 and one in 2011 but three in 2012 for example. There was one last year and this year there are three – February, March and November."

"Lucky one of them isn't an exam day!" Katrin observed. "I'd probably forget my gown or something!"

The Oxford students told Rita about the requirement that to take an exam they had to wear full academic dress, known as 'sub fusc', meaning dark brown. She learnt this didn't just mean wearing a gown but that they must have a mortar board, a dark suit with a white shirt and black tie or ribbon and a carnation; a white carnation for the first exam, a red carnation for the last one and a pink carnation for those in between. It all sounded like extra stress to her and she was glad not to have to do this at Warwick. "Some students are objecting" Priya told her.

"Yeh, while others support the idea." Katrin added.

"They may seek a vote on it later this year." Ayeesha said.

Then the conversation turned to the pain of being ID-ed.

"I just never expected it." Katrin was telling them. "The assistant in the shop was like, 'You don't look like your photo' and I was like 'OK' and she was like 'Do you have a bank card' and I thought do I? And if I do how exactly does that help? And there was an old lady behind me rummaging in her bag for her driving licence in case she needed it to buy her bread and jam or whatever it was she was getting and then the manager came over, took one look at me, and said to the assistant, 'let her have it' so. I dunno…"

"Perhaps she was having a bad day." Ayeesha suggested. Then they all crowded round to look at Katrin's photo and offered opinions on whether she looked like her picture.

"You do look young in the picture."

"Well it is an old one, but it's what I look like now that counts isn't it? I only wanted to buy vodka. It's not like I committed a crime!"

"So the murder you're looking into was at the cricket ground?" it was Priya who brought the conversation round to the physiotherapist's death.

"That's right" Rita confirmed, "And the information from Dr Hopkins was very helpful. I've been to look at the ground at Grace Road…"

"Yes, why is it called that?" Priya asked her friend, "Anything to do with W G Grace, he was an old cricketer wasn't he?"

"No, nothing like that." Rita explained. She had asked Rohan the same question.

"It was the surname of a local property owner. The fact that he was called Grace is just a coincidence."

"Do women play cricket?" Ayeesha suddenly asked.

"Yes they do!" Lauren knew this, "Most counties have a women's' team. There is talk of a new women's competition." she told everyone.

A few round the table raised their eyebrows in surprise.

"The England's women's team is finally getting recognition." Lauren added. "Their Ashes games will be shown on Sky Sports. And did you see Charlotte Edwards, the England Captain, getting her CBE from the Queen for services to cricket? She was the first woman to reach 2,000 T20 international runs."

"Now we have to see what the England women's football team can do in Canada!" Katrin said enthusiastically, "I hope they get through the group stage!"

Conversation flowed on and never got back to Rita's investigations until she and Priya were settling down to sleep, several hours later.

Rita told Priya the story of her sighting of Rashid with the woman and young child at Leicester station. Priya suggested they try to find an address for him and together they searched the electoral roll, noting down the details given against his name. Rita decided to check out the location when she had the opportunity.

Saturday 14th February 2015 9am

Priya and Rita talked into the night about Rita's father's condition. Priya suggested that Padma might find on-line support helpful. She thought her efforts were a manifestation of her worry and concern. Eventually the pair had fallen asleep but when the young women rose at about 9 o'clock they were still tired and not ready for much conversation.

"Sleep ok?" Priya asked her friend.

"Yes thanks" Rita replied, not troubling to tell her friend about her recurrent dream, the one where she was stuck in a darkening room.

Rita saw she had a text message from Mohal, ironically applauding the England cricket team for beating Afghanistan in the World Cup, a rare win apparently.

"Afghanistan and Scotland! Well done! I'm sure the Aussies are quaking in their boots over the Ashes trophy, ha, ha, ha!"

Leaving the house and crossing the road, they sat in the Howard Street Community Gardens, quietly enjoying each other's company while they waited for Ayeesha to appear. Priya had explained that Ayeesha was on the same course as herself. Rita wondered if she was working as hard as her friend. They stood up when the figure of Ayeesha was seen, walking along the street, her bag swinging at her side. She waved eagerly at Priya and hugged Rita when she arrived, even though they had only recently met.

"Oooh, it's going to be soo great to get to know you! I've heard so much about you!" Ayeesha bounced round the gardens like Tigger.

The three set off, managing to walk alongside one another some of the time, dodging other pedestrians and walking in the road on occasion, being wary of bikes which were a constant potential hazard. The February day was cold but bright and Rita could feel the sun on her face from time to time, reminding her of the walk along the sea shore with Rohan. Priya stayed in the middle of the group, Ayeesha by the kerb and Rita nearest to the houses, so that she could peer into the front gardens and wonder what lay behind the doors and windows. Priya was prodded into life by Ayeesha's energy and the medical students entertained Rita with tales of strange tutors and obscure medical subjects. Rita told the other young women about 'Lost' and what exactly happened to Rohan to cause the injury she had told Priya about.

"You raised a lot of money" Ayeesha was impressed.

The threesome crossed Iffley Road, Priya and Ayeesha pointing out the Coop store where they bought day to day supplies. The young women were headed for Iffley village. There the pavement was very narrow so they frequently fell into single file. Rita noticed some old houses, to her delight, including some with thatched roofs and one which said it had been a school in 1822. Ahead of them lay the church which was where, surprisingly, Priya wanted to take Rita before they headed for the river.

"What does she want to show me?" Rita asked Ayeesha, breathlessly trying to keep up with her as she bounded down the church path. "Search me; she hasn't let me in on it." Ayeesha shrugged her broad shoulders. At almost six feet tall, she was several inches above the other two.

The church sat peaceably beside a grave yard, the path to the entrance curving to an open green area with a hedge round it. The doorway was a large arch which Rita knew to be Norman in style; it had a typical zigzag pattern and was encrusted with carvings of strange beaked figures.

"It was built between 1175 and 1182" Priya told her. She had been doing some historical research, Rita noticed approvingly. She imagined the inside would be beautiful if the doorway was anything to judge by, and she was not disappointed. A still, welcoming, silence engulfed them as they pushed open the heavy door and crossed the threshold. They steeled their eyes to adjust to the gloom but in fact the sun was quite bright at that moment and shone colours on the walls through the stained glass windows. To their right was a magical window with pictures of speaking animals.

"That's by John Piper" Priya told Rita.

In the centre was a square construction with a beautifully decorated grey lid. Rita knew from RE lessons that this must be what was called the font, where people, usually babies, were baptised and welcomed as Church members. Above the font to their left was a stupendous glass picture, mostly in blue. A man, presumably Jesus, was hanging on a tree; the tree was in blossom, a river flowing round it and sheep frolicking in the grass. Rita thought she could look at the picture all day, it was so beautiful. But Priya was urging them on to the main part of the church.

"You're sure it's OK for us to be here?"

"Of course, it was unlocked wasn't it?" they exchanged.

There were rows of wooden seats - which Rita thought were called pews - either side of them and the stone walls bore various plaques and memorials, including one to local men who were killed in the First World War, on which a wreath of poppies lay. In front of them were more pews and, at the far end was an area partially fenced off by a wooden rail, at the back of which was a covered table- this was the altar, Rita remembered- with a golden cross on it.

While Rita was taking in the scene, Priya was tugging at her sleeve and dragging her along a particular pew to look at a picture which hung on the wall near the First World War plaque.

"Look at this!" her friend said proudly to Rita who crouched to see what it said.

It was a family tree of John de la Pole, Duke of Suffolk, whose dates were 1442 to 1491 and the picture, it seemed, explained a small coat of arms which was in coloured glass in an otherwise clear window above them. The information told them the coat of arms was put there in about 1475.

Now Rita saw why Priya was so excited. John de la Pole was the second duke of Suffolk. His coat of arms had leopards and lions on it. He was shown as having married Elizabeth of York, daughter of Richard of York and sister of Edward IV, George Duke of Clarence and- Rita gasped as she read this- Richard III!

"I knew you'd be amazed!" Priya was pleased with the look of pleasure on her friend's face. "I couldn't believe it when Katrin brought me in here and I saw it! Who would think there would be a reference to our Richard here?"

"Exciting!" said Rita, taking photos with her phone of the plaque and the coat of arms, including a selfie standing by the family tree. Thumbing through her phone she quickly checked on John de la Pole. The entries included a picture of the very coat of arms they were looking at. It appeared he had fought in the Wars of the Roses with the Earl of Warwick for Edward IV at the battle of Wakefield and in the second battle of St Albans in 1461. When Edward was King he was made a Knight of the Garter and became high steward of Oxford University. On the death of Edward IV, he offered support to Richard III but transferred his allegiance to the victor, Henry, after the battle of Bosworth, and remained loyal to him, although some of his sons later rebelled. His tomb was at Wingfield in Suffolk, she read, where he died. She learnt that two windows to the nave- that is, the middle- of the church she was standing in were put in by John de la Pole in his role as Lord of Donnington Manor and that the coat of arms was displayed to make clear that he was the donor. A sort of early form of sponsorship or advertising, Rita thought.

"Thanks. That's awesome!" Rita said as she relayed some of this detail to her friends.

"Clever Priya!" said Ayeesha, "She told me how much you like history."

The three left the Church to continue their walk along a narrow path which led eventually to the river. Walking along the bank, the young women had to step around errant toddlers and wandering dogs. There were also geese to negotiate, who gathered expectantly, presumably used to being given bread or other treats. They walked past a building which looked like a farmhouse but turned out to be a pub.

"It's lovely to sit out here in the summer" Ayeesha said pointing to the picnic tables on the grass in front of the pub as she ran ahead of them and then back, her behaviour not unlike that of the toddlers they had seen. The quiet flow of the river to their right was broken by the sights and sounds of various craft. Fours and Eights were rowing determinedly, single sculls fitting in between them. The good crews looked and sounded like machines, Rita noticed. There was efficiency about their energy which turned them into a well-drilled operation, moving the boat as one. She saw to her pleasure that there were female as well as male crews and coxes.

On the bank, runners sometimes passed them or came towards them, one dressed in Rosie Hunter green. There were bicycles to be contended with here too. The tinkling of a bell behind them signalled to the three that they should step aside and make way. Some of the riders were simply travelling along the tow path; other riders were coaching crews on the river and shouting instructions or encouragement.

"The women will be rowing against each other in the university boat race for the first time this year!" Priya reminded Rita as the trio passed under Donnington Bridge and continued on towards the town centre, laughing and talking.

"About time!" Rita retorted.

The college boat houses came into view, and then, on

the other side of the river people could be seen strolling through Christ Church meadows against the backdrop of the grandeur of Christ Church college, originally called Cardinal College and started by Cardinal Wolsey, Rita knew. At Folly Bridge they saw the pub called The Head of the River, where several people were brave enough to be drinking outside.

"Probably smokers!" said Ayeesha who had explained how much medics oppose smoking and the damage it does.

Leaving the riverside, the students walked up to the High Street. There were crowds in Queen Street and Corn Market but the trio were able to order herbal tea at a Caffe Nero and descended a steep set of stairs to sit and enjoy their drinks and some of Rita's favourite wafer biscuits while they checked their phones. Rita was surprised to see that at several tables there were people working on laptops or school age children being tutored; a place for recreation had become another place of work and study it seemed.

Continuing their circuit along the High Street after their refreshment break, Rita saw in a shop window a child's version of an Oxford sweatshirt and she dived into the shop to buy one for Priya's nephew, Theeran, as a 'thank you' to Meera for arranging the meeting at the Alternative Health Clinic.

The purchase made, the young women came to the spired church of St Mary the Virgin, the University Church.

"We need to go in here" Rita said. Priya shrugged - two churches on one day? she thought. Why do we need to go in here?

Chapter

12

"I think a captain is someone who captains on the cricket field, but most of the leadership that happens is off the cricket field."

Gautam Gambhir,
Indian international cricketer

Saturday 14th February 2015 11.30 am

"Come up here! You get a great view of the church and look at that window!" Ayeesha had scampered ahead of Rita and Priya, through the porch with its unusual twisted stone columns, like bent Mediterranean tree trunks, and into the church. Collecting a printed guide on the way, she had climbed a staircase. Now she indicated the large window in bright colours which was behind her.

Looking around as they followed Ayeesha, it was clear to Rita that this church was several times bigger than the previous one they had visited and had a less intimate, more official kind of atmosphere. There were several rows of pews, all facing the altar area which was in the middle and fenced off with rope. The pews to their right had doors to them

"Box pews" Ayeesha told them as they joined her, suddenly an oracle on the subject.

From their vantage point on this higher level the three could see there was also a place to preach from – "the pulpit." Ayeesha said, noticing their interest. There was a long flight of steps up to this speaking platform which towered over the pews.

"Some famous people have preached here," Ayeesha told her friends, reading from the brochure. "Heard of John

Wesley or John Henry Newman?"

"No." said Priya.

"One started a new Christian church – the Methodists. The other was something to do with reforming the Church of England, but then he became a Catholic." Ayeesha replied, skimming through the booklet.

"It was a good church to do it in, come and look at this." said Rita, who had led them down the stairs and across to a large memorial on the wall to the left of the altar. It was a dark rectangle with gold decoration and bore a list of names and dates.

"Martyrs." said Priya sombrely as she began to read what was inscribed.

The young women saw that it was a modern plaque to honour martyrs of the Reformation, both Catholic and Protestant, who lived in Oxford or were brought there for execution. The Inscription said it was it there for 'THOSE WHOSE NAMES ARE KNOWN AND FOR ALL WHO SUFFERED'.

"It's good that it reflects both sides." Rita said.

"Some of them were actually tried here! In this church!" Ayeesha read excitedly "Three bishops!"

Priya read aloud some of the names and dates, "Hugh Latimer, Nicholas Ridley, John Philpott, all 1555. That must have been a bad year."

"'Fraid so. Mary was on the throne, so the ones killed were Protestants." Rita said, "It explains the 1556 entries too, Thomas Cranmer and Julius Palmer. The anniversary of the burning of Cranmer is coming up soon – 21 March – I understand there is often a wreath on the martyrs' memorial in St Giles to mark the date."

"1581, John Campion and Ralph Sherwin." Priya continued.

"That was during Elizabeth's reign. So they must have been Catholic martyrs." Rita told her.

"Dreadful, isn't it?" Ayeesha joined in on her way to explore the entrance to the tower.

"1589 also seems to have been a bad year. There are three more." Priya observed.

"It goes on beyond Elizabeth the First, doesn't it? There's William Laud, 1645. He was responsible for that fancy porch we came through according to the guide book!" Ayeesha added.

"Yes, he fell out with Charles the First," Rita told them, "The last one is Stephen College, 1681. That was under Charles the Second, presumably Stephen was a Catholic."

"What a waste," said Priya, "It seems so pointless. They all get on ok now don't they?"

"Better" said Rita, "There have been problems in Northern Ireland, of course, and tempers still flare at sensitive times. But I think most people would say, as is often the case, that the Troubles there were more about power than religion. And Christians don't make martyrs of people for their beliefs any more, not in this country anyway. Look at the reburial ceremony being planned for Richard III; the Anglican Church and the Catholic Church will both take part. This country has moved on."

"Yes, I guess the worry is that divisions between other groups will lead to violence." Priya put in.

"Different Muslim groups, you mean?" Rita asked her, adding, "Yes, I think that is a genuine concern. There are about 300,000 Shia Muslims in the UK and 2.3 million Sunni Muslims. There are signs that some of the extremists may target the minority Shias in British towns."

"I hope not" Ayeesha contributed. "We don't need another set of martyrs."

"No, enough people are going abroad to fight as it is." Rita agreed.

Priya nodded, knowing that Rita was thinking about a friend of her younger brother, Nayan, who had disappeared to Syria over the previous summer and had not been been heard of since. From what the friends had learnt from their on-line explorations, the fighting there was between different Muslim factions, although the organisation calling itself ISIS also seemed to be attacking non-Muslims, such as the Coptic Christians, who had lived in the area for two thousand years.

"Why are we here anyway?" Ayeesha asked, her attention span waning.

"We need to go in here." Rita led the way to the place at the end of the church where there was another altar, above which was a large picture of a woman who Rita guessed to be Mary, the mother of Jesus, since the Church was dedicated to her. Walking across the stone floor, with wooden seats either side of them - "They are for the choir" Ayeesha told them - they came to a railing. Beyond the railing were some steps - "chancel steps" Ayeesha helpfully informed them - and on the steps were various inscriptions, which were difficult to read as they were upside down from where they were standing.

This part of the church had been renovated, probably in Georgian times, Rita thought, judging by the white and black pattern on the floor and the dates on most of the memorials. So the inscriptions were not original, which disappointed Rita, but still she pressed on, twisting her head and looking for one in particular.

"There it is!" Rita gasped with excitement.

Priya rolled her eyes and left her examination of a memorial written in Latin to join her friend.

"Amy Robsart" Priya read aloud, none the wiser.

"Exactly!" said Rita triumphantly. "Amy Robsart, she was Robert Dudley's first wife, the Earl of Leicester, the one Elizabeth the First had a soft spot for. Her death put paid to any chance they could marry. She fell down a staircase in suspicious circumstances and, although it was never proved that the Earl was linked to the death, the scandal of it meant they could never be together, it would have looked as if they had plotted to have her put out of the way."

"And why was she buried here?" Ayeesha asked.

"She died near here. At a house called Cumnor Place," Rita told her.

"So sad." said Priya. "What does the writing say?"

Rita read out the inscription:

"In a vault of brick at the upper end of this Quire was buried AMY ROBSART wife of LORD ROBERT DUDLEY KG on Sunday 22nd September AD 1565."

"Come on!" Ayeesha was impatient to be moving again. "Let's go up the tower!" and she set off across the church to the visitors' desk where they purchased tickets from a tiny grey haired woman who advised them to take care on the 124 steps to the tower gallery.

"Mind you don't fall!" Priya joked.

"What happened at Cumnor Place?" she asked Rita as they climbed.

"You have to remember that there was a lot of rumour at the time, which suited enemies of Dudley, like the Catholics who resented him as a powerful Protestant and did not want him to marry Elizabeth and produce an heir, and like Lord Cecil, her main adviser, who was jealous of the influence Dudley seemed to have over the Queen. The scandal haunted him all his life." Rita warned her.

"What a shame." Priya was sympathetic, "But what exactly happened?"

"Amy and Robert married when they were young, about seventeen or so, but they never set up house together. Elizabeth wanted Robert at court all the time and Amy stayed with friends and relatives. Dudley was put in charge of Windsor Castle around the time that Amy moved to Cumnor, which might explain why she went there. Before Cumnor Place, Amy was living at the house of Richard Verney, at Compton Verney in Warwickshire, and before that she lived in Throcking in Essex. So it wasn't odd that

Amy was living in someone else's house, when the accident – or whatever it was - occurred, or that she and Dudley had not seen each other for several months before she died, it seems."

"But how did the accident happen?" Ayeesha called down as she was several steps ahead of Rita and Priya.

"One day, Amy sent the servants away to the fair at Abingdon. She was quite adamant about it. Only two women stayed at home with her. When the others returned they found her dead at the foot of a staircase. Later gossip suggested she might have been expecting a visitor, or that a stranger might have called while she was alone, and that this unknown person might have pushed her down the stairs. Or she might have fallen, perhaps by accident, or perhaps she meant to do it."

"And the fall killed her?" Priya interrupted, "That's pretty rare these days." she said, thinking of NHS ambulance response times and the equipment they carried to treat accident victims.

"When the Queen heard the news she told the court, in Italian, that Amy had a broken neck, but the medical evidence at the time – the original coroner's report was found in the National Archives only a few years ago - said she had two wounds to the back of her head. Some people say that suggests it wasn't an accident, others that the wounds might have been caused by hitting her head on the stone steps. Anyway, there was a coroner's inquest at which the matter was looked into by a jury. They decided it was an accident, but, of course, even if they thought it was suicide they would have been reluctant to say so; it was considered a terrible thing in those days."

"They had coroner's juries even in then?" Priya was surprised.

"Yes, that practice goes back a long way." Rita confirmed. "The foreman was Robert Smith and, although Dudley was said not to know him, there is evidence in Dudley's accounts that he paid a Mr Smith for black taffeta and velvet in May 1566. It is hard to know if that was gratitude for a verdict that saved his wife's reputation or a bribe to protect his own. Certainly Dudley asked the jury to be 'discreet' and one member of the jury was his employee."

"But there was no evidence against Dudley, or the Queen?" Ayeesha called down, intrigued.

"No. Only speculation. Unfortunately a few days before her death Lord Cecil had told the Spanish ambassador that Dudley's supporters were planning to poison his wife to clear the way for him to marry the Queen. That wasn't very helpful to his reputation."

"Of course not." Priya agreed.

"Elizabeth sent him away from the court while the inquiries took place. She could see how bad it looked."

"And Dudley? How did he take it?" Priya asked as they climbed.

"He was shocked when the news came and determined to find out what had happened. Later, the Spanish Ambassador accused him of not showing much grief, but he had reasons for wanting him to look guilty, as I said. Dudley sent a man called Blount, a relative and a business associate, and told him to use all "means you can possible for the learning of the truth" about Amy's death." Rita pressed on with her story and the stairs to tower gallery.

"He asked Blount to make sure the coroner's jury was made up of "the discreetest and most substantial men"; and he asked Amy's half-brother, Appleyard, to watch the proceedings." Rita went on.

"But of course a guilty person would do that too?" Ayeesha put in as they caught up with her.

"Maybe." Rita conceded, "But I think he was genuine. It seems Amy was ill - probably she had breast cancer - so her bones may have been weakened, which would explain why the fall was so devastating."

"OK" Priya was trying to follow her friend's train of thought as well as her steps.

"The jury's verdict was that she died by what they called 'mischance'. Dudley seems to have been assured by the foreman that as far as he could see the death was a 'very misfortune'." Rita continued.

The young women were approaching the top of the steps now.

"Appleyard, Amy's brother, subsequently confirmed he was bribed to keep the rumours going. And later, long after the event, there was an attempt to blacken Dudley's name by the Spanish, who desperately wanted a Catholic monarch. There was a paper published called Leicester's Commonwealth which alleged Dudley, or at least his supporters, were responsible. The publication was destroyed as quickly as Elizabeth could manage."

"So you think he was innocent?" Priya asked. Rita nodded.

When they left the staircase, and before they started to admire the rooftops of Oxford below them, Rita read out from her iPad,

"William Cecil, who advised Queen Elizabeth, said that Dudley was 'inflamed' by Amy's death but Cecil did not allege he caused it. Dudley himself said, 'The greatness and suddenness of the misfortune so perplexes me' and 'how this evil doth light upon me, considering what the malicious world will buit' – that means gossip – 'as I can take no rest.'"

She turned her iPad to take pictures of the view. Some of the buildings were easy to name. In front of them were the round Radcliffe Camera, the distinctive Sheldonian Theatre designed by Sir Christopher Wren and the Bodleian Library. The college to the right, with magnificent towers, was All Souls, together with Hertford College and New College, while Exeter and Brasenose Colleges were to their left. The next balcony afforded them a view of Magdalen College.

From the south balcony they could see the spire of Priya's college, Merton, as well as Christ Church and Tom Tower. Standing on the west balcony, Ayeesha pointed out in the distance the tower of Nuffield College and closer to them was the tower of the library at Lincoln College. The students stopped talking to take in the sight. All the 'dreaming spires' were laid out below them as they discussed the fall to her death of Amy Robsart.

"So Amy sent the servants away? That might indicate she planned to kill herself?" Priya suggested.

"Yes, that's possible. She might have been depressed about being childless, or her illness might have affected her." Rita conceded. "The construction of the staircase adds to the mystery." she added.

"How so?" Priya was pulling at her hair as they talked. Ayeesha was leaning over to get a better view of the rooftops.

"Well, research suggests there was a dog-leg design in the stairs at the north-west corner of the building which gave access to the upper rooms and it seems likely there was a pair of such stairs. But, if so, each flight would only have been relatively short." she paused to see if Priya had understood.

"So there was not one long flight of steps, but two short ones, turning onto each other?" Priya tried to describe what she could see in her mind.

"Exactly!" Rita was pleased. "So you see in that case it could not have been a very long tumble, if it was a fall. Of course, there may have been other stairs in the house which were a single flight, but they don't seem to be the ones implicated."

"Mmmn" Priya nodded, grasping the point. "So she might have planned to kill herself, or she might have fallen? But then she might have been pushed down the stairs by a stranger or by someone she knew, someone she invited into the house, which would give her a motive for dismissing the servants?" Priya concluded. "We will never know for sure."

The young women descended the steps of the tower, still thinking about the mystery of the death of Amy Robsart. When they were almost at the bottom, Rita's phone rang, the Bollywood tones bringing them firmly back to the current century. She almost didn't answer it. Whoever it was could probably wait while she enjoyed her time with Priya, she thought. But she saw it was her mother's number, so she decided to pick it up.

As Rita heard her mother's words, she stopped walking and time slowed down. It was as if she could feel the words moving from her ear to her brain and, inside her head, shooting towards sensors that triggered alarms and set off reactions in the rest of her body. Her stomach felt like it might turn to jelly, her hand started to tremble as it held the phone.

"Oh Rita! It's your father. It's bad news I'm afraid." Padma said hoarsely.

Chapter 13

"You learn from cricket because there are more bad days than good."
Nicole Browne,
New Zealand international cricketer.

Saturday 14*th* February 2pm

Rita closed her eyes, as if she could blot out what her mother, using a strange, strangled, voice, was about to say to her.

"He's had another heart attack."

Rita could hear her own heart beating loudly now, the rhythm pressing into her ears.

"It was a bad one." Padma managed to say next.

"Oh no" Rita heard herself speak although she hadn't meant to say anything as she stumbled down the last of the steps.

"I'm afraid your father has died, Rita!" Rita could hear a catch in her mother's voice. It must have cost her a lot to make the call, to keep herself together to communicate this news to her daughter.

"I'll come home as soon as I can." Rita told her.

Then, "Nayan is with you?" she checked.

"And Mohal, too." Padma assured her.

"See you soon, darling." her mother hardly ever called her 'darling' these days. It was a term of endearment she had used when Rita was little. It had faded out of use once she was at secondary school. Padma's use of the word was almost more than Rita could bear. She clutched her phone tightly in her trembling palm as she jabbed at it to end the call. She was standing in the entrance to the tower, blocking the way for new visitors. Rita became aware that these strangers were diverting round her.

How can normal things be going on? she thought as she walked onto the High Street. The cars were moving, other people, oblivious to her devastating news, were shopping and talking, a child was crying, and there was the sound of laughter coming from an open upper window. Why was everything going on when the bottom had just fallen out of her world?

"What's wrong?" Priya caught up with Rita, noticing her friend's stillness and bewilderment. Even Ayeesha had stopped hopping up and down and was looking concerned.

"What's wrong?" Priya had to repeat; Rita was seemingly paralysed.

Rita chose her words carefully.

"It's my father," she said slowly; she was still fighting to get her phone back in her pocket but her hand was shaking too much to achieve this easily.

"My mother was ringing to tell me, to tell me..." but Rita could not get beyond that beginning. Instinctively, Priya put her arms round her friend and hugged her.

"Is it bad Rita?" she whispered in her ear.

Rita nodded.

"Do you need to go home?" Rita nodded again, feeling foolish at not being able to speak but sensing, suddenly, that her throat was a well of tears and if she tried to make a noise she thought the tears would flow, like that river in the beautiful glass window in the church in Iffley, the church they had looked round gleefully only a few hours ago.

"OK" said Priya, interrupting her thoughts, "Let's go and collect your things. We can get a taxi to the station." and she steered Rita in the direction of her student house, Ayeesha trailing sympathetically behind them.

"I'm sorry" Rita managed to say, shaking her head, as they crossed Cowley Road.

"He had another heart attack. He's died Priya!" and tears streaked down her cheeks, dropping onto her jacket, falling so fast she didn't trouble to wipe them. It felt like a release in some way. Reaching the sanctuary of the community garden, they paused for a moment so Rita could collect herself before they went into the house. Rita took the opportunity to dab a tissue around her eyes and managed to smile in a watery way to her friend who grimaced with sympathy.

"I'm sorry," Rita apologised, "I think it's the shock."

"Your mother's at home with your brothers?" Priya asked. Rita nodded.

"I expect your aunt will be there too." Priya knew how close Padma and her sister, Jaina, were.

Rita nodded again in acknowledgement.

Back in the house, Priya helped Rita to gather up her possessions while Ayeesha called a taxi for her. Rita could also hear her telling Lauren in subdued tones what had occurred and heard Lauren's gasp of sympathy. When they were nearly ready to leave, Ayeesha put her head round Priya's door to pass on information about train times, which she had gathered from the internet.

"The half past four train will get you back by quarter to six." she told Rita. "So sorry about your news."

Tactfully, she left the friends alone. Priya descended the stairs with Rita and followed her through the front door. Rita looked surprised.

"Oh I'm coming with you to the station. I wouldn't let you do that on your own." Priya said, taking charge as if Rita were suffering an illness.

Rita did not take in much of the car journey, her mind's eye was with her father, picturing him in his hospital bed, the last time they had had a long conversation and then, later, in the chair in the kitchen at Elm Drive.

"Be happy" those were the last words he had said to her as he patted her hand before she left for Priya's, too distracted by thoughts of train times and tickets to pay much attention.

"We always think we have more time" thought Rita, "More time than we have. We should learn to make every second count."

Her stomach was feeling less queasy now, but a strange heaviness had settled round her heart. Rita pictured it like the ripples in a pond when a rock was dropped into it. Padma's news had landed on her heart like a large stone, she thought.

Priya paid the taxi driver, talked to the ticket seller and sorted out the best journey for Rita. All she had to do, zombie-like, was put her PIN into the machine to pay. Then Priya propelled her to the ticket barrier.

"Platform 2, change at Birmingham. You'll be alright?" Priya held her friend by the arms as she spoke, looking into her face for signs of the old Rita instead of this stunned, paralysed version.

"I'll be fine, thanks so much." Rita shook herself and managed a half smile to reassure Priya.

"Let me know what's happening and if there's anything I can do!" Priya made Rita go through the barriers and pointed her to the stairs to platform 2 down which passengers were moving precipitately.

"Take care!" she called as Rita waved and turned towards where the Cross Country train, which was being announced, would shortly be approaching.

Sitting on the train by a half window, Rita felt she was seeing the passing scenery through a porthole. This was pretty much how she felt she was operating at that moment; she felt she was peering at the world, able to see some of it, the rest of her vision clouded and obscured by the enormity of what had just happened to her family.

Her father was gone. He had moved on to another life. She tried the phrases a few times in her head. It didn't seem to make much sense. She and her brothers had lost their father. Her mother - oh dear - that thought caused a stabbing pain in Rita's heart – how would her mother cope? Her parents had been married for how long, 24 years? They might have had their differences, but they were devoted to each other. Jahi had supported all Padma's building projects, even though he had grumbled sometimes, and Padma had been a loyal lieutenant at the dental surgery they had built up together. Their lives were entwined at home and at work. Neither of them could have envisaged it would end like this. Her mother would be lost without him, Rita thought, staring out at the encroaching urban landscape of Birmingham.

Stirring herself, Rita became aware of her own breathing, which was shallow, as if her body had slowed down to absorb the news. Sluggishly, she picked up her pink satchel bag and black backpack and climbed from the train, looking around her on the platform for an electronic board to tell her which platform she needed for the Leicester train. When she saw the information, she texted Mohal, in case he was able to pick her up from the station when she arrived.

Saturday 14th February 2015 5.45 pm

The red Peugeot was waiting in Leicester station car park by a poster advertising the Acorn Group of Care Homes, proprietor R. Massood. It bore a picture of a grey haired lady smiling up at a kindly faced care worker who was bringing her a cup of tea. 'Peace of mind' the poster proclaimed. Rita thought fleetingly that her father never had the chance to live to that sort of age, and then she swiftly dismissed the idea; people die all the time, don't they? People of all ages? It was not anyone's fault if they had long lives and others didn't. Look at Mr. Gregson; he had lived into his nineties. No one knew how long they had here. Trying to dismiss these morbid thoughts, Rita stepped into the car.

"Hey, sis" said Mohal quietly, "How are you doing?" and the two exchanged a clumsy embrace of solidarity over the gear stick and handbrake.

"Can't believe it" said Rita, releasing her brother.

"I know." he answered, taking up the car keys, "None of us can".

As he drove them out of the city centre, Rita saw that her home town, too, was unchanged, although everything had changed for her family. London Road, just outside the station, was full of traffic. Waiting in the traffic queue on Waterloo Way gave Rita time to examine the state of the inside of the Peugeot; how did Mohal manage to get it in such a mess? she thought.

When he had threaded his way through the lines of cars,Mohal told Rita what had happened.

"He was in the kitchen, getting some breakfast, I guess. I was in the living room. We all heard the crash. He must have knocked something off the counter as he fell. Mum was upstairs, so I was first to see him." he paused.

"Oh, Mohal!" Rita said in sympathy.

"He was lying there and I kind of knew, you know, that it was serious? I shouted to Mum who came running down the stairs so fast I thought she might fall. Mum said, "Call an ambulance, tell them he's had another heart attack" she was very efficient, really, must be her medical training or something. She laid him flat and checked his pulse. Then she tried CPR. But I think she knew it was no good. The ambulance came quite quickly – Nayan was in the kitchen by then, he'd heard Mum and me shouting about what to do. He let the paramedics in, they went through the procedures. All three of us were standing in a huddle in the kitchen by then. We just couldn't take it in. No way. The paramedics shook their heads but took him in the ambulance anyway. They tried everything, Rita, adrenalin, defibrillator. Mum went with him. I drove Nayan and me to the Infirmary. By the time we got parked, Mum was waiting by the reception desk. It was no good, she said, it was a bad heart attack. No one could do anything." Mohal finally got to the end of his tale.

"How's Mum now?" Rita asked as they approached 10 Elm Drive. She was trying to prepare herself. The sight of the house itself caused the heavy feeling over her heart to rise up across the whole of her chest and into her throat. Her father was no longer there. He would never be there again.

"She's coping pretty well, I think," Mohal said. "Aunt Jaina's there which is a great help. Nayan and I just don't know what to say."

"No" said Rita," I'm not sure any of us does."

Saturday 14th February 2015 8pm

"Well, what <u>are</u> we allowed to do?" Rita asked.

It was evening. Padma and Rita had clung to each other for a while in mutual sympathy. Mohal and Nayan had looked on awkwardly, changing their balance from foot to foot. Padma had taken Rita through the details. This seemed to be a ritual that she needed. On the phone to relatives in India, Padma had repeated the story several times already. It was as if by re-telling it her husband's death became more real.

Jaina, Padma's sister, was in the house too. She was staying in Nayan's room, so the 'boys' would share Mohal's. Rita was relieved. She doubted her mother would sleep much, she seemed quite wired, and Rita did not know how to cope. She had never seen her mother like this before.

It was not that Padma was out of control. Far from it. Apart from the occasional outburst of rage- "Why? Why?"- spoken as she screwed up a paper tissue in her hands, she seemed to have assumed command of herself and the situation;she issued orders on a frequent basis.

They were all sitting round the table in the kitchen, Jaina having brought a simple meal which they had dutifully picked at, all except Nayan who had been hungry and ate his quickly, looking guiltily at the others when his plate was empty.

Padma had been directing her rage at her husband's death towards the authorities in general and the coroner's office in particular.

"It's ridiculous! Even if we could register the death we couldn't do it until Monday! And I have to make an appointment!" she spat out the words, "But we can't get on with anything as the matter is being referred to the coroner! The death was unexpected they are saying! They are only saying that to cover themselves! All this means we don't know when we can cremate him!"

Jaina had promised to help with the phone calls and the visit to the Town Hall for registration, when that was possible, and had contacted her husband, Bandhu, who had said he would find out if the coroner's office really needed to carry out an invasive autopsy, which would be distressing, or whether they could satisfy themselves with scans. Everyone in the family understood the urgency of getting on with the cremation, but the powers that be seem unable to respond as quickly as they wanted.

Having said all she could on that subject, with her sister trying to apply soothing words, Padma had turned her attention to her children.

"And we will all have to observe mourning. It's only right and proper." she told them.

Hence Rita's question, what were they allowed to do during mourning? She had already emailed the Admin Department at uni to let them know the situation and her tutors to ask for extensions on her essay deadlines. Although she had not been enjoying her time at Warwick particularly, she did not want to be away too long and get behind with her studies.

Typically, Padma had started to make a list-
'1.Funeral Director

2. Puja
3. Post Mortem
4. Registration
5. Crematorium
6. Flowers
7. Incense
8. Garland
9. Charity
10. Ashes

Carefully she explained the steps to her children, scarcely believing that she was having to do so. It was as if she were watching herself. The words and the events she described brought back memories of her father's funeral. Nothing much changes where death is concerned she thought. As she spoke, her sister held her hand for support.

Padma told them about the process for the funeral, a process which had been adapted to fit the arrangements which were possible given the local crematorium facilities which did not permit, for example, space for family and relatives to circulate the coffin or for a family member to set light to the body unshackled by a wooden box. Jahi's body - "when the authorities finally release him to us" - would go to the funeral home of a firm of undertakers recommended by Bandhu and then to the crematorium. The family would go to the funeral home where there was more room for several of the ceremonies to take place. Mohal, as chief mourner, would help wrap a cotton sheet around the coffin. Rita nodded at this; she knew the idea was to act as a boundary round the soul so it would not return to earth to haunt the living. A flower garland would be draped round her father's neck and relatives and friends at the funeral home would offer a flower to say goodbye. Mohal looked serious as Padma laid out what needed to be done. Nayan swallowed hard as he tried to picture this scene. It was going to be a very strange experience he thought.

Then the coffin would be closed, Padma told them, and would be brought to the chapel in the crematorium, an incense stick placed on the top. An effigy of Shiva would be taken with the coffin. When the mourners were seated- historically women did not attend cremations, as their tears were seen as polluting, but Rita knew her family had not been observing this practice since they lived in Leicester and that they would be present - a puja would read verses from the Bhagavad Gita which describe the nature of the soul and advise mourners not to grieve because death is natural to all who are born.

"The puja will chant the name of Rama as the coffin…" Padma had to pause to collect herself, "as it disappears. The puja will tell everyone about the medical charity we want to support; I am going to suggest the British Heart Foundation. Mohal will make sure that the funeral home send the ashes to your father's relatives in India to be scattered there." The siblings knew Padma meant that the relatives would deposit their father's ashes in the Ganges.

"We will offer pindas" Padma told them. Rita remembered these from other funerals; they were balls of cooked rice moistened with milk and water to help the deceased acquire a new body for their next existence.

"Since we do not know when we can hold the cremation we will start the mourning now. We will keep mourning until 13 days have passed after cremation." Rita tried to calculate what this meant. She had looked at her phone for dates. It could mean that mourning would go on until the end of February. But it did not seem possible that the rest of the days in the month would pass easily. For the mourning period the family were supposed to stay at home and receive visitors. A photograph of Jahi would be displayed and a garland of flowers placed over it. A year after his death the family would perform a memorial event called 'shraddha' and pay homage to Jahi. So this time of year would always remind them of her father Rita thought.

"We will wear white. We will not cook." Nayan, who had rather been looking forward to missing school, now wondered what food would be available while they were in mourning; how would he survive?

"Relatives and friends will bring you food." Jaina spoke to reassure her nephew.

"Do we have to stay in all the time?" this was what was on Rita's mind.

"Behave with decorum if you go out." Padma conceded she could not keep her children locked up, "No temple and no festivities." she added warningly.

Mohal and his sister raised eyebrows at each other. He was thinking that he might escape to do some journalist assignments. She was thinking that if she was careful she might as well use the time in Leicester to do some more checking up on Rashid, Farah Ahmadi's brother.

Chapter 14

"I am very emotional. It took me many years to recover from the death of my father. Even when I was playing cricket, I wasn't happy. I would just sit and cry. I was very young. He was too young; he shouldn't have gone. Cricket is all right. We all play sport. Good and bad days come."

Harbhajan Singh,
Indian international cricketer

Monday 16th February 2015 11am

"Manor Gardens Dental Surgery, Rita Patel speaking." Rita was trying to sound helpful as she picked up the latest call to the surgery which her parents had run jointly until her father's sudden demise. There was not much she could say about cavities, extractions or fluoride treatment but her mother wanted her to explain her father's absence and to reassure patients that their appointments would be rescheduled with a locum. It was marginally better than being at home all the time. The regular receptionist, Sunetra, was on the other line; Rita could pass any complicated oral questions to her.

The three siblings were coping with the situation in their own way. Nayan had shut himself in his room and found solace with box sets and catching up on programmes on the iPlayer. Apparently, he told his family when he came down for snacks, a contestant from Coalville called Sheena had got support from all the judges on The Voice on Saturday. "Good for her" Rita had said, thinking to herself that singers on The Voice did not have the advantage of a contract with Simon Cowell at the end of the process, if it was an advantage. She had caught the news on-line that his company had recently dropped Sam Bailey, the Leicester winner of X Factor in 2013.

Nayan had also informed them, less than tastefully Rita felt, that Eastenders would run a show on Thursday revealing who killed Lucy Beale. He told them the favourite with the bookies was Abi Branning. Rita, who could not have cared less, had noticed how when Nayan did emerge from his room it was to spout endless, pointless, trivia, as if this would somehow fill the empty space they were all sensing.

Mohal, who was required to stay in by his mother – "Friends and family may call, they will expect to see you" she said- had spoken to Rita despairingly in the car as he escaped to give her a lift to the surgery on Uppingham Road.

"I don't think I can stand much of this. At least if I keep the car I might be able to get out later." he said.

Then he surprised Rita by showing her a poem in his phone. It had been sent by his friend Husna Mohammed who he had got to know when he was working for an MP at Westminster.

"Muslims think life on this Earth is a preparation for the next life when the soul, which has been lent by Allah, will live on." her brother had explained. "They think when you die the day was appointed by God."

Rita had rocked her head back, startled and not sure she wanted to hear this.

"It's a lovely poem." Mohal assured her. So Rita read it. It was by Suliaman El Hadi and said,

'Oh my people, what is your worth?

What is your worth, what is your worth, child of the earth?

Are you like silver, diamonds or gold increasing in value as you grow old?

Or are you like the dew at the start of the day like smoke in the wind, slowly fading away.

You cannot be measured in dollars and cents. You can only

be measured in your deeds and intent.
And what you achieved and how you relate.
And what are your virtues and if you are great.
And in your assent you will find that it's true.
There is no treasure more precious than you.
Oh my people, what is your worth. What is your worth, what is your worth, child of the earth?'

"It's great, I suppose." Rita had said cautiously, not wishing to upset her brother.

"You are still in touch with her then?" she ventured to ask, worrying what the reply might be. She thought Mohal had abandoned the friendship, which was carried out in secret from Husna's family and about which her own parents, when they found out, were very unhappy.

"We still text sometimes. Not often. I told her about Dad." Mohal offered as he turned right into the town-bound traffic.

"Good of her then." Rita conceded, seeing that the contact had brought her brother some comfort.

After all, she was not in a position to criticise. She had messaged Sammi to say she was interested in the room, but there was a delay as her father had died suddenly. He had replied instantly, offering solace in her bereavement. Later, when they exchanged further messages, he had explained that Sikhs do not mourn at the death of a Sikh as they see it as the progression of the soul. Sammi sent her a line from Guru GranthSahib 'The dawn of a new day is the herald of a sunset. Earth is your permanent home.'

Sammi sympathised with her mother's objections to an invasive post mortem. He said Sikhs objected to this too, although they were not opposed to organ donation if that was appropriate. In a Sikh ceremony, when the coffin was burnt, he told her, the evening prayer – the Kirtan Sohila- was said-

"God has determined the time for my nuptials; come pour the oil of joy at my door. Bless me, my friends, that I find that

sweet union, dwelling as one with my Master and Lord. All must receive their last call from the Master; daily he summons those souls who must go, Hold in remembrance the Lord who will summon you; soon you will hear his command."

Rita decided not to share any of this with her brother. They would each find consolation where they could she thought.

Looking round her while she sat in the reception area of her parents' practice, Rita noted that the surgery had been impeccably decorated under Padma's direction. The walls were cream and lined with restful framed prints of fields, flowers and foliage. The dark blue carpet sank reassuringly under the feet and the receptionists' desk was in warm pine. In the waiting room, swimming in circles, were three fish who watched the anxious patients with calm indifference.

Rita had taken up the phone reluctantly; she was having difficulty finding phrases to convey her father's death which allayed the annoyance of patients who were inconvenienced and which reassured them that a locum would be found to fill the gap. On reflection, Rita thought this an unfortunate phrase and reworded it to 'step into her father's shoes'.

Scrolling down the list of patients to check who needed to be contacted, a name leapt out at Rita: 'Rashid Ahmadi'. Rita, although knowing this was strictly not allowed, could not help noting the address and phone numbers given. Surely this was too much of a coincidence? This must be Farah's brother? But Rita had already checked his address when she was with Priya, using the electoral roll. Now she stared at the address he had given to his dentist. It was not the same. What was going on? Had he just not updated one of the addresses? Or did the duplication support her theory that he really was leading a double life? She determined to try to find out.

Monday 16th February 2015 6.30pm

In the evening, Rita had escaped the oppressive closeness of her family with Padma's permission.

"You really don't mind?" Rita had asked.

"Do what you need to do; your father wouldn't want me to stop you. Just don't let any of our relatives see you." was her mother's resigned answer; it was as if she could only fight so many battles at once and could not take Rita on at that moment.

She was jogging through the streets, her backpack strapped to her, which reminded her fleetingly of the Marines they had seen training on the road to Exeter. She tried to run proudly, like the woman in the 'This Girl Can' video. Most joggers pounded the roads wearing earphones, surrounded by their own favorite sounds, but Rita had not chosen to do that. She wanted to stay alert, to be alive to any noises or voices round her. Rita was thankful that her long T-shirt covered her black leggings well down her thighs. She had not realised how worn through they were until she put them on. Time to buy some new ones, when she was allowed, she reminded herself. It was a relief not to be clad entirely in white at least.

Being early evening, this was the time for joggers, who always seemed to emerge at dusk. Occasionally, a runner went past Rita, who was alerted to their imminence by heavy breathing, and thumping steps, as if a large dog or horse were approaching. Some runners were pushing themselves; others were well within their range of comfort. Rita thought maybe some were in training for the London marathon which would take place in a few weeks.

Unlike most joggers, who had no destination in mind and simply jogged between A and B and back again, Rita had an objective. As she reached it, carefully examining the house numbers to make sure she was in the right place, Rita slowed down, and then stopped. She put on the jacket from her backpack and took a swig from her water bottle to give herself a reason to be standing on the pavement on the opposite side of the road to 31 Woods Lane. The houses in the street looked like concrete boxes, she thought, probably they were put up quickly after the Second World War. The owners had taken pride in them; some of the walls were painted in bright colours – green, blue and yellow – and all the gardens which had not been sacrificed to parking spaces were well tended and tidy, although it was too early in the year for much to be growing.

At the house she was looking at, while pretending not to look, a buggy was sitting by the front door, and some shopping was slung underneath the seat. At a bedroom window, Rita could see a mobile hanging from the ceiling and stuffed toys on the window sill – a giraffe, a bear and a sheep. This must be the child's room then, Rita deduced, and was gratified to see at the window a brunette haired woman bouncing a toddler up and down in her arms.

She had not planned what to do next. Knock on the door with a lame excuse? Take a picture for the police? What good would either action do? Rita decided to take a photo anyway, it might come in useful, and she had just put her phone away when her endeavours were rewarded. Round the corner, a lap top bag on his shoulder and a plastic water bottle in his hand, came Rashid. He put a key in the front door of number 31 and entered. Rita would like to have filmed him doing that, but she thought this would be too obvious. She stooped instead and pretended to tie the lace of her trainer, while she kept up her surveillance.

"What are you doing?" Rita had not heard Rashid approaching, he must walk softly she thought.

"I said, what are you doing?" he repeated, more vehemently.

Rita stood up to prevent him from towering over her. Even so, he was quite tall, about 6 feet, similar in height to her older brother, Mohal, and so several inches taller than she was, especially in her flat running shoes.

Rita had prepared for this.

"I'm a student and I'm doing a project, I wonder if you would help me?" she said confidently.

Rashid looked wary, checking up and down the street as if expecting a trick and possibly TV cameras to record it.

"A project?" he repeated.

"It's about trading," Rita said, taking out her notebook and tearing out a piece of paper from it.

"Do you have anything on you – of no value, I don't want money," she said this to reassure Rashid as a look of concern crossed his face, "Anything that you would be willing to trade for this blank piece of paper?" Rita produced what she intended to be a hopeful look.

Rashid was now distracted and intrigued. "I can give you this?" he said, offering her the empty plastic water bottle he was carrying as he came over to her.

"Great!" said Rita and offered him the sheet of paper, taking the bottle from him in the same move.

"So now I have a piece of paper?" Rashid said, checking the sheet to make sure there was nothing written on either side, still unsure whether this was a trick.

"That's right," said Rita, putting the bottle into the plastic bag she had brought with her. "Have a good evening!" and Rita turned and walked away, feeling the puzzled eyes of Rashid staying on her. Only when she got to the corner did she dare to stop and look back. Rashid was just going into the house again. Jogging home, Rita puzzled what it could all mean?

Monday 16th February 2015 7.30pm

Rita arrived back at 10 Elm Drive, her jacket back in her bag. She was puzzling over Rashid and anxious to call Priya to discuss. Entering through the front door of her home, she became aware of a voice she didn't recognise. It was a male voice, and it was not one of her brothers, or her uncle. Who could be visiting? she thought.

Rita followed the voice to the living room where, usually, Mohal or Nayan would be sprawled, playing a computer game or watching endless episodes of Top Gear. Neither of her siblings was prone on the sofa, but, instead, a man she didn't know was sitting with a very straight back, his bent legs slightly splayed, his weight tilted forward, one of Padma's best china vessels balanced carefully in his hands.

"Rita!" her attention switched from the stranger to her mother who was sitting in the armchair positioned facing the sofa. The stranger must feel he was being interrogated, Rita thought - ordeal by Earl Grey.

"This is Dr Sharma. He's joining the practice as a locum. Just to tide us over while we adjust to your father's.. your father's..." Even the usually controlled Padma could not bring herself to use the words. Dr Sharma stepped into the breach.

"I am sorry for your loss, Miss Patel" he said, standing to acknowledge Rita when he had put down his cup.

She nodded and said thanks quietly. She hadn't found a way of dealing with this yet and the sympathy of strangers was hard to bear with equanimity. Rita was also conscious that, compared to the man in front of her, smart in his best suit and wreaking of cologne, she must look unprepossessing in her sweaty jogging clothes, her springy brown hair awry having escaped the band she had used to clamp it down.

"Dr Sharma qualified in Delhi before coming over to this country. He's been practising in Derby." Padma explained. Her interrogation seemed to have yielded results.

"We want to move to Leicester," the locum dentist offered some explanation for himself.

"Dr Sharma has a family" Padma said pointedly, as if in reproach that none of her children had taken the step towards matrimony and parenthood yet.

Rita groaned to herself silently. Padma had been starting

to hint about "the future" before their father died. Was she going to get worse now? Rita wondered.

"I'll get myself a drink." Rita said, wishing to escape and thinking the two of them wanted to discuss business.

"We've finished talking business" Padma contradicted her daughter's thoughts as Dr Sharma settled back on the sofa, looking more relaxed, "Come and join us."

"OK" Rita agreed uncertainly; did she have to take part in this threesome? she asked herself. There were so many other things she would like to have been doing. Like talking to Priya about Rashid and his two households. Could that have played a role in Farah's death? Did she find out and threaten to expose him? Or deny him access to her son because of it?

In the kitchen Rita got herself a glass of orange juice and then she popped to the downstairs bathroom to flick her hair about with her hands and don the jacket she had screwed up in her bag. It would have to do she thought, wrinkling her nose at herself in the mirror and spraying Marc Jacobs Daisy in her general vicinity, as if smelling of perfume would disable Dr Sharma's sense of vision.

She was leaving the kitchen with her drink in her hand when Rita noticed, by the table, a small black suitcase. Who did that belong to and why was it here? she wondered. It was not a case she recognised. Perhaps her aunt Jaina had left it after her stay with them and was fetching it later? She dropped her backpack onto one of the kitchen chairs, checked her phone for missed calls or messages and walked back to the living room.

"You must have a lovely garden" The lean figure of Dr Sharma was standing to look out of the window, although it was too dark to see much of the flower beds and the lawn, until recently so carefully tended by Jahi.

"Yes, my husband…" but again Padma had no words to continue.

Dr Sharma turned, his face obscured in shadow.

"I am so sorry, I did not mean..." he began.

This time Rita came to the rescue.

"It was Dad's pride and joy," she said, sitting in the other armchair. As the dentist sat back on the sofa he was trapped between the two women.

"More tea?" Padma offered.

"No thank you Mrs Patel. I will go and unpack in a few minutes if that is alright with you?" he added.

Rita sent a surprised look in her mother's direction. Unpack? What did that mean? she asked herself.

"I said that Dr Sharma could stay with us for a few days while he gets settled in. His family are in Derby, you see, and hotels are so expensive!" Padma told her daughter.

"Oh" said Rita, taking a gulp of her orange juice to hide her surprise.

"He'll be in Nayan's room." Padma went on.

Rita thought, Nayan will be pleased about that – not!

"The boys are upstairs now sorting it all out, so Nayan and Mohal can share." Padma finished.

"It is only temporary" Dr Sharma nodded at Rita proudly. "I hope to make arrangements to rent somewhere very soon, but this opportunity came up unexpectedly..." once again there was an awkward pause as they all contemplated the tactless remark.

"I want you to go into the surgery again tomorrow, Rita" Padma said.

"Really?" Rita found it hard to disguise her disappointment, even though she had resolved to support her mother in any way she could. The surgery was boring and she was tired of explaining to strangers that her father had died and couldn't fill their teeth any more.

"You can help Dr Sharma to settle in." Padma added.

Rita looked doubtfully across at the composed figure on the sofa. She was not convinced he would need much help in "settling in".

"Great" she said, trying to sound enthusiastic.

"I will sort out my things and see you in the morning" Dr Sharma said.

"You're sure you won't eat anything? There's plenty in the fridge we can heat up. People are bringing us food all the time. Our friends have been very kind." Padma offered. Rita knew that Jaina had left them enough food for several days, and that other families had called by with various dishes.

"No, that is very kind of you but I am practising the 5:2 diet. And I don't eat after 6pm." Dr Sharma said.

That explained why he was so thin, Rita thought. Look what that diet had done for Colin Firth, he of the scene in the lake in Pride and Prejudice that used to make Padma swoon. His face was very thin these days.

"We'll leave at 8" Padma told him. "I'll come along to introduce you to everyone. Then I'll leave you to it."

"Very well. Good evening." Dr Sharma bowed his oiled head to both women and was gone.

Great, thought Rita. So I have to travel to the surgery with him and spend all day with him hanging around.

As soon as Dr Sharma had disappeared up the spiral staircase, presumably with his black suitcase, two pairs of feet- sizes 11 and 13 respectively – came clattering down. Rita's brothers were talking animatedly about a computer game and how to get to the next level.

"Hi Mum" Nayan nestled on the arm of Padma's chair and put his arm protectively round her.

So he did understand how difficult this all was, thought Rita, draining her glass. It's just that her brothers put up such a front it was hard to know what they really felt.

"I'll get us some supper" Mohal said, putting his head round the door.

"You?" Padma looked up, astonished.

"I'll heat up something." Mohal told her.

Rita smiled and rose to help. Really, her brothers were full of surprises, she thought.

"What do you make of Dr Sharma?" Rita managed to say quietly to her older brother as they watched a vegetable dish spin round in the microwave.

"Seems a decent bloke" was all her brother offered.

"How did Mum find him?" Rita wanted a full report.

She was disappointed.

"Dunno." her brother said.

Did Mohal have no curiosity? Rita thought.

"I expect there's an agency." Mohal offered as he took the vegetable dish from the microwave and checked the bread which was warming in the oven.

"But if he's staying in our house.." Rita's voice trailed off. She didn't want to accuse the stranger of being an axe murderer but what if…

"Not everything's a mystery, sis," Mohal said. "Of course Mum spoke to his last practice and to his family in Delhi. They know Aunty Gee." Mohal referred to a relative of Jahi's who lived in Neasden in London. Rita knew she would be at the funeral with her son, Rakesh.

As they arranged the food together, and called Nayan and her mother to the table, Rita felt reassured by Mohal's words. Let's see what tomorrow brings, she thought.

Chapter 15

"If you play good cricket, a lot of bad things get hidden."
Kapil Dev,
Indian international cricketer

Wednesday 18th February 2015 2pm

"Hi" Giles' fine features filled the screen as he ran his fingers through the top of his golden head.

"How's Leicester?" he asked Rita jocularly. "Not much chance of surfing there!" he added.

Confined at home after a couple of days helping at the surgery, Rita sat in her bedroom, the one that had been Nayan's before they swapped in the autumn. It had blue walls with scars where paint had peeled away when he had taken down his Star Wars posters. He hadn't put those into his new room. Instead, Rita had seen, disapprovingly, his walls were adorned with female celebs in various states of undress. She thought she would cover up the marks; if she put up some interesting pictures it might help dispel the frightening dream which persisted to haunt her sleep. So she had a plan for the walls, just as she had to continue her investigations into Farah's death, if she was careful. She had been exchanging text messages with someone she hoped would be able to visit, since her mother was being funny about her leaving the house.

While she waited for the person to text back, Rita had skyped Giles, Morwenna's boyfriend, who had lent her the pass to the gym at the cricket ground. There was something she needed to find out from him. Giles was a keen surfer and spent many of his weekends travelling from Exeter to whichever of the Cornish coast lines had the best waves according to the forecast. Polzeath was a favourite.

"Not many opportunities, no." Rita conceded, recalling Rohan's fall on the sand at Exmouth and thinking this might be no bad thing. She explained she wanted Giles's help.

"Fire away" he said, rolling his shoulders and reaching forward for a bottle of water which he lifted to his mouth as if in preparation.

"What do you need to know?" he asked, readying himself in his chair like a contestant on Mastermind.

"It's about Farah Ahmadi," Rita began.

"Oh yeh?" Giles was interested.

"I want you to tell me exactly, exactly" Rita stressed the word. "What happened when you last visited her in the summer, for your shoulder?"

"OK" said Giles, jutting his chin out a little as if this would reboot his memory.

"I put my head round her door" he began.

"This was in the treatment room at the gym at the cricket centre?" Rita made sure she was getting the picture.

"Yeh, that's right." Giles confirmed.

"So I put my head round her door and she said, 'Hi Giles, I've been expecting you!' Giles said this in a sauntering manner as if Farah had been flirting with him.

"Did she?" Rita asked with narrowing eyes. Giles needed to take this seriously, she thought.

"Ok, well maybe not." Giles sighed. He was not used to having to make a lot of effort.

"Shut your eyes" Rita told him. "Shut your eyes and imagine you are back there."

Giles started to comply.

"Imagine you are at the gym and you're just going through the door to the treatment room."

Rita slowed down her speech so that her intonation became a little hypnotic. She hoped no phones rang to disturb the calm she was trying to create.

"Was the door from the gym to the treatment room closed?" she asked.

"No" said Giles, responding slowly and deliberately as if he were concentrating.

This was good, thought Rita.

"The door was open. I stepped through and closed it behind me……I said my name, Giles Cookson, and Farah-"

"Where was she?" Rita hated to interrupt but she wanted to picture the scene accurately.

"Sitting down" said Giles, "Facing the door. Facing me. She replied 'Come on in; let's take a look at that shoulder of yours.' She had an iPad and she'd obviously been looking me up in her records, getting familiar with my details, recalling what treatment we'd done so far."

"Good, Giles" Rita thought positive feedback might encourage Giles in this useful vein.

"She said, 'Take off your top.'" Giles managed to say said this in a sensible voice, not the sing-song sound he had been using earlier. "and your shoes, and stand on the mat."

"Stand on the mat?" Rita aimed for a neutral tone, trying not to betray excessive interest in this detail.

"Mmmn" Giles' eyes were moving beneath his closed eyelids, Rita could see; he must be trying to envisage the situation. "She had a mat she carried around with her, sort of like a large yoga mat. She'd cover it over with paper for each client but she said she preferred to treat people on it and not on the treatment table. She said it was more natural and would help clients to learn the exercises they needed to do at home." he paused a moment, then went on,

"I stood on the mat and she worked around me. She took her shoes off – they were some sort of sandal- and stood on the mat with me to check the shoulder from the front and the back. She felt it and asked me to do a few movements, raise my arm, put my arm out straight, so she could see what improvement there had been and think what might help me next. She made a few notes on the iPad when she'd done that."

"What did she think might help?" Rita asked.

"She had some exercises in mind and she showed me what to do. She also rubbed some cool gel into the muscle." Giles winced at the memory. "It hurt a little when she did that, but as soon as she'd finished the shoulder felt looser. She was very good at what she did."

"Then what?" Rita prompted.

"Then what?" Giles seemed to be having trouble moving on from the memory of how the pain in his shoulder had been taken away by the skillful therapist "Then she told me to put my top and my shoes back on. We made another appointment, but of course that never happened because it was made for after she.."

Giles opened his eyes when he started to speak of Farah Ahmadi's death. It didn't seem right to keep them closed.

"And what else did she do?" Rita queried.

"Do?" Giles echoed. He screwed up his forehead in thought. What did she do? he asked himself.

"Well I did up my shirt and pulled on my jacket."

Trust Giles to be well turned out, thought Rita.

"While I did that" Giles was continuing, "she scrunched up the paper cover and put it in the bin, and then she rolled up the mat."

"She rolled up the mat?" Now Rita was echoing Giles.

"Yeh, it rolled up like a yoga mat, like I said, it had handles and a bag or something, so she could carry it over her shoulder. It made it easy to carry about." he confirmed.

"And then you left?" Rita asked.

"Yeh. That's right. Farah invoices – sorry, invoiced- my private health company directly. That's another reason I need this shoulder to get better quickly. The health plan only allows a certain number of sessions and I'm near my limit!"

Giles said this as if the terms of the health plan represented the biggest obstacle to resuming his cricketing career.

"Anything else?" Rita wanted to know.

"I said something like 'see you next time' and she said 'take care and remember to do the exercises'. The last I saw of her was as I was going out of the door to the gym. She was sitting at the desk, probably updating what we'd just done."

"Yes, she was meticulous with her records." Rita agreed.

"And you didn't notice the door to the fire escape?" she asked next.

"No. I guess I didn't." Giles was mystified as to how this could be. "I didn't take in the room much to be honest. I just wanted her help with my shoulder."

"And the blinds? To the room? How were they when she treated you?" Rita wanted to know.

"Oh they were down, closed," Giles said this if it was obvious. "They were closed all the time, so we had privacy." he sat back in the chair as if an ordeal was over.

"Thanks, Giles, you've been a great help," Rita told him and the pair said goodbye, Rita wishing him good surfing for the next weekend and Giles offering belated condolences on the death of her father.

Wednesday 18th February 2015 4pm

"Rita!" her mother's voice carried up the spiral staircase and through the door to Rita's room. "A visitor for you." Rita put down the blue tac she was using. She was carefully positioning various posters over the marks on the wall left by her brother's icons. She had spotted some old Bollywood posters on a stall in the market in town when she had last passed through. They were colourful and lively, amusing in the seriousness of the poses, 'a bit camp' she was sure Sammi would say. They added colour, life and interest to the blue walls. Rita thought that sticking up posters might not be against the rules for mourning, but she had not checked in case it was.

Now her visitor had arrived. This was another welcome distraction from the tedium of being stuck in the family home she thought, guiltily remembering the essays she needed to finish – surely uni would be compassionate in the circumstances and not expect too much?

"Coming!" she called, pleased the visitor had arrived as agreed by text.

She bounced down the stairs enthusiastically, despite her white salwar kameez, forgetting for a moment that she was supposed to be in mourning and, according to her mother, to show some decorum. She received a disapproving look from Padma as she arrived at the foot of the stairs and assumed a serious expression. Towering over her mother was a slim woman with short blond hair. She was in her late thirties, wearing a pair of black designer frames on the bridge of her nose; she looked like an elegant star of a Scandinavian drama. She wore a black biker jacket over a black top and her legs were encased in what Rita took at first to be a diaphanous black skirt but on closer consideration turned out to be flared trousers in a light black material, beneath which she had on black shorts. The outfit showed off her long legs to advantage. She wore canvass shoes on her feet. A large black bag was hanging over her left shoulder and an infant was sitting on her right hip.

"Hi" said Rita. "So glad you could come…And you!" she added this as she bent to talk to the little girl who glanced shyly away and nestled further into her mother's side.

"Mum, this is Maria Finch." Rita made the introductions.

"Pleased to meet you I'm sure" Padma remembered her manners. Who was this stranger, how did she know Rita? she wanted to ask. Was it one of the new friends she had taken up with since she had been at university? If so, Padma was not sure she approved. It was much better when her daughter had spent her time with that nice girl Priya, she thought, the one who wanted to be a doctor.

"Can I get you some tea?" Jaina, who was with them again that day, offered as she came through from the kitchen.

"You can sit in the living room. The boys are in the garden running off some energy." Padma said this as if her sons were children kicking a ball around outside. In fact, they were in Jahi's shed, puzzling how to operate the lawn mower. Fortunately, much of the garden was under decking, which simply required sweeping and cleaning, an easier task than looking after the grass.

"Thank you so much for seeing me," Farah Ahmadi's partner began when they were sitting down, the baby placed on the floor with a book and a ball, both made of material. The little girl seemed to like banging the ball on the carpet while putting the book in her mouth; Rita hoped she would learn to behave better before she got into a library of real books.

"I am sorry that you are experiencing a loss," Maria went on.

"Well, you know how it feels, I guess," Rita replied, adding, "But losing a partner, and in such circumstances, must have been much worse."

"I was so shocked when they told me," said Maria, nodding. "She just went off to work, a normal day, and never came back."

A sudden death, like her father's; Rita thoughts were momentarily paralysed at the memory.

"Then I was angry. How could she do this? How could she choose to leave us?" her hands were screwed tight at the memory of the anger.

"You thought she'd killed herself?" Rita checked.

"Yes, that's what they said at first. That she might have fallen by accident – that would be bad enough. But that she might have thrown herself down the stairs, on purpose. That would be worse!" the older woman gasped. "She wasn't unhappy or anything. There was no reason to think she might have done." she added.

Jaina came into the room at that point with their tea. She put it down and then stroked the baby on the head. "Such a pretty little girl" she said appreciatively.

"Lucy. That's what we decided to call her. Farah loved her to pieces. Lucy misses her. I can tell. Hopefully she's so young that she won't suffer for it. I will make sure she knows all about Farah when she's older. She will always know she had another mother."

Jaina's smile became a little frozen and stiff at this. "Yes, well I'll get back to your mother." she said to Rita and left for the kitchen, to pass on this latest information about Rita's visitor. What would Padma make of it? she thought.

"So now the inquest has decided she was killed, I want to know who did it, and why. I want to know for Farah's sake, and for Lucy's. That's why when Inspector Bridge mentioned you, I thought, why not? Why not see if you have any ideas? I remember reading about you in connection with that death at the Space Centre, how you and your friend helped the police."

"Oh, I don't know about that!" Rita tried to put in modestly, although she had downloaded the Leicester Mercury article headlined 'Local Girl Helps Solve Space Death Riddle.'

"Inspector Bridge said there was an entry in Farah's diary for the day she died." Maria went on.

"Yes, tell me more about that day." Rita asked. "You say she left home as usual?"

"That's right. On Mondays she did a stint at a care home."

"Do you know which one?" Rita interjected.

"It was the name of a tree - Oak may be?" she offered.

"Go on" Rita urged her.

"Then she was going to grab a sandwich in the car and go over to the gym at the cricket ground. A lot of clients make appointments there to fit around their work. That was her trouble. She was too nice! Always fitting in with other people, and listening to their troubles. It's amazing how people open up when someone's trying to make them feel better. She never betrayed confidences, of course, she never told me which patient she was talking about, but she used to have some pretty amazing stories her clients had told her. People who do sport can be very driven, very competitive, and this seemed to spill over into their professional and personal lives. There were heart-breaking stories about divorces, for example – people throwing their spouse's things out of the window in bin bags, or tales of terrible child access disputes between separated parents. There were stories of fathers who abducted their children from the school gate, or mothers depriving fathers of access at the last minute just to spite them. People can be very cruel when their emotions are involved. And, of course, as Farah would say, they failed to see what damage they were doing to themselves in the process."

Rita thought this sounded an interesting line of inquiry. "Did any of the stories suggest a motive to kill her?" she asked as gently as she could. "Did any of them sound like the person might have said too much and regretted it?"

"I've been thinking and thinking" said Maria, trying to distract the baby who was starting to wail.

"Farah would not act on anything she heard from a patient. She was clear on confidentiality." Maria said firmly.

"What about anything else she might have seen or heard?" Rita pressed.

"Well, she had a very clear sense of right and wrong. She couldn't bear injustice. I don't know if you knew she was Baha'i?" Maria suddenly put in.

"Oh" Rita had not known this; she filed the information away in her head. She thought she might have guessed this. Farah's family was Iranian but she had not picked up any signs that they might be Muslim, so Baha'i made sense.

"It was a comfort to me, when we buried her, that she believed the soul was relieved of its physical bonds on death and entered the spiritual world." Maria spoke seriously.

"What else do Baha'is believe?" Rita was curious.

"Well, I am not religious myself so I can only tell you what I gathered from Farah. They believe in a single God, they aim to seek truth and treat all people the same; they aim for the oneness of humankind and work for the elimination of extremes of poverty and wealth. Farah told me they would like a single financial and economic system for the world, to eliminate differences between rich and poor countries. The religion came out of Islam, actually, as a sort of antidote to the Shi-ite branch. They oppose violence and they don't seek to impose their laws and rituals on others."

"Did her family have a tough time in Iran?" Rita asked her; she had heard about persecution and forced conversions when the revolution took place in 1979 which led to the establishment of the world's first Islamic state. Baha'is there had been systematically persecuted in all aspects of their lives as a matter of government policy she knew.

Maria nodded, "Farah and her brother were sent away to schools in England. Her parents had a difficult time. She always wondered about their car accident."

"Oh dear," Rita sympathised. "And, if you don't mind me asking, what about your relationship? Did that accord with Farah's beliefs? I know some religious groups are more accepting than others." Rita asked her.

"You're right." Maria conceded, "It wasn't easy for her to come out as gay. Her friends and members of her meeting group were very supportive, but I gather there is some ambiguity within the hierarchy. It seems some members have a strong belief that sex and marriage are for one man and one woman. We never experienced any discrimination, don't get me wrong. I think there were issues for others around the world, though, as there are with a lot of religions; it takes time for belief systems to catch up I guess. Farah used to read out stories that people had posted on a LGBT Baha'i online site which a member in the United States started."

The baby was getting restless now. It was clear that most of Lucy's patience had been used up.

"Oh dear, time for her bedtime routine I think." Maria said, finishing her cup of tea quickly.

"So you don't know who 'R' was? The person in Farah's diary?" Rita remembered to ask as time was running out.

Maria was collecting together the baby's toys, distractedly. "The police asked me that. No one came to mind, she didn't usually refer to people by a single letter."

"Not her brother then?" Rita ventured thinking she might as well bring up the subject.

"Oh, I doubt that" said Maria dismissively as she scooped up her child, avoiding eye contact with Rita as she did so. "She wanted him kept at arms' length. They had a regular arrangement to meet once a month. She liked to compartmentalise her life."

The baby's wailing was increasing in volume, although her voice was nothing like as piercing as that of Priya's nephew, Theeran, Rita noted. She needed to take lessons if she wanted to achieve his level of decibels.

"About the inquest..." Rita started, wanting to ask about the argument which Mohal had witnessed.

"I really must go" Maria interrupted her, apparently anxious to leave with her protesting offspring. "Let me know if you have any ideas."

Wednesday 18*th* February 2015 5 pm

Rita had just shown Maria out through the front door when her mother called her from the kitchen. Oh dear, have I broken some rule by having a visitor? was her first thought. Or did she not approve of Maria? Rita was fairly sure that

Jaina would have passed on the information that Maria was Farah's partner.

Anxious, Rita walked to the kitchen. She passed Mohal in the hall, who failed to give her any clues and added to her worries by raising his eyebrows and shaking his head slowly. Jaina had absented herself from the kitchen, Rita noticed. This was another bad sign.

"We need to have a talk." Padma's words were ominous. Rita feared the worst.

They two of them sat together at the large white table. Rita noted her brothers were keeping clear. She could not even hear them elsewhere in the garden or the house. What had her mother to say to her?

"It's about your future." Padma came straight out with it. Rita swallowed hard; here we go! she thought. Was everything she had feared about to be said? How could she argue with her mother at a time like this?

"Your father and I discussed your time at uni, of course, before he died." Her mother seemed very composed and determined, Rita noticed.

"He did not want you to be unhappy." Padma continued, placing her hands on the table and looking at her daughter over her brown designer frames.

Rita shuffled uncomfortably on her chair, desperately trying to guess where this was going.

"He knew of course that you wanted to change your accommodation." her mother went on.

"And in light of that I have decided he would want you to move to the shared house, if that will make you happier." Padma concluded.

Rita found she could breathe again, she had stopped for a second or two, worrying that her mother was going to say she should leave uni altogether.

"Really?" was all she could manage.

"Here is a cheque. Fill it in for the deposit and send it to

Sammi." Padma was business-like as she passed the paper across the table.

"Thank you so much, Mum!" Rita was genuinely relieved and breathed her thanks. She came round the table and kissed her mother's upturned cheek.

"That is not all we have to discuss." Padma went on, to Rita's consternation. Oh dear, perhaps she had relaxed too soon, Rita thought.

"If you are to get to Leamington you will need a car. There will be some money from your father's life insurance, so I will get you one. You should have a car of your own." Padma was firm.

"Wow!" Rita found the breath taken out of her. This was such a great surprise! "That would be amazing!" she managed to say.

"Your father would want you to be happy." Padma said. Rita nodded. She recalled those were his last words to her." And I want you to be safe." her mother added.

Rita kissed her again. Now, when she was allowed to return to uni in a few days, she had something to look forward to.

Chapter

16

"I understand cricket - what's going on, the scoring - but I can't understand why."

Bill Bryson,
American author

Sunday 22nd March 2015 10am

Over a month had gone by. A month in which they had carried out the funeral of Rita's father and observed the mourning period; a month in which Rita had returned to uni and been busy catching up with her studies; a month in which she had given notice on her student room and arranged with Sammi to move into the shared house in April. Holi celebrations had come and gone without Rita taking part; she had not seen Priya since the funeral. Now she was back in Elm Drive for the Easter holiday.

"Where are you going?" Padma called when she heard Rita leaving the house.

As Rita had complained to Priya on FaceTime the previous day, her mother did not seem to have adjusted to the fact that the mourning period was over and Rita was free to go where she pleased again. Yesterday, Padma had questioned her daughter when Rita was leaving for De Montfort Hall to see the Bollywood dance celebration; Rita knew some of the students involved and was excited to see their achievements.

"She doesn't treat the boys like this!" she had wailed to her friend. "She doesn't get that I'm an adult!"

"Maybe she wants to make up for your Dad." Priya had offered, "Perhaps she thinks she has to protect you."

Rita tried to bear in mind her friend's wise words.

Probably her mother meant well. So she called brightly, "To see Richard III!" and closed the glazed front door behind her to prevent any discussion, making for the blue Toyota that Padma had purchased for her as promised.

Nayan had said, "It's not fair! Why don't I get a car?"

Padma thought that although he had just started lessons with Mr Patel's 'SUCCESS SCHOOL OF MOTORING' he was not yet ready to have a car of his own. Indeed, judging by the reckless speed with which he drove on his lessons she wondered if he would ever be ready.

Rita headed for the University. Parking a few streets away she joined a growing crowd of people aiming to be sombre in their appearance but suppressing their excitement at the events about to unfold. It didn't do to exude enthusiasm when what you were waiting to see was a coffin. Even if it was the coffin of the last King of England to die in battle, 500 years ago; a coffin which had been designed and made by one of his few known living descendants. This was the first ceremony in 'interment week' which would culminate in the reburial of the remains of Richard III in Leicester Cathedral. Among the rows of watchers, many carried white roses, which were available in abundance that morning, as if a planeload of flowers had landed onto the city. Rita had put a rose in her car already, together with sandwiches and drinks, so she could follow the processions and events around Leicestershire that day. These would end with the coffin being handed over by the University authorities to the Cathedral dignitaries and then there would be a service in St Martin's, which had been carefully choreographed, according to the local news. The weather was playing its part in greeting the last Plantagenet King. Although only March, the signs were it would be a fine, bright, sunny day.

At noon the golden coffin, which emerged to gasps from some of the crowd, turned out to be a simple box of oak, crafted by his 17th great grandnephew, Michael Ibsen. Rita knew the body - or, rather, the bones - had been packed in woollen fleece and linen and arranged in a lead ossuary. A rosary and piece of Irish linen had been placed inside the coffin with him, everyone concerned being keen to reflect what may have been the expectations for burial in Richard's time. Michael Ibsen, a cabinet maker born in Canada and a descendant of Richard III's sister Anne of York, would have fixed on the lid. It was his mitochondrial DNA which had helped to confirm the skeleton found in the car park was indeed that of the King. The words on the lid read "Richard III 1458-1485, Reinterred 26-03-2015".

Rita saw the slim and unassuming figure of Canadian-born Mr Ibsen, dressed quietly in a pale grey suit and coat and carrying a white rose, moving at the back of a small procession which walked through the doorway. Next to him was the other known descendant, Wendy Duldig, a lady from Australia; she wore a black coat with a white scarf and also held a white rose in her fingers. The coffin was carried by six pall bearers and was taken past various officials including the Mayor, who Rita could identify by the shiny gold chain, a rare piece of finery on a day when everyone was respectfully dressed to honour the King. The crowd stood still and solemn. It was a breath-taking moment. Various members of the party were invited to place their roses on the coffin. These included some of the discovery team, who Rita recognised from their press conferences, and Philippa Langley from the Richard III Society, whose drive and determination had propelled the theory of the whereabouts of Greyfriars Abbey into a dig and then the amazing discovery on the first day of exploration, under the letter 'R' in the infamous car park. Now, as she said she had hoped, his body's journey was coming to a dignified end, and he was being reclaimed as a person and not an archaeological enigma.

The coffin was escorted away to a shout from one member of the crowd of "Long live King Richard"; perhaps not the most apposite of statements, Rita thought to herself, but somehow it captured the awe and raw emotion of the crowd. The first destination was Fenn Lane Farm which had been identified as the likely spot where Richard fell at the Battle of Bosworth. This was for a private ceremony before the coffin would be taken over for public acclamation at Bosworth Field and then toured round the city to the Cathedral. Rita had studied the route and planned to watch the progress from a number of vantage points. As she returned to the Toyota and got ready to head for Bosworth, Rita got a text; it was from Rakesh.

"Hi I'm in Leicester next weekend. Can we meet up?" Rita made a mental note to text him back with some possible arrangements. It would be nice to see him again she thought, he had been so kind.

* * *

Driving to Bosworth, Rita cast her mind back to her father's funeral, reminded in part by the sight of the King's coffin, but also by the text from Rakesh. He had arrived at their house the night before the funeral with his mother, Aunty Gee, and had proved an indispensable help throughout the next day. Rakesh had helped Mohal with his duties as chief mourner, he had cleaned Nayan's shoes, which Padma said were "a disgrace", and he had helped Rita when she thought for one awful moment she had left her phone in the crematorium.

Somehow, when someone close to you died, she found, your brain got a bit clogged up. You were thinking about them even when you didn't realise it. You looked out of the window and imagined their soul travelling soaring to another life and the next thing you knew half an hour had passed and you'd lost track of what it was you were supposed to be doing. That's how you made mistakes, mislaid and forgot things, imagined things that weren't really happening.

Your reality was not quite in tune, she thought.

Rakesh, whose father had died 12 years ago when he was fifteen, seemed instinctively to understand all this and was able and willing to help the siblings while they adjusted to this new feeling and life without one of their parents. After the funeral, Rakesh had also been a source of good advice on how to handle her mother and had made Rita laugh with tales of how he let Aunty Gee think she was controlling him when really it was the other way round. Altogether, Rakesh had made the proceedings bearable and she had been a little sorry when the time came for him to leave.

In order to attend the funeral, Rakesh and his mother had stayed at Sundial, the bed and breakfast run by Morwenna's mother, Athena Maitland, where Rita and Priya had sometimes worked in the holidays. Before Rakesh and Aunty Gee had left for London, Priya had driven over to Elm Drive and taken Rita to Sundial, getting Padma's permission first.

"As you're seeing relatives I'll let you go", her mother had said.

The three of them had sat amiably on the sofas and chairs in the guest lounge while Aunty Gee took an afternoon nap, sipping mint tea and talking of general subjects, not the gloomy prospect of life without Jahi. Rakesh, a chef at a London hotel, had to return to the kitchen the next day.

"Those vegetables won't prep themselves!" he joked.

Priya said he should go on Master Chef; Rakesh said he couldn't stand the pressure, He liked to be familiar with his kitchen and equipment and to repeat dishes until he was absolutely sure he could deliver them to the same standard all the time, he told them. "Slow but steady wins the race." he explained. The same goes for your feelings when someone has moved on, he had told Rita, seriously; take each day at a time and one day you will wake up and feel better about it.

* * *

Rita had let this advice echo in her head when the day came that Padma had calculated it would be acceptable for Rita to return to Warwick. Rohan had gone back after reading week, coming to Leicester for the funeral and then returning again, so he was not available to give her a lift. Mohal wanted the red Peugeot for one of his journalistic assignments and, in view of the mourning period and constant visits by relatives, there had been no opportunity to buy a car for Rita. So she had opted to travel back to uni by train, packing everything she thought she might need until the end of term into a large suitcase and her backpack. Dr Sharma had driven her to the station;his wife and family were now installed in a house they were renting in Syston.

"It's no trouble, it's the least I can do" he had said. He had been quiet on the journey, allowing Rita to think her own thoughts, which she was grateful for.

Arriving back on the campus, it was with a heavy heart that Rita had entered the accommodation building again. Her father's absence weighed on her heart, worry about catching up with her work and dislike of her room weighed on her head. Strangely, given that they were pretty annoying, she missed her brothers. Nayan in particular had provided some distraction from preoccupations and concerns about what life would be like after their father's death. He had been very excited to read that Kevin Pieterson, an England and IPL cricketer with a flamboyant style, he explained, might join the Foxes, as the Leicestershire cricket team were known, at Grace Road. The story had appeared in the press and been scotched pretty quickly, but it had not stopped Nayan from speculating that other high profile players might come to rescue the County from a moribund period. Rita thought the idea of injecting an exciting and well-known player into the mix might fit with the new Chief Executive that Rohan had told her about. Wasim Khan seemed keen to find ways to get the club moving forward, she thought.

She had been cheered by the cards she found when she opened her mail box. Insensitive as her fellow in-mates might appear to be when it came to social and catering arrangements, it appeared several were genuinely touched by the news of her father's death and had sent condolences in various forms. There were cards with pictures of trees and flowers. There were scribbled notes on pieces of paper. There was a small box of shell-like chocolates.

'May peace and comfort find you during this difficult time'

'We want to express our sympathy and let you know that our thoughts are with you'

'To everything there is a season, and a time to every purpose under the heaven'

She had scattered the cards around her room, put a garland by her elephants, and lit incense burners there. She added to her corner some words which Ben Cohen, the Jewish friend from school who Priya had gone out with over the summer, had sent-

'O Lord, show me the way and give me the will to live and work so that I may reflect honour upon my dear father's memory. This will also glorify Thy name, for Thou are the father of the fatherless, and in thy keeping are the souls of all our dear ones.'

There had been so much to catch up on once she was back that Rita had little time to think about her father. She had missed a few lectures and a couple of seminars, so she had arranged for another student to email her their notes to help her catch up. She felt confident about the introduction to historical skills, as this included an online skills programme which she had been able to access from home, and about the Italian course she was taking, as she had skyped an Italian post graduate student for language practice. Her essays had needed finalisation, using a variety of source material as required, but she had delivered them by the agreed revised deadlines.

In many ways, being so busy was good for her, she thought. It reduced the amount of time she could notice the things she disliked about her accommodation. Also, knowing her time there was coming to an end helped her feel better. She could count down the days she would have to share that kitchen and listen to the cries and giggles of her neighbours in the early hours of the morning. Working also stopped her brooding on how life would be now her father was gone. Would her mother expect her to go back after uni for example and not leave home for a career? Would she pressurise her into marriage? It had not escaped Rita's notice that Padma and Aunty Gee had exchanged looks when she and Rakesh were talking together. Were they planning something perhaps? Would Mohal or Bandhu, as senior members of the family now, see it as their role to persuade her to take a husband? Her father had always championed her and her plans to have a career, but, with him gone, things could take a different turn, she thought.

When she felt overwhelmed with her thoughts, and when she felt she had done enough work to earn a break, rather than feel stuck on the campus she took herself out. Strolling the streets of Warwick and looking at the old buildings provided a kind of comfort. The town had been established by Ethelfleda, leader of Mercia, daughter of Alfred the Great and sister of Edward the Elder, as a defence against Danish invaders. Rita knew about her; there was a statue to Ethelfleda in Leicester, in the grounds of the black and white half-timbered medieval Guildhall which stood near the Cathedral. It commemorated her repelling the Danes from the city in 918.

The magnificent castle dominated the town of Warwick on one side, and was operated as a major tourist attraction. As well as the church, which she had told Priya about, there were interesting medieval buildings which had survived the great fire in the town in 1694. These included the town's own

Guildhall, now the Lord Leycester Hospital, and timber-framed buildings including the Elizabethan house which was now the Thomas Oken Tea Rooms. People from the past had suffered loss just as she had. In fact, they had often suffered worse deprivations, losing loved ones being part of everyday existence when the life span was so short, Rita thought. From Warwick she caught a bus to Leamington to call in on Sammi's house. She didn't expect anyone to be in; she just liked the idea of looking at it, thinking that, very soon, she would be living there. It was a bit like trying on new clothes she thought, imagining what it would be like to actually wear them properly. As it was a bright day and she didn't feel like returning to the confines of the campus just yet, Rita had caught another bus, to Kenilworth.

"You went where?" Priya asked later, unsure what her friend was talking about.

Finding the way in after a ten minute walk from the bus stop, Rita had paid the fee to enter the English Heritage castle site and followed the path to the café and exhibition in the stables, which included references to the visit by Elizabeth the First. Then she had walked to inspect the contents of the gatehouse, which included more information on the 1575 revelries, and on to the reconstructed gardens. These could be inspected from an elevated walkway in the shadow of the castle ruins. Rita climbed the steps cautiously – they were quite steep- and was rewarded with a good bird's eye view of the carefully laid out geometric patterns which formed the gardens. Between the beds were sculptures like tall thin brown pyramids, an idea apparently borrowed from Renaissance gardens in France and Italy. The precise arrangement of the beds reminded Rita of the Elizabethan knot garden which she had seen at Hatfield House.

The gardens were a faithful recreation of the private gardens which Robert Dudley had constructed for the Queen's visit in 1575, complete with a reconstruction of the magnificent fountain in the exact place, as the archaeological investigations had proved, where the original had been. At the top of a pillar, rising from an eight sided base, and all in white, were two Atlas figures, holding up the world on top of which was a ragged staff, part of Dudley's coat of arms. Robert Lineham, keeper of the council chamber at the time, had described the white marble fountain – "whence sundry fine pipes did lively distil continuous streams into the reservoir of the fountain" and its decoration, which included "Neptune with his trident ….and Thetis in her chariot drawn by dolphins".

Rita looked up at the castle walls behind her. What was left of that building required imagination to create the vision of its former glory in the heady days of 1575. The Earl had renovated the castle in the manner of a French chateau within the old medieval defensive walls, using English workmen and an Italian engineer. He had put in large glass windows, which in the candlelight would have given it a romantic appearance. Dudley had spent a fortune on the restoration and luxurious decoration, which included Flemish tapestries, Turkish and Persian carpets. The furnishings were frequently embellished with bears and ragged staffs – part of Dudley's coat of arms- and with his motto 'droit et loyal' (honest and loyal). Rita had seen in the gatehouse a fireplace from the period which bore his initials and these words. From the descriptions, Rita could see the castle must have been magnificent and every inch worthy of a Queen. The Earl could not have tried harder, she thought.

Recalling his efforts, and climbing carefully down the steps from the viewing area, brought to mind the tragic death of Robert Dudley's first wife, at the foot of the staircase in Oxford; that reminded Rita that her preoccupations with her degree work had prevented her from spending much time mulling over the events surrounding the death of Farah Ahmadi. She had put the bottle she had inadvertently acquired from Rashid safely in a cupboard in her bedroom at Elm Drive and she had resolved to contact Inspector Bridge to see what progress the police were making, and to outline her theory, when she returned to Leicester at the end of term.

Sunday 22nd March 2015 2pm

Rita was standing, among a crowd of two thousand people, in the visitor centre at Bosworth; they were waiting for a service to be conducted by the Bishop of Leicester. She had watched as members of the army cadet corps had towed the coffin of Richard III up Ambion Hill, across the battlefield, under a golden sky. It was fortunate that the weather had been fine for a few days so the ground underfoot was relatively dry, enabling the wheels of the carriage to turn easily. The actual site of the battle had been confirmed by archaeologists a few years before; they had uncovered not only cannon balls – forming the largest such collection in Europe- but also a gilded silver badge in the shape of a boar – the personal emblem of the King. The ceremonies taking place managed to be both solemn and reverential, she noted approvingly, to observe the King's demise on that land, but also a pageant, for the area to celebrate the King and his return.

Two knights in armour had led the cortege at Fenn Lane Farm for a private ceremony which had taken place there. Three soils had been put together in a wooden box made by Michael Ibsen, which was like a miniature version of the coffin he had built. The soils were from Fotheringay, in Northampton, where Richard was born, Middleham, in North Yorkshire, where he grew up, and Fenn Lane where he had died.

As she waited for the service to begin, Rita recalled her unsatisfactory conversation with Inspector Bridge the previous Friday as she made good her resolve to pass on what information she had about Farah Ahmadi and to find out how the investigation was going.

Friday 20th March 2015 11am

The weather on that Friday had been overcast with intermittent sun, which was annoying to Nayan who had mumbled complaints as he left the house early. He had wanted a good view of the partial solar eclipse. Various schools were conducting projects on it, including his. Rita had decided she preferred to watch the highlights on the television. The eclipse was total to the far north, near the Faroe Islands, and the BBC were filming it from an aircraft.

"Imagine!" she had said to Priya on the phone the day before, "An eclipse just before they bury Richard III. What would they have made of that in medieval times?"

A feeling that matters were being seen only partially had extended to Rita's telephone exchange with the Inspector later that day.

"How is the investigation going into the death of Farah Ahmadi?" she had tried.

"You know I can't tell you that, Rita" had come his short reply.

"Well, have you any leads, anything to go on?" Rita had pressed.

"Are you sure it's your brother who wants to be the journalist and not you?" Jamie Bridge had replied, laughing, "You are very persistent."

"I just want to help that's all" said Rita, regretting the words as soon as she had said them.

"You know I take a dim view of that." Jamie Bridge had chided, "Ideas are fine, but don't start meddling." he warned.

"No, but I thought..." Rita tried again.

"What is it?" Jamie Bridge asked in a world weary way.

"Her brother, Rashid, he's behaving very suspiciously." Rita had ventured.

"Suspiciously? How? And how do you know?" Inspector Bridge had queried, his ears attuned to Rita's level of concern. After all, she had been useful in previous murder inquiries so she was worth listening to, he thought.

Jamie Bridge was not going to tell Rita that the investigation was stuck like a vehicle in mud. The wheels kept going round but they seemed to be making no productive progress. It felt like they were going deeper into the ground and not going forward. Many investigations were like this. If there were no leads or suspects in the first 48 hours or so then the chances of finding anyone responsible started to diminish. It was like drawing a series of concentric circles round the victim, each circle representing a period of time from the death. The centre, the bull's-eye, the first 24 to 48 hours, were the most productive. A perpetrator might be identified from the victim's immediate circle or last acquaintance, for example. Many women victims were 'last seen' in the company of a man whose DNA was found on the body of the unfortunate woman when found. Or a stabbing might be carried out by an aggrieved spouse, or by a driver in a moment of madness or road rage. Then there were mercy killings by a caring but desperate relative.

Farah Ahmadi's death fitted no such pattern and had yielded no such clues in the early days. When she died, her partner, Maria, was with their child at a mother and baby session in a ball pool at a leisure centre on the Loughborough Road, with multiple witnesses from the group who had been to antenatal classes together and bonded over their children; so she was eliminated. Those at the Grace Road ground at the time had been interviewed and everything they said checked out. The spectators could vouch for each other; no one had left the stands in the time frame in question. The archery course attenders had been occupied with hitting the targets and their trainers had been on the field to assist them. This included her brother, Rashid, although Inspector Bridge was prepared to concede that if he had a good enough motive he might be worth looking at again, to see if the witnesses could have been mistaken or, perhaps, had been persuaded to give him an alibi. He was certainly the only one they had interviewed who was at the ground and had a personal connection with the dead woman. Caterers and ground staff had been exhaustively background-checked in the hope that some link might emerge, but with no reward. The care sector conference members had also been looked over carefully, but, as with the archery course, they could alibi each other as they were all attending the same training talk at the time of the 'fall'. So the circle widened and time went by.

Were they looking for a stranger perhaps? Someone who Farah may or may not have been expecting;someone who had got into the gym and out again and had not been picked up in the CCTV? After the inquest, a review team had gone over all the steps taken in the investigation and suggested a few extra lines of inquiry, but nothing solid had resulted. Jamie Bridge had been secretly hoping that another detective would be appointed to take over the case. He disliked failure, but he felt he could recite by heart most of the statements they had taken and none of them was helping to solve the case.

Frustrated, he thought it would do no harm to listen to Rita, and perhaps ask one of his Constables to look into whatever she was saying if it seemed it could be useful. Of course, officers were thin on the ground at the moment, most being deployed on traffic and crowd control, as well as security, for the procession of the remains of the last Plantagenet King.

"You remember the diary entry? It said she was meeting 'R' at 2.30?" Rita reminded him.

"Yes, but we don't know that R meant Rashid." Jamie Bridge replied,

"No, but say it was him. Have you checked for his DNA,

on the shoes?" Rita asked.

"We can't go doing DNA tests randomly, whatever you've seen on CSI!" the Inspector objected "For one thing, it's expensive, you know, we have to justify every test nowadays, and of course there are human rights considerations. We don't have Rashid's DNA on file and we wouldn't have a reason to seek it, not at the moment." He paused for a moment, and then another thought occurred to him, "What shoes anyway?"

"The ones I brought in. The shoes from the charity shop." Rita said in a slightly annoyed tone; had the Inspector forgotten?

"I don't know anything about shoes, do I?" Jamie Bridge replied honestly, calling up on his computer screen as he did so the log of evidence for the Farah Ahmadi case.

"They were Birkenstocks. Like Farah's. I think they were Farah's. You should have tested them?" Rita sounded quizzical.

"So where are the shoes now?" Jamie Bridge did not seem to know.

"I gave them to one of your officers. Constable Gardner." Rita told him exasperatedly.

"Well, I'll chase that up then." Inspector Bridge said, not willing to admit his ignorance of the matter entirely. "But as for DNA..."

"I have his DNA." Rita said to his surprise.

"Excuse me?" Jamie Bridge was astonished.

"He gave me a water bottle. It's bound to have his fingerprints and DNA." Rita said.

"Yes, but we can't use them. It's not police evidence. You might have planted the prints or the DNA." the Inspector argued.

"Oh yeh" Rita adopted a sceptical note, "I go round doing that all the time! But seriously, even if you can't actually use the results in court it might help to identify whether Rashid was involved or not?" she pleaded.

"And why would he have been involved? What's his motive? What's this suspicious behaviour you know about?" Jamie Bridge was listening now, even though as he spoke he had the phone jammed against his chin so he could type out an email to Constable Gardner.

"He had two addresses and two women, wives or whatever. He is leading two lives." Rita told him.

"I'm not even going to ask you how you know that." Inspector Bridge had said, sighing. "You should know that your curiosity can get you into trouble."

But he had taken down the addresses and details of the two women and the child whom Rita had seen. "I'll get one of my officers on to it." he promised.

"And I'll bring in the bottle with his DNA" Rita told him. "I'll do it when I go to the Cathedral on Monday to see Richard."

Sunday 22nd March 2015 4.30pm

After the service at the battlefield, Rita took a route across the outskirts of the city, avoiding the signs that read "King Richard III Route Sunday 22 March Expect delays", to a parking space near the down-at-heel Saint Matthew's estate, now home to a recent influx of migrants from Somalia, the women identifiable by their colourful costumes. From there she planned to walk to the Cathedral, passing from the Clock Tower through the fashionable Lanes area, at the back of the market, with its up-and-coming cafes, wine bars and boutiques.

Rita arrived at the Cathedral in time to see the four black horses drawing the gun carriage, which bore the coffin of the last English King to lead his forces into battle, arriving from the opposite direction. She was at the back of a crowd which was seven or eight deep so her view was obscured, but she could see enough to know that the wooden box was being given to the care of the Cathedral by University officials; and then Richard disappeared inside the building.

As she walked away with the crowd, to catch the television coverage of the service which would take place in the Cathedral later, Rita's mind was buzzing with the excitement of the day, but she was also impressed with the solemnity which had surrounded the events. Rita thought how sad that Richard would be reinterred on Thursday with so few family members around him. In a way, the Richard III Society had become his family, or, at least, champions of his cause, she thought. That led her to recall Mr Gregson, who had died leaving only one living relative behind as far as she knew, his son in New Zealand. She had never heard him speak of grandchildren. Perhaps his family line would die out, just like Richard's, and like Robert Dudley's she thought.

With Mr Gregson in her thoughts, and driving past a sign to Thurmaston, where the Oak Trees Care Home was, Rita was reminded of the conversation between the care workers which she had overheard a few weeks ago. Was there anything in what they had been saying? Did Farah know something about Ramlah Massood's business? Something she might have gone to the authorities about? And what could they have done? she wondered. Aiming for home, where her uncle Bandhu was due to call in on them, Rita formulated a plan to find out more.

Chapter

17

"I delayed my father's funeral because of cricket."
Virat Kholi,
Indian international cricketer

Sunday 22nd March 2015 7pm

"Are they going to bury him again - the King dude - today?" Nayan asked, wording his question in a way calculated to annoy his sister.

In the living room at Elm Drive, Rita had, for once, overcome the claims of her brothers and obtained use of the large screen TV for the Channel 4 coverage of the evening service at the Cathedral.

"No" Rita told him. "This is more of a welcome. Then the coffin will stay in the Cathedral so people can visit it. He goes in his tomb on Thursday"

"Creepy!" was Nayan's verdict. "And what do you mean by 'visit it'?"

"It's called paying your respects." Rita said seriously, "I'm going tomorrow."

"Woohoo!" her younger brother was not impressed.

"Ssh!Look!" Brother and sister watched the screen as a young girl wearing a brown and yellow uniform placed a crown on the coffin which had been draped in a cloth embroidered to reflect the King's life. An old Bible had already been placed on the coffin, a link with the past. There was some singing and some speeches before the service ended.

"There will be someone standing at each corner of the coffin" Rita told Nayan, who was not even feigning interest.

"Just like for Royalty today."

"Oh, OK" Nayan said.

"Any luck with solving your murder? Find out how that physio came to fall?" Nayan changed the subject.

"I have some ideas." said Rita "I've told the police, but they don't seem to be taking much notice" she sighed.

"Pity there's no video" her brother sympathised. "Look how many people have watched Madonna's fall at the Brits last month!"

"Yeh, very embarrassing." Rita agreed. "It was a cape malfunction wasn't it?"

"So they say." Nayan smiled, "She was singing 'Living for Love'. It is kinda funny, watching it on YouTube; she goes tumbling backwards in slow motion. She couldn't see what was happening. She was sort of pulled from behind." He paused, and then added "Since there's no Top Gear after that Jeremy Clarkson business, can we catch up with the football? I don't know why I want to watch it. City haven't had a win for so long!"

"Still doing badly then?" Rita decided to take an interest. "They haven't sacked the manager though?"

"No, Nigel Pearson is still there." Nayan answered her question, and then, as she suspected he might, he continued at some length.

"There was a rumour last month – well the papers reported he had been sacked after the Crystal Palace match – but it wasn't true. That was another 'fracas' according to the press, like the Clarkson one but less violent. Pearson was supposed to have held on to one of the players on the touchline. Bizarre. Anyway, he is still there and a good thing too, I think. It's not as if we are being hammered. There have been lots of close games. We had two good draws, with Everton last month and Hull this month. Yesterday we lost to Spurs, but four goals to three! It was well exciting"

"Do they have good players?" Rita wanted to know.

"We signed Estaban Cambiasso from Argentina last August and he has been an important player for us, but I really think we will go down again to the Championship. A team that's bottom of the Premier League in January rarely survives. It's been a good year, anyway." Nayan was philosophical, "We've seen all the top teams at our ground."

"And what about women's football?" Rita asked her brother, "Does that ever get on television?" She thought if it did she might watch.

"The Women's World Cup will be on BBC 3," he said to her satisfaction, "and their FA Cup Final will be played at Wembley for the first time and televised, too."

* * *

Richard's service over, and the Premiership highlights asserting their usual pride of place on the living room TV, Rita walked into the kitchen where, as she had expected, she found the reassuringly comfortable looking figure of her uncle. She had seen his car outside the house when she arrived and had heard him talking with her brother Mohal. She thought they would be together, exchanging 'man' talk – probably about golf handicaps or cricket averages.

"Richard in the ground yet?" Mohal asked. He was as bad as Nayan! Rita thought.

"No, that won't be until Thursday." she told him. "Am I the only one with a memory round here?"

"That reminds me," Mohal said, "Since I couldn't watch the football" he did not succeed in taking the sense of grievance out of his voice, "I finally got round to cleaning out the Peugeot while you were watching the Richard thing on TV."

"Great!" said Rita who had remembered how the car had been gradually filling up with plastic water bottles and pizza boxes.

"I found this." Mohal held up a USB memory stick. "Is it yours? I don't recognise it."

"Oh, yeh" Rita reached across to take the memory stick from her brother, "It's photos from Mr Gregson. You remember the old black and white ones I showed you?"

"Mmmn" Mohal indicated his recollection.

"Bandhu" Rita addressed her uncle as Mohal left the room to join his younger brother in catching up on the Premier League action.

"I was wondering what you could tell me about care homes, how they are inspected and so on." Bandhu, who worked for a hospital trust, looked up with a slight jolt. The conversation had taken an unexpected turn all of a sudden. What was his niece up to now? Bandhu thought.

"Oh" her uncle tried not to sound surprised, "Well, let's see. An outfit called the Care Quality Commission rates the homes. Alternatively, if something goes very badly wrong, the home can be prosecuted. There was a case recently, for example, where a home was fined £100,000 with £35,000 costs for the death of a man of 85 who got serious burns from a scalding hot radiator pipe."

"Ouch!" said Rita, "The poor chap!"

"Exactly" Bandhu sighed, shaking his head regretfully "He fell and was trapped between a wardrobe and the radiator; he couldn't reach the emergency buzzer."

"Oh no!" said Rita, horrified.

"The pipe should have been boxed in or insulated." Bandhu said, nodding in agreement with Rita's shock.

"And was the Home closed?" Rita wanted to know.

"Oh, no" Bandhu's reply surprised her. "The company running the Home had a good safety record, so it was treated as a 'blip'"

"Some blip!" Rita was not impressed.

"I know." said Bandhu, "But to be honest no one would take on these businesses if they had to be completely free of incidents." he tried to explain.

"Even so..." Rita tried to argue.

"Well, it was accepted what the company said, that it was not a cost cutting exercise, just that it was a risk they had not appreciated." Bandhu went on.

"So much for the inspections then." Rita was not impressed.

"Well, I agree. Perhaps we place too much reliance on the inspection regime. Obviously the inspectors didn't realise the risk either." Bandhu nodded thoughtfully.

"And a grandfather was lost. In terrible circumstances." Rita said sadly shaking her head. "How do the Home owners get taken to court?" she wanted to know.

"Offences have been prosecuted under the Health and Safety at Work Act." her uncle told her, used to Rita's strange curiosity, "But sometimes the police are called in. In another case an old lady died when a bannister gave way and she fell down the stairs. The inquest jury were on your side Rita. They said it was gross neglect. It was only after their decision that the police investigated."

"It seems you are safer on the streets than in some of these Homes!" Rita was amazed.

"What else can people do? If someone is frail and cannot look after themselves, what choice is there?" Bandhu countered, thinking of discussions which happened daily at the health trust. "Don't forget, hospitals are constantly being criticised for not discharging people quickly enough into care homes. The system cannot afford for us to start being too picky about the safety record of the Homes."

"Well it seems a sad end to valuable lives." Rita observed, "I hope I never need to go into a Home."

"Marry well and have children who can care for you!" Bandhu advised, lifting up his hands in an imploring gesture. Rita felt her cheeks go hot. She had been hoping to avoid conversations about her long-term future.

Bandhu saw her discomfort.

"I'm only joking!" he said, lowering his arms. "Who knows what the future holds for any of us? I am relying on Shona and Shreya to make their fortune and look after the two of us!" he added.

"What about that Commission you mentioned. What can they do about bad care homes?" Rita checked.

"They issue ratings. New rules mean the ratings will have to be displayed on their websites and on the premises." her uncle said.

"Sounds about time." was Rita's opinion.

"Yes. Of course not all providers have been rated yet" Bandhu added, standing at the sink to fill a glass with water and taking a few gulps.

"How come?" Rita queried.

"Well it takes time and resources. The CQC can only do so many at a time." he told his niece.

"I wouldn't put a relative of mine in a Home if I could possibly avoid it and I certainly wouldn't use one that hadn't been rated" Rita affirmed.

"You say that, but you might not have any choice. Or you might know people using the Home and feel it's ok. You can't make rules about these things." Bandhu said reasonably, putting down the glass.

"So what are the ratings anyway?" Rita wanted to know, thinking about the conversation she had eavesdropped and starting to make sense of some of the things which had been said.

"Outstanding. Good. Requires improvement. Inadequate." Bandhu recited, standing now facing Rita, his back to the sink.

"And how can you find out if a Home is rated as poor?" Rita wanted to know.

"You can go on the CQC website. All their reports are there, together with their recommendations for improvement." her uncle replied.

"Mmmn" Rita thought she might look up the Home where Mr Gregson had been, in the light of the discussion she had overheard.

"And what about - whistle-blowers are they called? People who tell the authorities if there's something going wrong?" was her next question.

Bandhu sighed and scratched his head, looking sideways at his niece. She never gave up!

"Well, of course, the Commission and the Homes say they encourage it. But everyone knows there's a price to pay. If you want to keep a job in the sector you might think twice. You might try other means before you put your name to any complaint. Obviously the proprietors wouldn't like it. They are trying to make money out of the Homes, not add to their costs with additional safety procedures or to lose residents because of allegations." he told her.

"It sounds ghastly." Rita said. "Just another business with overheads and profits to think about. I don't like the idea of elderly people being a commodity."

"I know. But that became possible once health and social care were split from each other. Politicians know there are limits to how far they can privatise the health care side but the social care side is pretty well done now. The providers are private. It just depends how well off you are whether you pay for yourself or the local authority pays for you" Bandhu replied. "Can I go now?" he added, "I need to see your mother before I leave."

Sunday 22nd March 2015 9.30pm

Before going to her room, Rita wandered into her father's study. She liked to do this. It still smelt of him, and it had his books and even some notes he had made and left strewn around the room. It helped her to think of him on his journey. She felt that although his spirit was travelling he was somehow watching over them. She didn't share these thoughts with her family. They would think she was losing it, she thought. Rita picked up Jahi's paperweight – the one he had brought back from his most recent trip to India- and rolled it round in her hand. Idly, she flicked on the lap top which he had used to update the records for the dental surgery. The receptionist had taken over that job now and used the surgery computer for the purpose. Having switched on the computer, Rita remembered the memory stick which Mohal had found in the car and thought it would be nice to see the photos on the computer screen. She inserted the USB stick and sat in her father's chair to look at the pictures.

What Rita saw was not what she was expecting. It wasn't pictures of arrivals to England in the 1970s. It was recent video footage. The footage was taken from a phone perhaps. The pictures were not very steady. But they depicted a sad scene. A scene Rita wished she had never witnessed. Behaviour towards the residents at Mr Gregson's care home that made her want to weep. Poor Mr Gregson, if only she had known! When she had last visited, in the summer, all had seemed well. It now appeared that with the change of ownership had come a new regime and one far from pleasant.

Some care workers were mocking a lady with dementia, copying the noises she made and calling her a witch. Another elderly lady was being prodded and taunted and told she was a 'silly woman'. Now Rita wondered if Mr Gregson did really die of pneumonia, or, rather, if that could have been prevented. Was he getting adequate care? There had been no one to stand up for him and she had let him down.

Rita stopped watching the video. It was too upsetting. What was it Bandhu said? The police can be asked to investigate a Home. She thought she would contact them. The dates and time of the incidents were included in the footage so they should be able to act on it, she thought. Meanwhile, she decided to look up the care home on the CQC site which her uncle had mentioned.

Oak Trees had been inspected, she found. It scored orange- requires improvement. Under 'who runs this service' it said 'R Massood'. The breakdown of the report was that the Home scored good for 'being caring', inadequate for being 'well-led' and 'requires improvement' for 'safe, effective and responsive'.

Essential work to make the home safe remained outstanding. Needs had been assessed but not all the residents had opportunities to pursue their interests and hobbies. There were frequent changes of personnel, the report said, meaning people were not always supported by the same members of staff. The quality of the food was not always consistent and there was no proper complaints system or clear leadership, governance and accountability to ensure the care provided was consistently good.

The report seemed to hide the plight of individual residents behind jargon. It did not seem that the inspectors had witnessed the sort of scenes shown on the memory stick. Presumably Mr Gregson had seen them often enough to be concerned and to want to get help. Sadly he had died before anyone could do this. Rita resolved not to let him down now.

Then a nasty suspicion grew in Rita's head like a fast-germinating seed. She followed a hunch and checked the list of people present at the cricket ground on the day that Farah Ahmadi 'fell'. Mohal had obtained the details from a friendly police officer. Rita looked through the names of those attending the care home conference. Yes, there it was, Ramlah Massood. She was at the ground that day. What if she was the R whom Farah was meeting at 2.30, and not her brother? She had a temper. Rita had witnessed that in the changing room at the gym. The conversation which Rita had overheard gave her a motive. What if Rita had been wrong about Rashid being implicated in his sister's death and someone else was responsible? She must alert Inspector Bridge.

Chapter

18

"Twenty20 is cricket on speed. In an era of hectic lifestyles and falling attention spans, it gives spectators more drama and intensity in three hours that they would get from a whole-day match. And even though it is a heady cocktail of money, entertainment and media, at its core it is cricket."

Vikas Swarup,
Indian author and diplomat

Tuesday 24th March 2015 3pm

Constable Constance Gardner was not a fan of neighbourhood policing. "We should be out catching perpetrators, not putting on a good show to reassure the law abiding!" was her view. She was also not a fan of the bicycle, the mode of transport being promoted by Leicestershire Police for community patrols. According to her training course, the bike made the officer 'more accessible and aware' instead of being 'cocooned and protected' in the environment of the police car. Constable Gardner had never felt 'cocooned' in a police car. It was a place of work like any other, it seemed to her, and populated by men and women you might not spend much time with if it weren't for the job. You tried to get your records up to date while you waited in the car for the next radioed call-out. You exchanged pleasantries about other officers' children and birthdays but you also shared information about what was happening in your area, characters who needed to be kept an eye on, gangs which were operating, and you could access the Police National Computer for information, provided you kept the engine running.

The patrol car was like a mobile police station, and the way the cuts were going it would be the only sort of police station soon. The rumour was that, in the next round of station closures, instead of desks the officers would be given tablet computers on which to record all their arrests and other information.

Going out on a bike with a fellow officer was an entirely different experience to being in a patrol car. Concentrating on the traffic and the road surface left little time for social niceties or information exchanges and there was certainly no chance of catching up on paper work. So, on days like this, Constable Gardner would ride along envisaging her in-box filling up unattended. Not that she had voiced any objection to the patrol when she had been sent out. She had seen the email from Jamie Bridge about the shoes which that girl, Rita Patel, had brought in. She had winced to herself. Oh dear! She had taken the shoes and put them away carefully but the idea that they were linked to the murder seemed so remote that, rather than be laughed at, she had only mentioned the diary at the briefing. Everyone had been interested in who the mysterious 'R' might be and they had speculated among themselves as to the significance of the entry.

After that, she had been busy on various inquiries- vandalism at a farm, a break-in at a golf club among them- as well as attending briefings on 'interment week'. She would be on duty at the Cathedral on Thursday. She felt guilty about forgetting about the shoes. Jamie Bridge had been tactful, but pointed, in his email of a few days ago which read, tersely, "We should get forensic tests done. If there is any usable evidence we may have some DNA and fingerprints to check it against."

Although she secretly thought this was a wild goose chase, Constance Gardner knew she needed to get back in the Inspector's good books by checking if there was anything in the madcap theories of Rita Patel. So Constance Gardner had set off with Constable Hann, with the idea of following up on Rita Patel's suggestion that Rashid Ahmadi might be leading a double life. As they had turned into Stonehill Road, Rashid emerged from number 3. "I'll call you when I've finished at the gym. We can get a take away!" he called before he closed the door; a woman had waved to him from the kitchen window which looked out over the road.

Hann and Gardner cycled past as if intent on reaching another destination and noted Rashid walking purposefully along Stonehill Road. He was probably going to the gym a mile away, Constance Gardner thought; he'll use the cut-through, the walkway between the housing estates. After all, he would not want to waste energy before he got to the gym. But the take-away sounded a bad idea. Should she warn him about the dangers of consuming too many calories after he'd burned some off at the gym? Better not, she was thinking, just as Constable Hann came to a juddering halt.

""Sh*t!" he exclaimed in un-PC manner. Constance Gardner slowed her vehicle and rode back to see what the problem was.

"Puncture! Just my f***ing luck!" It seemed Constable Hann was just as much a fan of cycling as Constable Gardner.

"I'll ride on to the gym" she said, not sympathetically. She had the feeling that extending empathy would make his temper worse. He needed to stay calm to fix the puncture. "Meet me there" and she set off again, taking the road route in case she passed Rashid on the footway. The officer crossed a bridge over-looking the motorway and travelled down a narrow but busy lane before coming out at a corner of the car park of the gym, where her view of the main entrance was annoyingly blocked by a green Rosie Hunter mobile home. Dodging round it, she was rewarded by seeing Rashid standing at a silver car, helping a brunette haired woman to take out a small child. Constance Gardner knew the woman he had left behind, the one who waved from the window, was a blonde. So Rita may be right about this, she thought.

The threesome passed into the gym. Constable Gardner locked up her bike - another disadvantage, this took far longer than clicking a car key - and entered the gym, looking to see where the three had gone. She spotted them heading for the changing rooms for the swimming pool. She couldn't follow them in as she had no swimwear, but there was a view of the pool from outside the gym, she knew, so she planned to exit and take advantage of that. It would be an opportunity to smoke a cigarette as well. The chances of doing so in working time were rare; such were the concerns these days for the health and safety of colleagues and members of the public. So this was a treat. As she left the gym, Constable Hann's whinges came over on the radio.

"I can't fix the bl***y thing. The puncture kit's no good!" he yelled.

"I'll see if I can get you some help." Constable Gardner said and walked over to the Rosie Hunter motor home. There were some bikes attached to the back of the van so it seemed possible that they might have a puncture repair kit. She knocked on the door. No one answered. Strange, she thought; she was sure she had seen someone moving around in the van earlier. She knocked again.

"Hello. It's the police. Can you open the door please?" she said loudly. There was still no reply.

Anxious not to miss Rashid playing happy families she moved away, noting the registration of the van in case it became relevant. Constance Gardner walked round the gym to the large glass window which gave a view of the pool. She found a raised, grassed, area with picnic tables on it – ideal for smokers, which was probably the intention – such hypocrisy by gym users! she thought. As she lit up, the Constable could see Rashid and the brunette woman carefully lowering a young child into the water at the shallow end. The child had water wings and was also floating in a large ring so it had plenty of buoyancy.

Rashid and the woman were laughing and smiling at the infant. Then Rashid went off to swim a couple of lengths of competent front crawl before returning to 'goo' over the baby some more. After about 10 minutes – during which time Constable Gardner had finished her cigarette and placed the butt in the bin provided – the woman took the child out and Rashid continued to thrash up and down for a few more lengths. Constance Gardner was intrigued to see how he would manage to leave this woman behind and re-join the other one for the promised take away.

The Constable strolled inside the building again and sat in the café, her head behind the gym's in-house magazine while she kept an eye on the doors to the changing rooms. The woman, the child and Rashid appeared at almost the same moment. Either they timed that well or they were in phone contact to synchronise, Constance Gardner thought. She watched as Rashid waved the infant 'goodbye' at the door to the gym. She heard him say "Sorry, I have to work tonight. I'll call you when I get back." And the woman and the child left the gym for the silver car.

So it looked like he <u>was</u> lying! Constance Gardner thought. To both women? Intriguing, she conceded. But it didn't mean it was a motive for murder. Meanwhile, where was Constable Hann? She was starting to get annoyed by his absence and bad temper over the puncture.

Just to be sure, Constable Gardner decided to continue the surveillance on Rashid; she unlocked her bike and took to the road, informing Control that she was retracing her route back to Stonehill Road. Part of the journey took her on the narrow lane, which could be used to get to the MI and down which traffic tended to speed in anticipation. Constance Gardner cursed her colleague for not being there, once again. Two police officers were more intimidating to speeding traffic than one. She kept near to the inside, noticing that the road was fringed with bushes and fly-tipped rubbish. Something else you didn't have to get too close to in a patrol car. The road curved to the left. She could hear a vehicle behind her. Either go past me or wait! she thought. Don't sit on my….

She did not get to think the next word. The vehicle clattered into Constable Gardner, sending her in one direction and the bike in another.

Wednesday 25th March 2015 11 am

The following day, Inspector Bridge was on the phone to Rita, "I expect I have you to thank for this." were his exact words when he had explained how his Constable came to be struck by a vehicle and knocked off the road the previous day while following a suspect suggested by Rita.

"I couldn't have known." Rita tried.

Inspector Bridge sighed. "Rashid is in the clear. Constance Gardner is in hospital – the Royal Infirmary. Are you satisfied now?"

"I don't see how…" Rita tried again.

Jamie Bridge took a deep breath.

"OK. I'm not saying it's your fault, Rita. An accident is an accident. Only Rashid couldn't have killed Farah, we have several witnesses from the archery training to say he never left the field, and don't forget I saw his reaction when he got the news. He was genuinely devastated. No one could have faked that." he paused for a moment to let that information sink in.

"What about the double life, and the argument with Maria?" Rita persisted; she might as well find out what she could.

"OK, you were right about him having two women. But he's not married to either of them, so although he's a 'love rat', as the newspapers say, it's not a crime." he answered her.

"And the argument?" Rita pressed.

"Look, I shouldn't tell you this, but, if I don't, you won't let it go. I know you." he took a breath before continuing, "When we spoke to Maria again, to check all the angles ..."

"You interviewed Farah's partner again?" Rita put in.

"Yes." he confirmed. "It turns out that the baby is his. Rashid's"

"Maria gave birth to Rashid's baby?" Rita repeated incredulously.

"Yes." Inspector Bridge was emphatic. "Farah thought it would be nice if the baby shared some of her genes. So he was the donor." he waited for Rita's reaction.

"So the baby is his?" Rita repeated the information.

"Technically, biologically, yes. Farah's intention was that that he would have no involvement but, especially after Farah's death, Rashid wants to see the child. That's what he and Maria were arguing about." the Inspector finished.

"Oh, I see." Rita let all this sink in. How had she missed it? Why hadn't she asked Maria about the argument with Rashid? But Rita knew the answer – her mind was still preoccupied with her father's death when they met, she had not got her thoughts straight.

"Whether he'll tell the other two women about this baby, I don't know!" Jamie Bridge managed to lighten his tone a little. "After all, he's keeping so many secrets. Why not one more? But even if he had an opportunity - which he didn't -" he emphasised, "I can't see him killing a woman who was not only his sister but the parent of his child."

"No, I guess not" Rita felt chastised. Her theory has been proved wrong and she felt badly for Constable Gardner, even if the accident was not directly due to her.

"Any news on the vehicle that struck Constable Gardner?" she ventured.

"No, and you should leave that to us please. In fact, leave the whole thing to us. We'll decide on our lines of inquiry without your help." Jamie Bridge, uncharacteristically short-tempered after little sleep, little progress with the case, and a seriously injured officer, ended the call abruptly.

Rita looked at her phone for a while, as if Jamie Bridge would call again. Rita had failed to see Inspector Bridge on Monday as she had planned; it took too long to queue to see the coffin of Richard III. When she had telephoned the station on Tuesday she gathered he was away until Wednesday. So when she had seen the news about Constable Gardner's accident on twitter, Rita had immediately worried that she should have spoken up sooner. Maybe Inspector Bridge was right. If she had not suspected Rashid, maybe Constable Gardner would not have had her accident. Rita decided to make amends by visiting the officer in hospital the next day. If it wasn't Rashid who struck Farah at the cricket ground and pushed her down the fire escape, who was it? Was it possible that Ramlah Massood was the mysterious 'R' in Farah's diary? If her temper tantrum at the pool was anything to go by, she was strong enough. But, Rita thought, undeterred by the inspector's words, how would she prove it?

Chapter

19

"What is human life but a game of cricket?"
3rd Duke of Dorchester, 1777

Thursday 26th March 2015 4pm

Rita's blood was pumping so fast round her body that her ears were throbbing and she couldn't believe that no one else could hear it. Peering through the keyhole of the walk-in linen cupboard in which she was standing, Rita could make out, lying on a hospital bed in the adjoining room, the body of the police officer- Constable Constance Gardner. She was attached to several monitors and had an oxygen mask over her face. Crossing Rita's field of vision, so close that all she could see was the fabric of a green sweatshirt, was a figure walking around the hospital room. Rita realised, as she held her breath, that this person had probably committed murder, attempted another, and was set on finishing the job. From her spyhole Rita could see in the person's hands a box of matches.

Rita had decided to visit the police officer in hospital once the TV coverage of the reburial of Richard III had ended. A cloudy day following rain in the night had seemed appropriate for the re-burial. She had taken in the formal music intoned in Latin by male choir voices, the readings and the words of the Bishop. She had watched as the box-shaped coffin was carefully moved to the area of the Cathedral where it was to rest. She had seen the coffin lowered into the hole prepared for it, the sprinkling of water, and the scattering of soil. It was hard to understand what it all symbolised, but Rita could see that efforts had been made to provide aspects of a service consistent with practice in Richard's time. Not enough efforts, if the scarcely veiled remarks and backhanded compliments of some members of the Richard III Society were anything to go by. One of them planned to sit by the tomb and recite the Latin prayers which Richard had left behind to be said over his grave, apparently. Now the cameras were waiting for the 'lid' of the tomb, a giant piece of carved stone, to be manoeuvred around the Cathedral and installed over the buried coffin. This was taking place with less ceremony and a great deal of engineering expertise. Rita couldn't wait to see the final tomb, but she knew there would be plenty of time once the stone was in place. So she had thought the least she could do, since she felt so guilty about what happened to Constable Gardner, would be to visit her, to see for herself how ill she was and, if the officer was up to it, to express her regret.

Rita had been shown to the side room where Constable Gardner lay and had been left at her bedside by a nurse from whom she had asked directions. The room was on the top floor of the Infirmary, in a corner at the end of a corridor; it was a long walk from the lift and opposite a flight stairs which were the fire exit. It gave the officerInspector peace and quiet, which might be beneficial if she were awake. But she was not. Rita saw she was unconscious. Presumably the nurses check on her every so often, she had thought.

It was at that point that Rita became aware of a figure approaching the room. They were not coming from the corridor end, which would be normal if the person had taken the lift, but from the fire exit stairs. Rita could not explain it- and wondered how she would ever explain her reaction- but she instinctively felt uneasy as the steps approached. She had looked around. Was there anywhere she could hide, to see the visitor without being seen? It was at that point that she had realised that the room was a little makeshift. It had been created out of a large store cupboard. The remains of the storage were situated behind a door, with space for her to walk in and wait to see what transpired.

Fearing the worst as she watched the figure move around the hospital bed, Rita reached into her pocket and was relieved to see not only that she had reception but that her phone was on silent. Hastily, she ran her thumbs over the electronic keys, texting for help, hoping it would arrive in time, unsure how best to protect the policewoman in the next room if not. If only she had not got it so wrong and misread the clues, she thought.

The figure was dropping a trail of liquid as it moved round the room. Then, with a quick movement, the person lit a match from the box, dropped it on the floor and exited the room. Quickly, yellow flames and grey smoke started to rise. Rita was frozen in horror. Was her frightening dream about to become true? Was she going to be trapped in a dark place with no means of escape?

Thursday 26th March 2015 3pm

Inspector Jamie Bridge of the Leicestershire Police took a deep breath before entering the interview room. He would need to use all his experience in dealing with this witness he thought. He tried to recall some of his training, and the words of various psychiatrists he had spoken to in the course of his police career-

"Keep your emotions hidden"

"Speak clearly and unambiguously"

"Just get the facts"

"Don't keep your eyes fixed on the interviewee"

Here goes, he thought, as he stepped through the grey door and into a room furnished with matching brown chairs and a sofa. These were all in faded leather-effect plastic so that the appearance was of furniture from a pub or club that had seen better days.

The interviewee was seated on a chair, an 'appropriate adult' in another. Detective Constable Hann occupied part of the sofa opposite the chairs.

Jamie Bridge decided to pull up another chair so he wouldn't be sitting directly across from the interviewee. He made eye contact with David Hann, who he had worked with before, and then with the appropriate adult, who was Jocelyn Howard, the manager of the hospice charity shop on Saffron Lane. She was a long-faced woman in her early sixties, Jamie Bridge would guess, She had white hair piled up on her head like one of those loaves you get from those fancy bakers in the Leicestershire town of Market Harborough.

She nodded back in recognition of the inspector - they had already had a preliminary chat - and settled her sleeved arms on the chair. She was wearing a long blue skirt over brown boots, the tops of which peeked out from under her hem, and a white jumper under a black waistcoat. None of her clothing seemed new; it was as if she had dressed from the shop's contents before she left.

Jamie Bridge said carefully.

"Good morning, Anton. It is 3pm on Thursday 26th March and we are in interview room 4 at Leicestershire Police Station on Mansfield Street. In the room are Anton Bromley, Jocelyn Howard as his appropriate adult, Inspector Jamie Bridge - that's me - and Constable David Hann."

The interviewee lifted his head at the mention of his name but did not look at Inspector Bridge, or at anyone; he kept his gaze at 45 degrees, as if examining in minute detail the dark brown table that lay between the sofa and the chairs.

"Do you understand what an appropriate adult is, Anton?" Jamie Bridge asked, mentally ticking off a series of tasks he must perform before he could try to prise out the information he needed. Trying to get the information was like opening a difficult can he thought. The opener had to fit the lip of the can perfectly; you had to apply just the right amount of pressure; you had to maintain the pressure. Then the lid would glide off as if it were the easiest thing in the world. Fail at any step – misapply the opener, fail to engage it properly, stop holding the opener tightly and the result would be a dangerous jagged edge and, exasperatingly, the contents would still be trapped, even though you knew what was in there and they were so close.

"It's Jocelyn" Anton replied, still staring at the table.

"Yes, that's right," Jamie agreed, although this was not what he meant by the question, but he had broken the rule about not being ambiguous. He decided to explain.

"So we all understand," he said - he was going to say "so we are all clear" and then realised that this itself was an ambiguous statement if you lived in a world where you took words literally.

"An appropriate adult sits with an interviewee to make sure they understand what is happening and to make sure that we, the police, act fairly. So Jocelyn is here to be on your side Anton." The analogy was out of the Inspector's mouth before he could stop it and he chided himself. "To make sure what we ask is fair and that you have a fair chance to tell us what you know," he paused, this was as exhausting as he had thought it might be. It was a real effort to self-edit his words as he went along.

David Hann meanwhile was making notes. All of the necessary steps to protect the interviewee had to be observed and recorded in writing.

Jocelyn Howard nodded encouragingly.

"Is that alright with you Anton?" Jamie Bridge finished.

"Yes" the young man said. He was afro-caribbean in appearance, a slight shadow on his chin indicating he had reached puberty; his black hair was soft and springy on his head. He was in fact 16 but his clothes – a tight-fitting check shirt and maroon cardigan with cream edging, worn with dark blue jeans, made him look younger, more like an overgrown school boy.

"We can stop any time if you want us to." the Inspector mentally ticked off another item in his list.

"And you are not required to answer any questions." Jamie Bridge gave himself another tick.

"You may be able to help us with a case we are working on". Just in time, Inspector Bridge had stopped himself from saying "fill in the details" which on reflection probably qualified as ambiguous; he congratulated himself.

"I am going to show you something, it is in a bag because we need to preserve any fingerprints on it. Can you tell me if you have seen it before?" Inspector Bridge produced from the carrier bag which DC Hann had put on the floor a clear plastic evidence bag containing a pair of shoes. They were ladies size 5 Birkenstock sandals.

Ignoring superstitions, which he was pretty sure would mean nothing to Anton anyway, as he was somewhere on the Asperger's spectrum, Jamie Bridge put the shoes on the table, more or less at the spot where Anton's gaze was directed.

"They're from the shop" Anton said.

"Do you know how they got there, in the shop?" Inspector Bridge asked gently and hopefully.

"Yes" said Anton.

Jamie Bridge cursed himself. What's the first rule of interviews? Don't ask closed questions! he said to himself.

"How did the shoes get in the shop, Anton?" that's better Inspector Bridge thought.

"She brought them in. With a bag of other things. T-shirts, towels, an exercise mat, sweat bands, water bottles and some weights."

Frustrating as this list was, Inspector Bridge let Anton continue until he was finished. It clearly mattered to him.

"Do you remember" he began, then started again, realising his mistake. "What kind of bag were they in?" he asked to check Anton's memory before moving to more crucial questions.

"They were in green bin bags. She always brings things in green big bags. Green's her colour." Anton told him, still addressing the table.

"When was this Anton?" Jamie Bridge said and held his breath, looking at Jocelyn Howard who lifted her eyebrows. What would Anton say? they were both thinking.

"July 14th, 4 o'clock." Anton replied.

"July, last year?" the Inspector checked, trying to sound matter of fact and not to betray the amazement and excitement he felt at this reply.

"Yes" the young man answered.

"Why do you remember that was the date, Anton?" Jamie Bridge coaxed, "Is there a reason or are you good at remembering dates?" the Inspector cursed himself for a longwinded question which was leading in its nature.

"It's my sister's birthday." Anton said. "July 14th. We went for pizza. I like pizza."

"Thank you Anton" Jamie Bridge said. That should be verifiable, he thought.

"And what did you do with the T-shirts and the other things in the bags, including these shoes?" was his next query.

"What I always do. What Jocelyn showed me." was the reply. Jamie Bridge waited a while for more but nothing was forthcoming.

"Which is? What is it you did with the shoes and the other items?" the Inspector prompted.

"I got her gift aid number. It's on the computer. I printed off the labels for all the goods. Gift aid labels. It's a bar code. It's so we can tell the person what we sold and how much money went to the hospice." Anton explained.

Jocelyn Howard was nodding. She had explained the system to Jamie Bridge earlier. Gift aid codes were associated on the shop's data base with a person's name and post code. The charity benefitted from claiming the basic rate of tax on the goods donated and sold. Higher rate tax payers could claim tax relief on donations. So a record was kept for each donor and they were sent a letter every year totalling the donations they had made to the charity.

"So you knew the gift aid code of this person and you applied it to all the items she brought in, on July 14th?" Inspector Bridge checked he understood what Anton was saying.

"Yes." the young man replied, reaching to touch the bag and show Jamie, through the clear plastic, the bar code label he had applied to each shoe.

"And who was this person, the lady who brought the goods in, the one with the green big bags?" Inspector Bridge waited patiently although he felt anything but patient.

"Rosie Hunter. It was Rosie Hunter." Anton said.

"Rosie Hunter, the runner?" Jamie Bridge checked.

"Of course!" Anton replied as if this was obvious.

Jamie Bridge did not have time to show his surprise. There was an urgent text message on his mobile phone.

Thursday 26th March 2015 4.15pm

The flames rising higher, Rita realised she had to act fast; there was no time to wait for help. She abandoned the false security of the cupboard and carefully crossed the room, circling round the flames, which were surrounding the bed but not touching it, yet. Rita looked desperately for a fire alarm, or a means of escape for them both, but she and the police officer were cut off from the alarm, and the door, by a tower of flame. What was more, flames were now rising outside in the corridor. The person must have set a second fire as they exited via the fire escape.

Rita reached the sink in the corner of the room and put the taps on as full as she could. She found a spot where she could step between the flames and set about stripping the bed of its sheet and covers and pulling down the curtains which hung around the bed. Meanwhile, Constance Gardner slept on, like sleeping beauty in the story, mercifully unaware of the life and death struggle in which Rita was engaged.

The trail of flames was almost licking at the bed, but Rita's action in removing the curtains and the covers had bought some time as they only touched the metal of the bed frame, so far. Rita put the sheets and the curtains in the sink and drenched them as much as she could in the cramped space. Then she hauled the dripping material onto areas of the flames, as well as over Constance Gardner, in the hope that they would save her from the worst if the fire could not be stopped altogether.

Rita was worried about the equipment which was attached to the officer. Should she detach it in case it caught fire? Or was it keeping her alive? There must be oxygen going into her mask she thought; was it better to leave the mask on or take it off? She kept the taps running and tried to use cups of water to douse the flames, too. At first it seemed she was making no progress, that the flames would leap all over the room and they would both be overcome, but her efforts yielded results and the soaked sheets had a dousing effect.

Exhausted by her efforts, Rita paused to survey the scene. The officer slept on, coughing disturbingly from time to time, but Rita could not do anything about that. The flames in the room had gone but there was a lot of smoke. Rita looked out to see if it was possible to get help from within the hospital. She soon saw this was hopeless. The trail of flame which the figure had left as they fled down the fire escape had filled the corridor with flickering light and billowing smoke. So they were stuck, she thought.

Should she try to open a window? Was that a good idea, she wondered? She felt it might help the officer if some fresh air could be admitted. As she struggled to work out how to move the window, Rita was relieved to be able to hear the sirens of emergency vehicles which she hoped were fire engines. Smoke from the corridor was starting to infiltrate the room and Rita was coughing too. She must find a way to get some fresh air. At last she saw the catch and raised the glass. But this only seemed to attract the smoke and the room in which she was trapped was getting darker. Was she destined to die here she wondered?

Just as Rita was starting to give up hope, she heard a mechanical whirring sound and a firefighter on a ladder appeared at her window like a crazy clown in a circus act. The firefighter looked like every cartoon incarnation that Rita could remember seeing, with a large dark jacket and trousers with yellow flashes and large black boots. The firefighter waved to Rita and only as they spoke did she realise it was a woman under the yellow helmet.

"How many of you?" she asked.

"Two" said Rita, "One's a patient"

"We have to get you out, it's not safe, can you prepare her to be transported?" the firefighter asked this as if Rita were a nurse or health care worker. Could she?

"I'll do what I can." she called back.

While the firefighter got in closer – "Keep away from the window!" she shouted - and broke the glass, Rita detached the somnolent patient from all her equipment. Mercifully, with the exception of the oxygen, this seemed to be for monitoring purposes only. Nothing untoward seemed to happen to Constable Gardner as a result of her actions, anyway. The oxygen seemed to come from a supply in the wall. Rita hoped it wouldn't help the fire get started again, but what else could she do? Presumably the fire brigade would have that covered when they got in the room.

When the police officer was no longer fastened to the equipment, Rita tried to slide her sleeping body out of the bed. Fortunately, at that moment two firefighters climbed in through the window. "Let us do that" and almost effortlessly they gathered up Constance Gardner and took her outside to another ladder which was waiting; this had a sort of cage at the top of it with a stretcher inside, so Constance Gardner would be comfortable on her journey down.

"There's a doc waiting at the bottom." the original firefighter, the one Rita had seen first, said to reassure her "Now let's get you out. Can you step up here?" and she guided Rita onto the windowsill and out onto the ladder. The last time she was so high above the ground, she thought, was when she went on a balloon ride after her A level exams. She had been nervous then, but soon adjusted and enjoyed looking down on the countryside below. She was nervous now, too, but the presence of the firefighter was very reassuring and her strength reliable as Rita wobbled a little, her legs weak either with the efforts she had been making or with relief at being rescued, she was not sure which.

They seemed to be miles in the air. It felt higher than the tower at the Church where she had climbed with Priya and Ayeesha at Oxford. Rita could see several fire engines below her, so small they looked like toys, and as she glanced across she saw water being directed by other firefighters at windows along the top corridor of the hospital.

"The fire escape is blocked by flames." the firefighter told her as they slowly descended. "My name's Teri, by the way .What's yours?" Rita tried to make conversation, but was struggling in these surreal circumstances. "We'll take you to hospital – another one obviously! - to get you checked out." Teri told her.

Rita thought she must present a rather bedraggled sight. She had black sooty marks on her arms and hands and probably had managed to get black marks on her face, too, she thought. Her brown curly hair was blowing about in the wind, which might help to get rid of some of the soot perhaps. Her clothes were soaked in the water she had used to douse the room. Rita thought she must look like someone from an advert; a warning of what might happen if you failed to use the advertised product.

Finally, the ladder reached the ground and, just as this happened, a familiar red-haired figure came running towards them.

"Rita! Thank goodness you're ok!"

"Glad you got my text." Rita said to Inspector Bridge.

Chapter 20

"The era of playing aggressive cricket and to have the mid-on up is gone. You now try to read the mindset of a batsman."

Mahendra Singh Dhoni,
Indian international cricketer

Saturday 25th April 2015 5pm

"Ssh everyone!" Nayan sought silence, no easy request from the gathered guests who were chatting amiably over food prepared by Rakesh.

He had arrived early for this purpose, putting together platters to pick from as well as a fruit cup and various smoothies to drink. Rita was sitting in the kitchen, watching him approvingly. Since her father's funeral they had shared a lot of their spare time and consequently she had seen less of Rohan, especially now that she had her own car and was not relying on him for lifts to Leicester. She had enjoyed the inventive picnics which Rakesh had prepared for the two of them when he visited her at uni, and she had looked forward to the late night telephone conversations they engaged in when the last diner at his restaurant had been served.

The pair had things in common, which made him easy company. They were children of Asian migrants from Uganda, with relations in common; they had overbearing mothers and their fathers had died. But while she enjoyed his company and, let's face it, his cooking, Rita thought Rakesh, several years older than her, was looking for something long-term, and every time she peered into the future Rita could not see that it would work. She had no interest in cooking –

everyone mocked her about it , and she knew that, compared to her mother, aunt and cousins, her efforts were always hopeless, either underdone or overdone and sometimes both at the same time. She would never survive in Hell's Kitchen, she thought, a programme she watched with her hands over her eyes sometimes, so badly did she feel for the kitchen staff.

So the fact that Rakesh wanted to have his own restaurant one day was a daunting prospect; Rita did not see how she could fit into that picture. Rakesh was also quite traditional when it came to women's roles; unlike Sammi, he had made clear he saw the woman's main job as bringing up children. 'Unlike Sammi'? Why did she think that? She didn't fancy Sammi did she? Rita shook her head to dismiss the idea. No, it was just that she had spent some time with Sammi and his views on equality were refreshing, she told herself. Watching Rakesh being so attentive, kind and courteous with her friends, Rita thought maybe she should tell him some of this.

"An Inspector calls!" Nayan tried to get attention again as Rita, wearing a turquoise kaftan top over black leggings, with flip-flops on her bare feet, placed Inspector Jamie Bridge's skyped head on the coffee table in the middle of the room full of guests. They were gathered in the student house in Leamington Spa, where Rita was now installed and where she was holding a 'housewarming' for her friends and family.

The party members had been mingling and getting to know one another. Priya, who sported a yellow top under a long sleeveless denim dress which gracefully skirted brown roman sandals on her feet, had helped by handing round plates of food. Apart from the house, Rita's recent adventures, and the next baby for the Duke and Duchess of Cambridge, which was due any day, a lot of the conversation had been about the Nepal earthquake, news of which was starting to appear. The common view was that, sadly, the number of fatalities would go up as the days passed. Hindu communities were trying to see how they could provide support and which charities could help the most.

The UK general election was another topic, campaigning for which seemed to have been going on for weeks. The common feeling was that politicians seemed to be out of touch with real life. There seemed to be lots of uncertainties.

"What if the Scottish National Party holds the balance of power?"

"Look what a strong campaign they ran in the independence referendum – they almost won it!"

"Will Nick Clegg keep his seat?"

"Will Cameron go if he loses?"

"I wouldn't mind Boris as leader, he'd be fun!"

"Did you see that Sandy Tosvig is joining a new party? It's for female equality and called the WE party."

Sammi said he had read an article which suggested that British Sikhs could hold the balance of power in the election. He told the room that there were 500,000 Sikhs who could vote in Britain and the Sikh Federation were saying that there were 50 constituencies where Sikh votes could make or break a party.

"They need our support! That is always good!" he said, "Wait 'til you see Cameron at a temple. That will clinch it!"

They all settled to get a view of the screen as the skype call began. Rita's cousins, Shona and Shreya, who had travelled from Leicester with Mohal, sat on the floor beside Rita and Nayan. Nayan was wearing his Leicester City goal keeper top -Kasper Schmeichel being a favourite player of his. The top was black with 'KING POWER' - a company owned by the club owner Vichai Raksriaksorn, after which the stadium was also named- in white writing with fox emblems above it. Rita thought that if her brother could wear goalkeeping gloves to the party he probably would. He had informed the room that Leicester City had continued the remarkable run of results they began at the start of the month by recording a one nil win against Burnley that day. That added more points following their wins against West Ham and Swansea.

"Too much to hope they might escape relegation," he had said, "But good to see City getting some rewards."

Priya and her medic friend, Ayeesha, together with Daz and Siva, who shared the house with Rita, and Sammi, were perched on kitchen chairs. Morwenna had arrived, with Giles, in her white Renault Clio, and was reclining on the sofa with Lauren and Katrin from Priya's student house, as well as Rohan, whose T-shirt today bore the legend "I am not all men"-where did he get them from? Rita wondered. Giles, Sammi, Mohal and Rakesh were standing at the back of the room, like a row of slip fielders, behind the sofa.

All eyes were focussed on the ginger-haired officer, his orange polo shirt and pale skin creating an interesting orange and white striped effect, reminiscent of a deck chair, or perhaps an exotic jungle animal.

"Hello" said Rita to him, "Everyone's here!"

"Hi everyone!" he returned, giving a mock wave like those politicians who were constantly on television, anxious for voters' approval.

"Hi" they all responded and waved in reply.

"How are you Rita?" Jamie Bridge wanted to know first, wrinkling his freckled face in concern.

"I'm fine!" she told him confidently. "No ill effects from the smoke at all!"

"Well, I'm pleased to hear it." the Inspector breathed out theatrically.

"When I got your text I thought the worst." he added.

"You'd worked out by then that Rosie Hunter was the killer? That she killed Farah Ahmadi?" Rita asked.

"Yes, we followed through on the shoes you brought in and found she had dropped them off with a lot of other stuff at the hospice charity shop. She often gave them left-over stock- T-shirts, sweat bands and so on. So she put the shoes in with the other things, after wiping them of course.

By chance, they were put in with the winter shoes; otherwise they might have been sold months ago."

"She could so easily have thrown them away!" Mohal pointed out.

"Yes, it was a stupid risk, but I guess even a trained athlete like Rosie Hunter doesn't think straight all of the time. She said she didn't plan to kill Farah – so everything she did after that was improvised."

"What else did she leave at the shop?" Rita asked to the surprise of the rest of the room. Why was Rita interested in charitable donations? they were all thinking.

"That's exactly it!" Inspector Bridge answered excitedly in admiration. "The volunteer who took her bags that day had an excellent memory, it turned out, and he was efficient in applying her gift aid code to everything she brought in. So we know that among the sportswear from her company was a pair of weights- according to Rosie Hunter, Farah was using them as part of the treatment she was giving Rosie. Rosie struck Farah on the back of the head with them when her back was turned."

"It must have been quite a blow" Sammi observed from his position behind the sofa.

"Yes. But Rosie Hunter is a strong woman don't forget, and a lot was at stake." Jamie Bridge replied.

"But where did the blood go? Why didn't the luminol test pick it up in the treatment room?" Nayan was intrigued. Shona and Shreya smiled at each other when they heard his question. Typical of Nayan! they thought. Others looked round the room nervously at the red chilli dip and raspberry smoothies which were suddenly looking less appetising than before.

"That's where Rosie was lucky. Farah was standing on the treatment mat. She'd taken her shoes off- the Birkenstocks- and they were on the mat, too. The mat and the shoes got spattered."

"Wasn't she afraid of being seen?" Giles wanted to know.

"Rosie says she knew they were alone. It was a quiet day with the cricket team away. There was no one in the gym. She took her chance, hit Farah then dragged her body to the fire escape and threw her down."

Everyone in the room shuddered at the vision this invoked.

"She knew Farah was dead?" Priya asked, horrified, her hand half covering her mouth with her braided hair.

"Oh yes, Rosie had first aid training so she knew Farah wouldn't make it. But she needed it to look like an accident." the Inspector confirmed.

"Which explains the shoes?" Rita kept them all reminded of the details.

"Oh, yes, well the sandals she put in her own bag, as they had blood on them, and the green shoes she took from Farah's bag and put on her feet before she moved the body. She said she hoped they might suggest she toppled on the heels, but I think she also guessed the blood on the sandals would indicate she hadn't fallen to her death like Rosie wanted to make it look." the Inspector told them.

"She's confessed to all this?" this was from Ayeesha, for once relatively still, just swinging her legs backwards and forwards as she sat on her chair.

"She agreed to tell us what happened if we recommended to the CPS a charge of manslaughter not murder. It may help when the time comes for her to be released on licence. We also have her for attempting to run over Constable Gardner." Jamie Bridge told the room.

"Really? That was her too?" Giles, who had not been following the details of Rita's investigations, was surprised.

"Yeh. I'll get to that." Jamie Bridge said, putting his finger to his head as if making a mental note.

"So the blood?" Rita brought them back to the point.

"Yeh. Rosie dragged Farah to the fire escape on the

treatment mat. Afterwards, she rolled up the mat and put that in her sports bag too. She went back to her motor home and left the ground before the body was found. When questioned, the security guys said they remembered Rosie arriving, but they must have been busy when she left. They didn't take much notice of her, they said; she was always in and out of the ground."

"How terrible!" Shona spoke and Shreya nodded agreement.

"Rosie Hunter knew where the car park cameras were, by the way, and she left without passing one directly. When we looked back at the footage you can just about make out a green vehicle in the background, but it's not good enough as evidence on its own. She parked up a few streets away, washed the blood from the weights, the sandals and the mat in the sink of the motor home - as much as she could anyway - and put them in the green bags with the charity shop goods. Only the shoes were still at the shop, the rest were sold or thrown away."

"How calculating" said Ayeesha.

"She was very focussed" Inspector Bridge said, "Focussed on protecting her reputation."

"What was the problem?" Morwenna stirred on the sofa to ask; like Giles, she was not familiar with the events, she had read neither the Leicester Mercury reports nor the social media outpourings on the subject.

"As a physiotherapist, Farah found out about Rosie's doping habits." The Inspector told them. "Her own and some of her team of runners'. She told Rosie she was going to speak out about it, that it wasn't fair to those athletes who don't cheat."

"Doping?" Giles was interested now. "Surely she couldn't get away with that? Not with random drug tests and everything?"

"I guess whatever the rules, there will always be people who try to find a way round them. They were using EPO as well as having blood transfusions to improve their performances." the Inspector said.

"What is EPO exactly?" Nayan was curious.

Priya spoke, "I can answer that I think. It stands for Erythropoietin. It's a hormone produced by the kidneys. Dopers inject it under the skin and it stimulates red blood cell production. It improves endurance, especially in long distance runners." she explained.

"But how does it help?" Nayan was still curious.

"It delays fatigue," Priya explained, "Meaning that the athlete can run harder and for longer."

"But what about the testing regimes? Wouldn't they be found out?" Giles was incredulous.

"Not if they were careful." Jamie Bridge explained. "Blood tests would show up an unusual red blood cell count and, if followed by a urine test, it would be possible to tell if the EPO had been produced naturally or artificially. The problem is that the tests are only positive if the athlete has taken EPO within five to seven days of the test. With careful planning, positive tests can be avoided."

"That's terrible!" said Shreya.

"Mmmn" the Inspector agreed, "Rosie Hunter not only doped herself, but she got others into the habit too, that way a conspiracy of silence grew around her. Everyone working with her closed ranks. It was in no one's interests to blow the whistle. Insulin was another of the substances she used; taken at the right time and in the right dose it's undetectable in testing. She was at the top of her game for a number of years and that takes its toll I guess. It's not surprising she might try to improve the odds in her favour and keep up the legend of Rosie Hunter, especially when her new business ventures, like the ready-meals, depended on it. So she resorted to more and more artificial help. And by encouraging team members to do the same she effectively bought their silence."

The Inspector paused for a moment as the idea sank in

across the room, that Rosie Hunter was a cheat. He told them Rosie had said that Farah saw something she shouldn't have when she was treating her at the motor home,

"That made her suspicious. I guess Rosie got careless. Or forgot that Farah wasn't in on it. Then another athlete that Rosie treated confessed to her that their methods were not entirely legitimate. Farah said she would go to the authorities if Rosie and her team didn't stop. Rosie literally couldn't afford for that to happen. Rosie said she just snapped when Farah threatened her that afternoon. She grabbed the weights, and bingo!"

"Phew!" Giles let out a long breath, "That's a hell of an ego!" he added, running his fingers through the golden locks on top of his head.

Priya said, "It makes you wonder if all the efforts she was taking didn't distort her personality. I don't think she saw reality anymore."

"Maybe" Inspector Bridge conceded, shrugging his shoulders, "But even so it's not enough to be a defence. We'll have to see what kind of mitigation arguments her barrister puts up."

"She's pleading guilty then?" Morwenna finally gathered this.

"Yes, to all the offences. Killing Farah and trying to kill Constable Gardner, twice." Jamie Bridge told them.

"Why Constable Gardner? Why was she such a threat?" Rita asked. Her cousins looked at each other with pride. They knew all about Rita's role in saving the police officer.

"Rosie Hunter thought she'd seen something she shouldn't, that history was repeating itself. I think she was getting a bit paranoid." the Inspector started to explain. He paused to take a sip from an energy drink can."Constable Gardner was following Rashid Ahmadi..."

"That was my fault," Rita interjected, putting her empty smoothie glass down on the floor under the table on which

Inspector Bridge's head was sitting. "I shouldn't have suspected him. I should have left it to you." she conceded.

"Pleased to hear you say that," Jamie Bridge grinned, "But it worked out ok in the end, thanks to you." he paused before continuing with the story.

"Constable Gardner disturbed Rosie Hunter while her mobile home was parked at a gym. She must have been up to no good in there; she thought the police were on to her. Constable Gardner left the gym, where she'd been trailing Rashid while he took his child swimming - that's the child from his second relationship, the one he didn't tell his first girlfriend about. Rosie Hunter followed Constance Gardner when she rode away from the gym and ran her off the road deliberately. It if had happened near the bridge over the motorway she would have fallen to her death for sure."

Shona and Shreya gasped together at this image.

"But she was thrown clear and sustained concussion and a badly broken leg." Jamie Bridge said, and then he continued,

"As you know,"- the Inspector meant 'as Rita knew'-

"she was in a side room at the Infirmary. Rosie Hunter often went to the hospital to cheer up the patients, as well as to promote herself, no doubt. No one batted an eyelid when she visited. She bestowed glamour on everyone in their hour of need. So her plan was to set fire to Constable Gardner's room and leave her to burn - a very nasty end - but, because you were there Rita, she didn't succeed."

"How long do you think she'll get?" Nayan wanted to know.

"It depends on the judge. The maximum penalty is life. The fact that the motive was financial as well as reputational, and that she succeeded once and almost succeeded again will count against her."

"So it was all about reputation," Rita said," I was right about that. But it wasn't Rashid who feared being exposed, or Ramlah Massood as I also thought, it was Rosie Hunter."

"That's about it" said Inspector Bridge, "If we'd tested the shoes when you gave them to us we might have got there sooner. When we did get the forensics it showed that there was blood on them-of Farah's blood type- and finger prints which were matched to Rosie Hunter."

"What a terrible waste," said Ayeesha.

"People don't want to let go" said Rita "They don't understand that if you do let go, something new comes in its place; you grow, people round you grow."

"Yes, I think Rosie Hunter is learning that even now." chuckled Jamie Bridge. "She's planning an on-line exercise class for women prisoners!"

Mohal laughed at this. "I don't believe it!"

"What about the care home?" Rita wanted to know," You are doing something about that?"

"Yes, Rita," Jamie Bridge said patiently, "Don't worry. We've made arrests based on the film you gave us. Everyone at Oak Trees is in safe hands now, and the Care Quality Commission are looking into Ramlah Massood's empire. The residents have a lot to thank you for!"

"Well done, Rita!" said Mohal grinning with pride.

The Inspector signed off.

"Thanks for your help, Rita. Glad you are ok. Come and see Constance Gardner some time when she's back at the station. She'd like to thank you in person. 'Bye everyone!"

The screen went blank. Rakesh raised his glass of orange juice. Quietly he had been making sure that everyone had a drink in their hand, everyone but Rita.

"Let's drink to Rita" he said, "Reading history and solving mysteries!" All her friends, her brothers and her cousins, raised their glasses.

In unison they said loudly "To Rita!"

Rita Patel returns in
Body on the Train

Other Books by Catherine Cooper

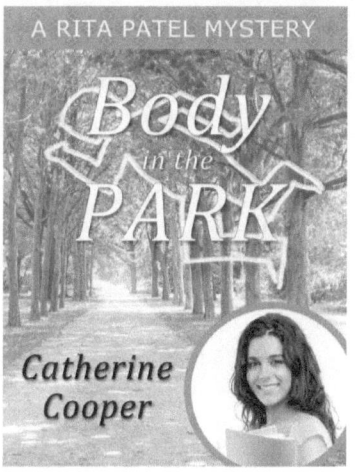

ISBN: 978-1-910779-68-2

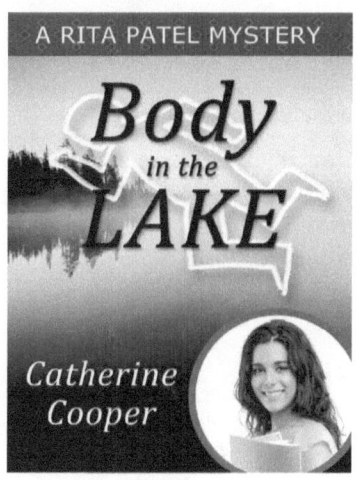

ISBN: 978-1-910779-69-9

ISBN: 978-1-910779-70-5

ISBN: 978-1-910779-71-2

ISBN: 978-1-910779-72-9

ISBN: 978-1-910779-73-6

ISBN: 978-1-910779-74-3

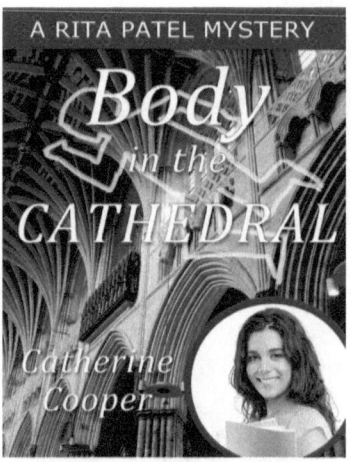

ISBN: 978-1-910779-75-0

www.ingramcontent.com/pod-product-compliance
Lightning Source LLC
LaVergne TN
LVHW091538060526
838200LV00036B/662